GIOVANIA & Jakeem

Married to a New Orleans Savage 2

A NOVEL BY

CARMEN LASHAY

Published by Royalty Publishing House
www.royaltypublishinghouse.com

Contains explicit language & adult themes suitable for ages 16+ only.

Royalty Publishing House is now accepting manuscripts from aspiring or experienced urban romance authors!

WHAT MAY PLACE YOU ABOVE THE REST:

Heroes who are the ultimate book bae: strong-willed, maybe a little rough around the edges but willing to risk it all for the woman he loves.

Heroines who are the ultimate match: the girl next door type, not perfect - has her faults but is still a decent person. One who is willing to risk it all for the man she loves.

The rest is up to you! Just be creative, think out of the box, keep it sexy and intriguing!

If you'd like to join the Royal family, send us the first 15K words (60 pages) of your completed manuscript to submissions@royaltypublishinghouse.com

SYNOPSIS

Did Giovania's mom really pull a gun on her? And who was behind the text messages sent to Ja's phone? Most importantly did Ashanti really kill Big John and Crystal? The finale of this heart-pounding, mind-blowing, series picks up right where it left off with Ja finding himself finally in the clutches of Detective Morris. Has he finally succeeded in bringing down Jakeem Carter in the hopes of avenging his brother's death? Or will Ja still have a few more tricks up his sleeve?

Giovania has had everything thrown at her in life that was designed to break her, but somehow she finds herself standing through it all. Will this new revelation be the one straw that breaks the camel's back? Or will she once again persevere through it all?

Shaken to the core by what happened that fateful day, Ashanti struggles to pick up the pieces and move on with her life. But will moving on prove easy to do with newcomer Lexx? Or will Yari blow back into her life and once again, shake things up? And where will that leave poor Danielle?

Known for shaking things up while joking around at the same time,

Sade jokes about a lot of things in life, but when it comes to his feelings for Kosher, Ja's cousin, his feelings are anything but a joke. Will he finally get her to see he wants to be more than lovers and friends? Or will his ways laugh her right out of his life?

Get ready to have your edges snatched and your life gathered together because part three will take you through so many emotions that you never saw coming. If you thought part one took you on a crazy ride and part two left you emotionally drained, you haven't seen anything yet. Strap back in and take yet another with Giovania, Ja, Yari, Danielle, Sade and Sage, and Ashanti as they battle through sex, lies, deceit, enemies on every corner, jealousy, and greed all to find a little thing called love.

Will Giovania finally get to experience her happily ever after? Or will she once again find out the hard way it's STILL not easy being Married to a New Orleans Savage.

ACKNOWLEDGMENTS

First, I want to take time out to give thanks to God who is forever the head of my life. With Him, all things are possible. I am so very thankful and blessed to be bringing you guys my fifteenth book, and I'm very excited to share it with all of you. It feels so surreal to even be able to say that I have successfully published fifteen books, and I'm so very thankful and blessed. I also want to take a few moments and give thanks to a few people who I love, admire, and that hold a special place in my heart. They go above and beyond to make this journey I'm walking an easy one for me with just the support they display.

To my parents, whom I love dearly, I want to thank you for just loving me and raising such a strong-willed and motivated young lady. To my wonderful husband, who is always my #1 fan, thank you for encouraging me daily to reach for the skies in my pursuit of my dreams. To my sister, Paulesha Hill, I thank you for staying on me when I want to give up and motivating me to keep pushing forward. I also thank you for always encouraging me to keep going when I start to doubt myself. To my longtime best friend, Keiaira Cooper, who is always there for me no matter what time it is, you are always ready for me to bounce ideas off you and offer me your honest, constructive criticism. You understand I don't always need a "yes man", rather someone to tell me if that doesn't sound right. You always read each and every book I write and put up with me during my meltdown moments. Our sessions always give me a burst of energy and motivation. To my entire Miller and Smith family, I love you all so very much, and just know I'm doing this for you guys.

Last, but certainly not least, I want to personally thank you, the readers. Without your continued support, none of this would be possible. I thank each and every one of you who took the time to read my books, whether you purchased it or borrowed it, I still thank you. As always, you can follow me on the social media links below and be sure to leave me a review on Amazon. I do enjoy reading them. They are the highlight of my day. Without further ado, I give you Married to a New Orleans Bully 3.

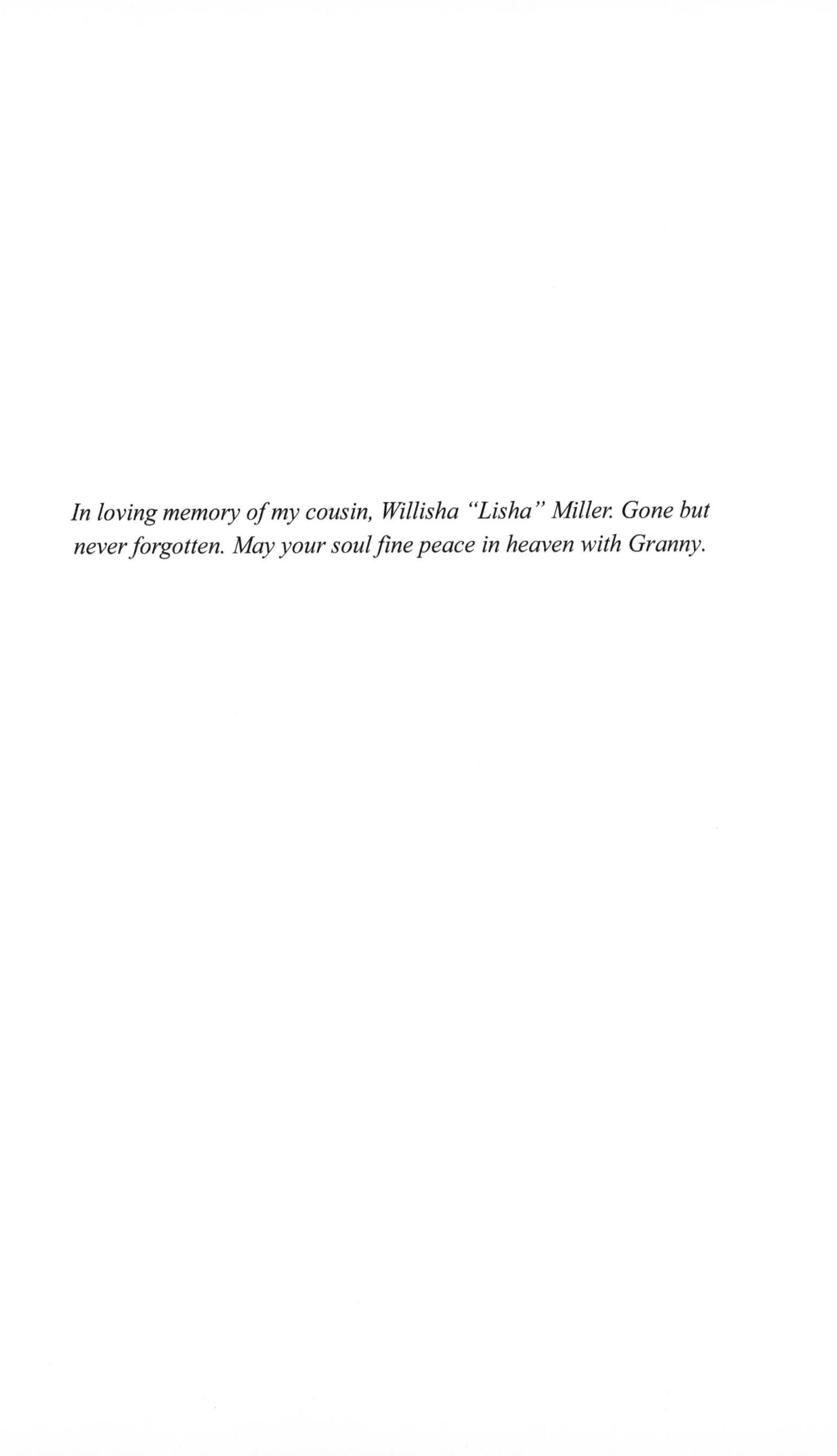

In loving memory of my cousin, Willisha "Lisha" Miller. Gone but never forgotten. May your soul fine peace in heaven with Granny.

GLOSSARY OF NEW ORLEANS "SLANG" WORDS

Joce=entertainment at the moment, typically refers to platonic/sexual companionship or someone you only fool around with when bored.

Trade=was originally gay vernacular but more so recent demographics have claimed it as meaning an attractive guy

Poo=trash, garbage, poorly put together

T-lady=refers to your mother

Toe up=dusty, crusty, unattractive, sloppy, poorly put together (whether it be an outfit, hairstyle, style of speech, behavior, etc.)

Buku=a lot, large quantity of; repeating telling someone something.

Down bad=refers to a fucked-up situation

Sweetie=term of endearment. Someone who is always there for you; your rider.

Duckass=insult, stupid.

Bucked up=excited, giddy, clearly expressing excess joy about something.

Throwed/Throwed off-crazy all over the place.

Maw=generally refers to a female.

Teedy=aunt or older woman you're really close with.

Cutting up/cut up=could mean you're doing too much and trying to be seen or you're doing something and it's being done really well.

Lil' yeah=refer to joce or sweetie depending on how it was used in the sentence.

Jakeem "Ja" Carter

Braylon's wife had been silent, and with so much other shit going on, I had no choice but to take her silence as a good sign. When all of this shit was over, for my piece of mind, I was definitely killing her ass and her fuckin' children. My main and only focus right now was Mateo's ass. I had a special death just for him. It's been awhile since I tortured anyone, but I wanted to make sure he died a very painful, very prolonged death. If I had to hire a doctor to keep the nigga alive for a few days, I would.

The fact that somebody else killed Big John before I could pissed me off. After everything he had done to my wife, I wanted to personally handle that situation myself. But if I couldn't get to him, I was definitely finding the muthafucka that shot my wife. Shit was getting crazier by the minute, but if you poke the beast long enough, he damn sure was gone respond.

Pulling up to go see if a package was still inside of Giovania's box, we all headed inside and began looking for the box.

"So what you think in the P.O. Box?" Sade asked me.

"Shit, I don't know, but I hope it's some shit that will be useful to me," I said.

"Maybe it's like a million in it," Sage said.

"That shit not useful to me," I said.

"Shit, it's useful to my ass, give it to me," Sade said.

"I asked about the shit, so technically, he should give it to me," Sage said.

"Neither one of y'all getting shit," I said stopping in front of the correct P.O Box.

"Baby, y'all the third guys that's been here trying to get into that box. I hope y'all get it, baby, because uh-uh, that's a mess," some guy said to us as he flipped his imaginary weave behind his head.

"My nigga, what is you flipping?" Sade asked as Sage burst out laughing. I literally could not take their asses no damn where.

"And have they gotten inside?" I asked.

"Shit, if I had my bundles in, I'd be flipping them inches, bitches. And, no, baby you gotta have a key to get in or be the owner of the box. Them trades tried everything to get in too, honey, let me tell you. They even tried to bribe a bitch," he said.

"Why you ain't take the money then and get yo' inches?" Sage said.

"Oh, you tried it. A bitch ain't getting fired for no damn hair. That don't pay the bills," he said. "Y'all have fun, I got work to do. Come to the front desk if you need me.

"Nigga, if we need your help, we gone be shit out of luck cuz ain't nobody coming to get your ass," Sage said.

"Don't front," he said, sticking his tongue out at Sage as he walked off twisting.

"Bro got him one," Sade said, laughing.

I'm glad his ass was finally gone just to case it was just crazy shit in this P.O. box. After he walked off, I stuck the key in the lock, and popped it open as I reached in and grabbed a small box.

"Shit, what you think it in?" Sade asked, damn near leaning on my shoulder to look in.

"Damn, Sherlock HomeBoy. How the fuck would I know?" I said, closing the box and walking off.

"We taking it with us?" Sage asked as he and Sade quickly followed behind me. Without saying anything, I popped the locks to my truck. and hopped in.

"Can't be no damn drugs, the damn box too small," Sade said as I pulled a pocket knife out and cut into the box.

Once it was open, I pulled out a stack of pictures. One was showing me getting off the top of a building, holding a case in one hand, and gun in the other hand. Next, it was a picture of some nigga, and chick shot up. The last thing in the box was a bloody ear.

"This gotta be a damn joke. This can't be what the fuck them niggas was after. Some damn pictures?" Sage said, confused as fuck.

I didn't say anything as I studied the pictures hoping something was gone jump off the pictures and speak to me. Grabbing my phone, I took a picture of the dead guy and chick and sent it to Danielle.

"Say this shit a joke. You think Giovania playing us? For all we know, her ass put them pictures in this damn box. I mean, the shit makes no damn sense, bruh," Sage said.

"Yeah, you on to something. I mean, think about it, she just magically shows back up," Sage was saying until I cut them both off because Danielle had just gotten back to me.

"Both of y'all niggas, shut the fuck up. Giovania ain't have shit to do with this. These pictures were taken the day old dude shot at me while I was on the roof, and these dead ass people are targets I was originally supposed to kill. Shit, nigga don't know who ear this is, though. But I bet I know who this box was supposed to be delivered to. These niggas was killed on US soil, but they a big deal back in Mexico.

"Somebody is trying to say I killed they ass, and they got me running off the building I almost killed them on with a gun. I bet my last dollar this box was intended for Detective Morris. But since I'm one step ahead of him, I already know what he gone try and come at me with next. He already popped up on me outside the hotel that one time," Ja said.

"Who the fuck knew to take pictures of you at that exact time?" Sade asked.

"The person who sent the hit in the first place. Mateo," I said.

"I don't understand the damn purpose of these pictures though; he couldn't come harder than that. Some pictures, my nigga," Sage said.

"They could spin these pictures any type of way they want," I said, tossing the box as I started the car up.

My first stop was gone be to my lawyer's office to give him all of this because one thing they ain't do, is catch a nigga slippin.'

* * *

Father forgive me, I fucked up a blessing
Whenever I fall, you the only one catch me
Let's change the subject; I gave a confession
You put me back in it, I bet I go extra

Listening to Kevin Gates's "The Truth", I was headed to the warehouse to meet up with Sade and Sage. I still had not heard from Yari, and I was starting to get worried about the lil' ugly ass nigga.

Ding! Ding!

Looking down, I noticed a text came through my phone from an unknown number. Unlocking my phone, I damn near swerved off the road because I couldn't believe what my eyes were seeing.

Is this your sweet, precious wife?

The text said with a picture of Giovania with her hands wrapped around a dick that I knew wasn't mines. At first, I thought this might have been from when she was kidnapped, but zooming in on the picture, I realized she was in a dorm room. Nothing but death flashed in my eyes the longer I looked at the picture.

I tried to calm myself down though because the last time I jumped to conclusions, I spiraled out of control. What I was doing differently this time, though, was asking her ass. Hitting an illegal U-turn, I made my way back home where I had just left her at.

Seeing blue lights flashing in my rearview mirror, I punched the steering wheel extra hard as I pulled over. I knew I was clean because I didn't ride with drugs, and my guns were licensed. Pulling my license and registration out, I sent a text to Danielle and Pops as I waited patiently for the officer to approach the window. About five minutes went by, before the nigga finally came over with about five police.

"Get out of the car and put your hands where we can see them!" one of them yelled.

I was so mad that I was eerily calm and laughed as I got out of the car with my hands in the air. As soon as I was out, they rushed my ass, quickly handcuffing me and all them walking me to a police car like my ass was an armed and dangerous criminal they had been searching for, for a while. The entire time this all this was going, I just laughed.

Once I made it to the police station, instead of being placed in a holding cell, I was taken to an interrogation room. I don't know who they thought I was, but I was gone play along with their asses until my lawyer arrived. I knew that by now, Pops probably figured out they got my ass, so it won't be long before I'm out. Not even twenty minutes had passed before the door opened, and Detective Morris walked in.

"Why aren't I surprised?" I said, laughing at his ass. "Nigga, I need you on my payroll as persistent as you are. That's hard to find these days," I said.

"I don't work for murderers," he said.

"I'm glad you don't. Neither do I, so we have something in common," I said.

"We have nothing in common."

"Shit, it has to be something you like about me as much as you harass me," I said.

"You think you funny, but I told you as soon as I found that crack, your ass was mine," he said.

"Those fake pictures you was supposed to be getting of me? That crack? Yeah, my lawyer has those already," I said.

"I have something else, something better," he said.

"Dignity and pride to let the past go, accept you will never accomplish this mission and bow out gracefully? Your father did," I said.

"You don't know shit about my father. My father was a better man than you and your drug-dealing, murdering family will ever be. I hope you get it all out because you won't be smiling after you see my secret weapon," he said as the door opened.

"Who?" I asked just as Trina walked in with a huge smile on her face

Jakeem "Ja" Carter

When Trina walked into the room, I stopped smiling, not because I was scared, but because the dumb bitch didn't have shit on me. She never knew Grim Reaper, nor did she know of anybody I've ever bodied. She knows I'm best friends with Yari, but only Yari and my crew know of my status in their operation.

As far as what she can testify to, she was a mule for Yari smuggling drugs into prisons and helping run a prostitution ring he put together a few years ago. His crew also used her house to cook drugs up and shit. Yari never stepped foot inside of her apartment personally, nor did he ever personally pay her, so she couldn't tie him into any of the shit, but a lot of other niggas would be caught in the crossfire because of this bitch. I couldn't believe the hoe had turned snitch. That was one thing I thought for sure she wouldn't do—try and rat a nigga out.

Yeah, I tried being nice to her ass, copping her that whip and crib so she wouldn't try and run her mouth, but if I'm honest with myself, I never thought the bitch would actually do the shit. I just got her that shit because I didn't want her ass telling Giovania we smashed because I had developed real feelings for my pretend wife.

"This your secret weapon? Shit, you did all of that, made that long ass speech, illegally arrested me, and had my black ass hemmed up like

America's Most Wanted and shit, and this all you came up with?" I asked as I burst out laughing again trying to show that I was unbothered, trying to keep my cool, but really I was trying to calculate how I could fix this for Sade, Sage, and all the rest of the niggas she could place everywhere drugs were at in her presence including locations to a few trap houses.

This is why I told Yari ass don't be involving these kick bucket ass hoes in too deep—for reasons like this. Granted, his switched up a lot of shit when I started fucking with Giovania hard as fuck and fell back from Trina, but the bitch shouldn't have known as much as she did from jump. Hell, that's how I met the hoe because she been working for us long before Pops retired. Who knows how long she been a snitch? Rat ass bitch. Somebody must never told her snitches get stitches. Not bothering to say a word to her, I just looked at her with a look that said, *I got you bitch.*

"How's your son, Antwon, doing Trina?" I asked her referring to the son in Texas she thought no one knew nothing about that she had at thirteen years old.

Lil' nigga stayed with her grandma out that way, and her deadbeat ass saw him about every three to four months but does send him money. I smirked at the look of terror on her face when I said his name. She thought I didn't know about him, but you can't hide shit from a nigga like me, not even a needle in a haystack because it's guaranteed I'd find that bitch as well.

"I'll help you with anything you need. Make sure he doesn't kill my baby please!" Trina said finally breaking her silence.

"Kill?" I asked putting my hands to my chest as if I were shocked.

"You have me confused, miss. I'd never hurt a fly," I said.

"Don't worry, Ms. Hill. With your testimony and evidence you provided, he will never see the light of day again," he said.

"You can't be serious about this being your witness?" I said again with a smirk, feeling myself regaining control over the situation.

"Ms. Hill has provided us with vital information about your drug operation, stash houses, and countless other things that's gone bring you and that murdering father of yours down. My brother will finally get the justice he deserves, and my father can rest peace."

"Naw, my nigga, your father's ass still gone be restlessly rolling over in his grave I'm sure because your ass ain't accomplished shit. If you basing your entire case off of this witness alone, then once again, you lose," I said laughing.

"And how do you assume that? What she provided will bury you, and mention my father again, and watch me fuck you up!" He snarled, banging his fist on the table.

"At no time of the day, on no day of the week, will you ever fuck me up, my nigga, but it's cute you think you could. Got a little bass in your voice and everything. Shit, I almost for a second believed that you actually believed yourself," I said with a little smirk before I continued talking.

"This witness though, Ms. Hill, did she tell you I used to bless her with this dick in every hole on her body until the day my wife put that pussy on me, and a nigga had to gon' put a ring on it. I broke up with her, and she became angry, deranged, and violent. She even took a group of females and jumped my pregnant wife outside of a Walmart, and it was recorded to Facebook. I'm glad you found her so we can press charges. My wife was two months pregnant at the time," I said, getting mad all over again thinking about them jumping Giovania, and she was pregnant.

Dumb ass hoes make me wish I could bring them back to life and kill their asses all over again. But oh, I got something real special planned for Trina's ass, and pretty soon, it'll be time for her to collect her price. An evil grin spread across my face just thinking about the shit. Killing excited me like a kid in a candy store. I'm a fucked-up individual, but I can admit that shit.

"From the look on your face, I take it Ms. Hill left out those details," I said.

"And you killed my best friend and cousins as well, you sick bastard. Why did you take them from me!" Trina cried out.

"I honestly have no idea what you are talking about, Ms. Hill," I said to her with a straight face.

"Wait outside for me Ms. Hill. That will be all," Detective Morris said to her, walking her to the door. The minute she closed the door behind her, he walked over to the wall, cut the camera and sound off to the room, then walked back to me, grabbed me by the collar of my shirt, lifting me up and slamming me into the wall behind me.

"You think you so tough because you scaring that bitch, but that shit won't work on me, boy. Let's see how tough your black ass is when I haul your ass to Angola and toss you in to the wolves. Then we'll see how tough you still are."

"Angola? Shii, all them niggas my peoples. I'll still be good," I said as he grabbed me off the wall and slammed me against the interrogation table. Being that I was still handcuffed, it wasn't shit I could do, but I was gone be his worst nightmare once I got free.

"You'll be good, huh? I hope that attitude holds up when your little pretty ass becomes someone's bitch in jail. She gave names, locations, dates, video recordings, and detailed accounts of things she's witnessed, dating back a few years. With her testimony, plus all the evidence I have from my newfound friend, it's enough to put you away for a very long time. I know for a fact I can place you on that rooftop," he said, referring to the hit that almost cost me my life. Speaking of which, I needed to find out who the shooter was. I don't give a fuck who killed dude and his ole lady.

"Become someone's bitch? Nigga, I give dick, and lots of it. I'll never take shit but pussy, and even that's freely given to me, so you wrong again. And I keep telling you I don't know what the fuck you talking about. What rooftop? I believe you have me mistaken with someone else," I said, laughing at him as he punched me in my gut hard as fuck, knocking the wind out of me.

Before I could recover, he was hitting me in the face so hard, blood instantly shot from my mouth and nose. He wanted to get a rise out of me, but I wasn't giving his ass shit but laughter. The only person getting mad here was his ass. I was cool, calm, and collected on the outside, even though I was a volcano threatening to explode on the inside.

"Don't know what I'm talking about, huh? That's cool, I guess you caught amnesia. Maybe your memory will come back to you when you and your father are doing fed time, and I find myself in his house, in his bed consoling that fine ass mother of yours. I never had black pussy, but I hear it's dipped in gold and comes with sprinkles on top. If she's sweet on me, I might work out a deal and get the both of you life in prison with the possibility of parole in fifteen years. That is, if that memory of yours comes back," he said with a smirk on his face as if he held the keys to my life in his pocket.

One thing I'll never play about is my T-lady, even though I know she'd kill his ass before he touched our front door—it's the principal of the matter.

"What's the matter, boy? I'm not good enough for your mother? Did that make you mad?" Detective Morris asked, taunting me as I snarled up at him.

Slightly sitting up, I spit blood out of my mouth onto his shoe, and I glared at him. My smile and laughter were gone, and murder danced in my eyes as I went to open my mouth to really let his ass have it when my lawyer finally walked his ass inside the door pausing me.

"Don't say another word, Mr. Carter," he said, storming in.

"Why is my client handcuffed and bleeding?"

"He slipped and fell. I was helping him up," Detective Morris said, mad that my lawyer had arrived ruining his poor attempt to break me down.

That's why they illegally stopped me and hauled my ass in here so fast. They thought they would be able to keep me a few hours or even a few days before they were forced to let me make a phone call and lawyer up. I guess the plan was to break me by any means necessary and get me to admit to some shit. I still don't know who the fuck Detective Morris got me mixed up with, but the nigga need to thoroughly do his research on Jakeem Cater.

"He fell, huh?" my lawyer, Stan, said, walking over to me. "I'm no doctor, but his injuries don't appear consistent with a fall to me. I will be sure to have him examined when we leave here to have a doctor confirm these bruises are related to a fall," he said.

"You do that when he is released. In the meantime, we holding him until we gather all our evidence together. He is the prime suspect in not only a murder case, but a huge drug case we have had under surveillance for a few months now," Detective Morris said with a smirk.

A lesser man hearing this would have probably shit bricks, but I paid Stan a hefty fee, and his ass knew like I knew that he damn sure couldn't walk out of here without me.

"If he is the prime suspect in a murder case, a warrant for his arrest would have been issued, so where is this warrant? As I recall, you arrested him on a routine traffic stop. What probable cause did you have to stop or arrest him? Were drugs found in his vehicle? I will be subpoenaing the body cams of the officers who made the stop and arrest," Stan said.

"He made an illegal U-turn—" Detective Morris began, but Stan interrupted him.

"Then he should have been issued a ticket, not taken down like a criminal. You are letting your personal dislike for my client cause you to play judge and jury, taking the law into your own hands, Morris," Stan said.

"We have an eye witness that can place—" Morris started, but again, Stan was on top of his shit as he pulled out printouts from Facebook of Trina saying shady and petty shit toward Giovania, tagging her in old ass pictures, and all of Trina's angry ass statuses.

I was on top of my shit way before the fight just in case I had to kill the hoe over her telling Giovania about us. I still can't believe the hoe turned snitch though.

"Are you referring to the witness sitting outside? The same one who was romantically involved with my client and outraged by their breakup? So outraged that she would say anything to get back at him for leaving her?" Stan asked.

"She is not lying," Detective Morris all but screamed. That cocky ass smile he was wearing a minute ago had quickly left because Stan was handling his ass.

"And the video of her attacking a pregnant woman doesn't exactly help her testimony of this sweet, innocent, law-abiding citizen either," Stan continued as if Detective Morris hadn't said a word.

"Bottom line, unless in the next five minutes you produce substantial evidence that will allow you to tie place my client at the scene of a murder or place drugs in his hand for this drug sting you also said he involved in, we walking. You know as well as I do those bullshit ass pictures you tried to forge won't hold up either because I have travel information, hotel receipts, credit cards, and about twenty-five witnesses that place my client in a totally different state during those murders," he said.

After I had turned the photos in to him, he got to work creating me an air-tight alibi.

"By tomorrow, I will have a lawsuit drawn up suing this department for harassment, wrongful imprisonment, racial profiling, assault and battery, and a slew of other charges. You already on thin ice. You need to stop while you are ahead because this vendetta you have with my client is bound to cost you your fifteen-year career you've put in with the department.

"You are holding a grudge against my client and his family because of your deceased brother's unfortunate passing. A passing, which at the time my client was a child, and his father, a suspect at the time was cleared of all charges. I will have papers drawn up and signed by a judge before daybreak tomorrow ordering you to stay within one hundred yards of my client because you are abusing your badge and becoming a danger to yourself and your job. Let's go, Mr. Carter. Those five minutes are up," Stan said to me.

Smirking, I stood up and turned around for Morris to uncuff me.

When he hesitated, Stan said, "Not only do I have Chef Bradley on speed dial, I play golf every Friday with the Major, so don't test my patience. I climbed out of some fresh, young pussy to come down here. I suggest you comply because you have no options left," Stan said, adjusting his tie.

His square ass surprised a nigga with that one. For one, I know for a fact I was at his wedding, so I knew he couldn't have been talking about his wife when he said fresh and young. And how in love he ass acts, always my wife this, my wife that, I just knew he wasn't knocking shit off on the side. Shit, that goes to show you that you can't put shit past anybody. With a growl, Detective Morris roughly freed me and pushed me toward the door.

"This ain't over, Carter, I don't care what your puppet says," he said.

"A puppet that makes your yearly salary in one day," Stan said, walking out as we headed toward the exit.

As soon as we jumped into a waiting black Yukon, Stan turned to me and said, "Trina, what all does she know? Tell me now so I can get ahead of this because he not letting this go. He will dig deeper and push harder. I know he knows I was bluffing about the restraining order, or if he doesn't know, he'll find out soon and then he'll be back at it."

"Man that hoe don't know shit about me or Grim Reaper. She used to make runs up north for Yari though, and she was a part of his way prostitution ring, getting the girls for him and shit. His crew used to cook up work at her crib and shit. She can also place the twins at a few trap houses," I said, being truthful with him.

He knew about Grim Reaper because I told his ass everything, that way he knew what he was up against if one of my kills ever went left. I wasn't worried about him telling anybody because aside from the high ass retainer fee we paid him, I was the reason he could afford the extra huge ass wedding he gave his wife, all the expensive suits he wore, the cars, clothes, and easy lifestyle he lived. With my income alone, he didn't have to take on other clients if he didn't want to, and since I wasn't one that had many run-ins with the law, he was just sitting back, collecting free checks.

Aside from the fact that he knew, even from behind bars I could and would have his entire family touched, turning on me wouldn't benefit his ass at all. It wasn't no money in that shit, and with me in jail, he would need to take on at least ten to fifteen more clients to even top what he was making from me. That meant more work, crazy hours, and a decrease in his lifestyle.

"As your lawyer, I'm advising you that killing her will definitely not be in your favor. With that being said, if she dies of a drug overdose, failed brakes, or something that couldn't possibly be proven to be your fault, make sure you far away from the state with a room full of witnesses, preferably doing charity work," he said.

"I'ma kill the bitch myself, and very painfully, because she touched my wife with my seed inside of her. The hoe not dying of no failed brakes, overdose, or shit like that," I said.

"You know that'll make you the prime suspect," he said as the car slowed down in front of my crib.

Opening the door, I said, "I never said I was killing her ass tomorrow, but the bitch will die, and they can't build a case without a body. Trust me, they'll never find the hoe because it won't be shit left to find. After I make sure she dies a very painful death, I'm chopping the bitch up and feeding her body parts to my pet alligators." His eyes grew big as saucers.

I don't know why his eyes was acting surprised like he didn't know my ass wasn't wrapped too tightly. Smirking, I closed the door and hurried inside of the house. I had another issue I needed to deal with right now, Giovania and this damn picture. Letting the garage up, I noticed her G-Wagon was gone, but I still walked past the rows of cars into my crib.

Kicking my shoes off, I walked past the living room, up the stairs, and into my bedroom. Stripping out of my clothes, I pulled up the tracking app I had installed on Giovania phone and car, which was how I knew which nail shop she was at, and saw it was pinged at the warehouse. Walking naked as the day I was born into the bathroom, dick just swinging from side to side, I stepped into the shower to wash the troubles of the day away as I let my mind drift to off to this picture.

Me and Giovania we're finally in a good space, and I would hate to have to kill her, because she was carrying my seed, but if she told me she willingly sucked another nigga's dick, she gon' find herself on the back of a milk carton. Stepping out the shower, I quickly got dressed in an all-black suit, went to my closet, and pressed a code in as the doors slid open, revealing my gun collection and my baby, my Katana.

Grabbing a desert eagle and my baby from her place on the shelf, I quickly grabbed the carrying case and closed the door so that it swung back shut, revealing my wall of shoes. Picking the perfect pair to go with my outfit, I was back downstairs and out the house in minutes. Giovania has never before seen Grim Reaper, but tonight was the night she'd come face-to-face with her worst nightmare.

* * *

As soon as I pulled up to the warehouse, I immediately sensed something was wrong before I even got out the car. My phone pinged Giovania's phone as still being here, but her truck was gone. It's no way she would leave her truck. Even if my workers went to get something for her moms or sister, they'd just take their own shit, which one of their cars was still here.

My gut never steered me wrong, so I quickly pulled out my gun as I walked into the warehouse. It's usually two men here at all times, but the shit looked eerily quiet. Walking further in, gun locked and loaded, ready to shot anything that moved wrong, hearing silent cries made me walk toward the conference room cautiously.

Just a few minutes ago, I was hell-bent on strangling my wife, but now, heart racing, palms sweaty, I simply wanted to find her alive and well. Nigga wasn't the praying type, but the closer I got to the room, I said a silent prayer to the man above that I didn't walk in to a crime scene with my girl dead. I would lose my fuckin' mind if something were to happen to Giovania and my seed.

No matter how much shit I talked, I loved the fuck out of that girl. My heart was pounding so damn hard as I rounded the corner only to find Giovani looking shaken up with a very distraught little girl that I knew from pictures to her sister.

"What's wrong? What happened?" I asked, telling by her face that something wasn't right. Surveying the room, I didn't see anything that stood out, but I still I wasn't letting my guard down.

"Where yo' moms at?" I asked her.

"She pulled a gun on me, threatened me, took the cash I had on me, my keys, and left after your men came back in shooting at her. Before she left, she said don't think this is over," she said with tears in her eyes.

"Why, Ja? Why does stuff keep happening to me?" she said, asking me a question that I wasn't sure I could answer. The real question was why them niggas ain't call me and let me know all this shit went?

Giovania

Looking at the woman in front of me that has always been there for me, who took care of me when I was sick, clothed me, fed me, and pushed me to succeed in life, I felt hurt to the core. My mother's love, and all the sacrifices I saw her making for me growing up is what kept me going in America. It's what made me even push myself harder to get to America in the first place. I couldn't and refused to believe this was the same person waving a gun at me right now.

"Give me your purse and keys," my mom said as I just stared at her. "Now, Giovania, I won't ask your ass again," she yelled, cocking the gun snapping me out of my trance as I quickly gave her my purse and keys. Snatching them from me, she just looked at me with pure hatred in her eyes.

"This a joke right, Mommy?" I asked her, stunned as I looked from her to the gun.

"If it's a joke, then the joke is on you. As always, little Giovania has to come to the rescue. You fucked everything up. You had one fucking job! One! And you managed to screw that up. You simply had to go with the flow, let us finish our plan in setting up Maxx Carter, and getting Ja out of the way. We would have been set for life and back in America living peacefully," she said to me, instantly pissing me off as I thought about everything I had been through these past few months.

"What are you talking about? I thought you were sick, that's why I even fucking agreed to that bullshit arrangement. Yes, I did everything I could to get out of it, including putting my life on the line for you and Camille! I was gon' do anything to protect you guys, and you standing in my face holding a fucking gun on me!" I screamed, more pissed right now than sad. I don't think it had really registered to me just yet what was actually going on.

"You so damn gullible. I really don't understand how the hell you Mateo's daughter. I knew if you thought I was dying that you would seek out your father to help with my treatment. Why did you think I told you exactly where to find him a week before you came home trying to get you to have a relationship with him?" she asked laughing as I just looked at the person who I would have died for.

"So you never was sick?"

"Yes, I was sick. I just wasn't on my deathbed like you thought," she said.

"If you wanted to form a plan with Mateo, why the hell didn't you just go to him yourself? What the hell purpose did I serve in all of this? Why couldn't you just contact him, tell him you wanted to set Maxx Carter up, and you guys figure that out?"

"Because he would have shot me on sight probably. We didn't exactly end things on the best of terms the last time I saw him. Shit, the only reason I'm still living and breathing is because of you. Besides, I had to let him think it was his plan, and I was merely making suggestions, when really I've been in contact with Chad for a while now," she said.

"Who the hell is Chad?" I asked her.

"Chad Morris, the Carter's worst nightmare," she said. That name sounded familiar to me. I just don't recall where I had heard it from.

"If you thought Mateo would have shot you, why did you tell me where to find him? What if he would have shot me too?" I asked her.

Her silence told me all I needed to know. She didn't care if he shot me and was willing to gamble with my life to carry out her plan.

Covering Camille's ears, I said, "You are one stupid, selfish old bitch, and when my husband finds you, because you should have done your research if you think Jakeem Carter won't find you, he will kill you. And I won't shed not one tear," I told her, meaning every word I said as I pressed tightly down onto Camille's ears, not wanting her to hear that this bitch would soon meet a fate worse than death when Ja caught up to her.

I thought I would do my usual Giovania and cry. But I was over the tears and had been betrayed by so many people, that I was numb to it all now. It seems like everything in my life except my husband was a lie. He may have been a lot of things, but Ja has never lied to me, or tried to intentionally break my heart. And for that, I'll love him forever.

"Oh, I see, so you done got a little bit of that black dick, and now, you feel like you bold enough to talk to me crazy," my mother said.

"Correction, I got a lot of big dick because it's damn sure nothing little about the dick my husband blesses me with." I shot back as she looked stunned that those words had come from me.

"And I don't know what the hell your problem is or what's gotten into you, but if you want to continue this plan with Mateo, you can die with him," I said, meaning every word I said. Nothing but death was waiting for anyone threatening the Carters.

"You so cute. You still think Mateo running the show," she said. "After you burst into his meeting that day, he called himself contacting me and threatening me to get you to work with him in marrying one of the cartel's sons to solidify his position. It was me who suggested he link up with someone powerful in the States because that would still give him a higher position, and it would keep you safe. I played the concerned-mom role, stressing that finding a powerful American family would work, even shed a few tears and begged for your life.

"Stating that you only burst in out of concern for me, and you had your entire life ahead of you in America, He believed me, and still probably believes that this whole thing was his idea, when really he's been my puppet this entire time. I suggested he call up Maxx Carter and told him about Ja being a hitman for hire. Who do you think even put the hit out on Jakeem?" she said, laughing, which made me want to beat her ass with that gun in her hand.

"You evil bitch!," I yelled. I almost said fuck it and charged her until Camille spoke up.

"Mommy has been really mean lately," Camille said.

"Shut your ass up, you little spoiled brat. At least I still chose to take care of you instead of selling you to the highest bidder," she said.

That's where I drew the line at. She would not harm my innocent baby sister. Before I could advance toward her, we heard voices coming into the room as a few of Ja's men walked inside of the room carrying bags of food. They must have left them to go get them something to eat. As soon as they took one look at her, she opened fire, causing them to dive behind a table as I grabbed Camille and hit the floor.

From the spot that I was at, I heard my mother yell, "This ain't over Giovania," before she ran out of the door as the men got up and followed behind her still firing shots.

The entire time, Camille was screaming at the top of her lungs in horror.

"It's OK, baby. It's over now," I told her, struggling to even believe that myself.

This was just too much to deal with, and at what point would it all end? When would Giovania Carter get her fairy-tale happily ever after without someone throwing a curveball at me? I just wanted my husband, my family, and a couple of forevers, is that asking too much?

"Why is Mommy doing this?" Camille said, asking me the one question that I could not answer.

"Mommy isn't herself right now, baby. The medicine is making her mean," I said to her, not knowing the proper way to tell an eight-year-old that her mother wasn't shit.

I know she didn't really fully grasp and understand everything going on, and it breaks my heart that she has to lose both parents at an early age, but I'll be damned if my mother gets her back after everything she said and did here tonight.

Shaking, I tried to get my nerves under control as Ja walked into the room with his gun drawn. I was happy to see him but still couldn't fully process what had just happened. My mom really pulled a gun on me, took my purse, car keys, and told me I messed everything up, but this wasn't over.

I just knew this was a horrible dream that I would eventually wake up from, but the pain in my chest, and ice in my heart told me it wasn't all a dream as I would hope.

* * *

"Y'ALL READY TO GO YET?" Ja asked with annoyance as he walked into the room. It had been a few days since the incident at the warehouse and things were struggling to get back to normal. The first two days, Ja lovingly doted on me, but after that, his entire mood had changed, and I don't know why.

The way he looked at me was different, and our interactions weren't even the same. This baby had my body on fire, wanting to be touched, caressed, and blessed with some bomb ass sex. However, Ja was even holding out in that department as well. I made a mental note to get down to the bottom of what was going on soon because I was done with drama.

Today, we were having our first family outing, heading to the mall to get Camille some clothes because she didn't come with much of anything.

"I'm coming, I'm trying to finish Camille's hair," I said, struggling to brush her hair into two big pigtails. The girl on YouTube made it look extremely easy when she had done this, but here I was failing miserably.

"Them ponytails look lopsided as hell," he said, laughing at me. Even though he was criticizing my work, I welcomed his laughter because it was a change from the attitude he'd reverted back to giving me.

"Well, that's the best I can do," I said as Camille reached her hands up to touch her hair.

One ponytail was much higher than the other, and both looked crooked as hell. It's safe to say, that combing hair wasn't my strong point. I was hoping for a girl though, so I was gon' have to learn.

"I'm ready," I said as Camille stood up, and I grabbed my purse and phone, and we all headed downstairs to put our shoes on.

"Camille, I'm baking you some chocolate-chip cookies for later on," Ms. Mary said to Camille as I helped her into her shoes.

"Yeah," Camille squealed in excitement as I smiled.

I was glad she was adjusting to her new life, and everyone was treating her as welcome as they had treated me. She still woke up some nights, screaming at the top of her lungs, but for the most part, she was fine. I was going to talk with Ja about having her go see a therapist once a week, so that whatever traumatized her won't haunt her for life like it did me. I still get scared when it rains, but I'm dealing with it, just like I dealt with my kidnapping.

Once we got to the mall, I tried to grab Ja's hand, but he pulled away from me and slightly walked in front of us. I didn't know what his problem was, or why he was intentionally trying to hurt my feelings, but I was sick of it at this point. We walked around for about an hour, and everybody was tired and ready to go, but I hadn't found exactly what I was looking for yet.

"Giovania, half an hour is all you got left. Nigga tired as hell and starving fuckin' around with your ass." Ja grouched as we walked through the mall.

"It's gon' take us that long to get to the store I really want to go to," I said, trying to reason with him because I knew his ass was serious.

"The last five stores we just left were stores you swore you really only wanted to go to," he said, looking at me annoyed as hell.

"I promise. I really, truly just want to go to this one. Those other ones were pit stops on the way," I said, pouting.

"I don't care about you pouting. I'm about to run to this sneaker store, and when I get back, we leaving. End of discussion.

"Can we stop and get some ice cream, GiGi?" Camille asked.

"Ice cream will spoil your appetite," I was saying until Ja interrupted me.

"Yeah, we can do that, lil' homie. Come on," he said.

That's another thing that's he's been doing, each time I tell Camille she can't do something or have something, he purposely comes behind me and gives it to her. Grabbing a seat, I watched them get in line and grab some ice cream and head back over to me.

"Here. We got you one, GiGi. It's your favorite too," she said with a gap-toothed smile.

Taking the ice-cream cone from her, my greedy ass immediately went to bite in instead of licking it.

Tasting nuts, I said, "I didn't know it had nuts in it."

"Really? Nigga could have sworn you liked nuts in your mouth," Ja said, causing me to almost choke on my ice cream as my eyes grew big as saucers.

"I like nuts in my mouth too, Ja," Camille said, oblivious to the double meaning of the term.

"No, baby, you don't," I said to her. I didn't even know how to correct her without having to explain why she couldn't like nuts in her mouth.

"Yes I do, GiGi. I do like nuts in my mouth, see," she said as she took another bite of her ice cream, then stuck her tongue out so I could see the nuts in her mouth.

Ja thought this was the funniest thing ever as he burst out laughing.

ROLLING MY EYES AT HIM, I got up, dumped my cone in the trash, and grabbed Camille's hand.

"Let's go, baby girl, so we can get you some clothes."

* * *

"HOW DOES THIS ONE LOOK?" I asked Camille as I head the shirt up in front of her. Ja had gone to the shoe store while me and Camille hit up a few clothing stores to get both of us some new clothes.

I was starting to feel like I couldn't fit any of my clothes anymore. This baby was already giving me hell.

"I don't think I like I like that one, GiGi. I like this," she said, holding a shirt up to her body.

It looked similar to the few outfits Ja had purchased her the other day. He clearly doesn't know quite how to shop for a girl yet because he had her looking like a little tomboy. Like now, she was rocking this blue-and-red Champion jogging suit with a pair of white Balenciaga shoes.

"That one, Millie? Don't you want to wear something more girly like this?" I asked again, holding the cute, pink shirt with glitter on the front that I planned to pair with some stonewashed jeans.

"Jakeem has the same one, and I wanted to dress like him," she insisted.

Laughing, I gave in to her demands because I couldn't wait to tell Jakeem about his little protégé in the making though. I thought it was cute when they came back from the mall with matching Jordans and shirts, but now that I know Millie's reasoning for wanting to dress like Ja just warms my heart. I wanted them to get along, but I never imagined this.

After racking up on both of us a few shirts, pants, shorts, and sundresses, we walked off heading toward I register because I knew Camille could fit hers, and I didn't feel like taking my clothes off. I swear at three months pregnant, my baby really hated my ass! Or hated this heat because my body disagreed with everything I did.

I got tired from walking, from driving, from sitting down; hell, I even got tired from doing anything other than eating! Momma Jackie said this was a girl, but I believe the baby was stubborn and mean just like his damn daddy, so he had to be a boy! My doctor says in about three more weeks, we can know the sex of the baby, and I'm beyond excited. Kosher and Kemari already talking about a gender-reveal party, and the only issue I have is, what family will I have there for me?

Yes, I'm married, and they are my family now, but I would give anything to have my mother and best friend experience this with me. I act like I'm OK most days, but I'm really not. I'm broken to the core from the betrayal of the only family I've ever known, but the only option for me was to be strong and push on. Paying for our items, we headed toward the shoe store to meet up with Ja and get some shoes for Millie since it was a lost cause trying to make her wear girly things.

Walking into the shoe store, I spotted Ja talking to a sales associate, and headed that way.

"Can I have some shoes like that, Jakeem?" Camille's spoiled ass asked, getting straight to the point as she pointed at the shoe he was asking the sales guy to find for him.

"Yeah. Aye, get these for baby girl in a kid's size three in every color," he said, without hesitation. Then he added, "And get a size seven in women's for my wife," he said, causing the hugest smile to appear on my face.

"Do I get every color as well?" I asked.

"GiGi, I need to use the bathroom," Camille said.

"We have one straight to the back," a different sales associate said pointing to a sign that said restroom.

"Come on, Millie," I said, grabbing her arm.

"No, GiGi! I can go by myself," she said taking off toward the restrooms before I could protest any further.

"She'll be fine. It's only one way in, one way out this bitch. Besides, I'll shoot this while fucking store up if something happened to her," Ja said, calmly texting away on his phone.

"I just don't like this," I was saying as I heard someone begin to speak.

"Look who they let out of jail. You done getting your booty rubbed on, bitch boy?" Turning around, I saw none other than Trina with a new set of friends. I guess she didn't get enough after the last time. How can you sleep at night knowing you are responsible for getting your friends killed?

"Where your son at? Shouldn't you have eyes on him at all times?" Ja asked her.

"Yeah I should because of your murdering ass, but see, he somewhere that you can't get to pussy," Trina said.

"Bitch, get beat up. You not about to keep trying *my* husband, hoe,"

I said as she looked taken aback by my words. *Don't let these hoes play you pussy*, I heard Ashanti's voice go through my head.

"Hoes sholl grow balls when they feel like it's somebody around to help them fight. Well, in Ja's case, pull the trigger. That's the only thing he knows how to do."

"He was around last time, and you still got beat the fuck up, so what's your point?" I asked her. I was sick of her and everybody else trying to push me around. I wasn't having it anymore.

"Bitch, them weak ass punches you got in. I bet you won't try that shit now," Trina said, getting loud.

"Ohh, this the hoe y'all had to beat up in Walmart parking lot?" her friend asked.

"Yeah, Rachel, that's her ugly ass," Trina said.

"Now, girl, you know damn well I'm not ugly. You just want me to be. Just like a weak hoe, always coming with a crowd. I go everywhere around the city unbothered, bitch," I said

"Man stop addressing this hoe. You funny as fuck, son. You want me to pop off or say something with that wire you wearing so the laws can burst in on a nigga again, huh?" Ja asked laughing.

"I'ma hoe now, but I wasn't a hoe when you wanted some ass."

"Umm, yes, you were, sweetie, because that's all you received was a wet ass," I said.

"Let's not act like you received that ring because he loves you. Yeah, I know all about the real, sis," Trina said, laughing slapping high five with her friends.

"Bitch, keep showing out in front of these weak ass hoes and watch how a nigga show his ass up in here. Don't make me embarrass you, Trina. Gon' head, bruh. This your last warning," Ja said with annoyance in his voice. From the tone of his voice, I knew it was the calm before the storm.

"Uh uh, nigga. You not about to be talking to her like that. Don't be showing out in front of no bitch because we'll beat you and that bitch up," the dark-skinned girl with them said.

"You better put that bitch ass on a leash, making all the idle threats. Let her ass know I'm with all that dumb shit. I won't ever hit a female, but I'll beat a bitch up real quick. My girl pregnant, so I'll never let her fight, but keep talking shit, and I'll call some bitches up here to hop on your ass," Ja said.

"Nigga, I ain't never been scared of nan bitch, and you already know this, baby, so call whoever the fuck you want up here. I want all the smoke, bitch. You know what's up with me, baby!" Trina yelled, clapping her hands loudly and rolling her neck.

"And ain't nobody gone touch her, and I put that on me, baby," Rachel said.

"Right," the dark-skinned one said. Right then, Camille came skipping back over to us, oblivious of everything going on around her.

"See, I went all by myself, GiGi," she said.

"Damn, this nigga went across the border and grabbed a whole family of illegal muthafuckas. When the hell Trump gone build this wall?" Trina asked, laughing.

"Oh, now you crossed the damn line, bitch!" I yelled dropping my bag trying to charge her as sales associates headed out way. Ja grabbing me around the waist and whispered be cool in my ear as I reached out and grabbed Camille's hand.

"Hey, I'm Camille," she said. She was such a happy, friendly child, but she didn't understand the world wasn't always nice in return.

"D-o y-o-u s-p-e-a-k e-n-g-l-i-s-h?" Rachel said, smirking.

"You funny as fuck, girl," the dark one said.

"This bitch must be dying of a sickness or some shit. This some 'just ten cents a day' type program," Trina said.

"Bitch, you stupid. That only applies to Africans, not Mexicans," Rachel said.

"The only thing that's just ten cents a day is that dead ass, deceased ass pussy," Ja said, wiping the smile off of her face as he turned to the sales associate who had just walked up.

"Bag all that shit up, and I'll be back to get it when y'all see these broke ass, cotton-pickin' field niggas out," he said, pulling me and a very confused Camille toward the door.

"Don't fucking try to keep playing me, Jakeem Carter, because every chance you got, you was calling begging me to suck your little dick wet, so don't flex on me for this ugly ass bitch. You already how I get down," Trina said.

"I see how you get down, hoe, and I'm not impressed you rat-face ass, snitch ass bitch. You talking about me, but you only talking that hoe shit because you know those police somewhere lurking around. You dusty-foot ass bitch, don't you ever fucking come for my sister!" I yelled trying to break free as Ja had a death grip on my arm. Hearing Millie cry paused my struggle to get loose.

"I'll slap all three of you hoes, bruh, and that's on my momma. Confidential snitch ass bitch. Aye, everybody, this hoe wearing a camera and fucking with the ops!" Ja said, pointing at her as people scattered like Moses parting the Red Sea. Nobody wanted to be near a snitch.

"Y'all better gon' head. Trina, why you tryna show out in front of these weak ass hoes? How about you tell them that every time I wanted to get my dick wet, I texted your ass off a burner phone, and you had to catch a taxi, bus, or get dropped off to a run-down ass motel. I wouldn't even fuck your ass in a two-star ass place. You wasn't worth that much. Must I go on?" he asked her as she looked like her feelings were genuinely hurt.

I didn't feel bad for her dumb ass though because no matter how many times he embarrassed her, she continued to poke the bear, and she would eventually bite off more than she could chew.

* * *

"You should have slapped the fuck out of him, not them hoes," Momma Jackie said to me. We were currently in Momma Bee's, and I was telling her about what happened at the store yesterday.

"Why would I have slapped Ja? They started with us first, and you know Trina jumped me," I said as I took a bite of my wings.

"Because from the beginning, he was supposed to have had them hoes in check to the point where they wouldn't approach you at all. Listen, I know Maxx used to cheat on me in the past; hell, maybe the present too." She revealed to me, which was news to me because I couldn't see Pops cheating on her. The love they had for one another after all these years was what I aspired to have in my own relationship.

"I can't even see him doing that," I said.

"Yeah, he did. He just think I didn't know about it, but chile, you can't pull shit over on me because I'm an old-school investigator. Anyway, in all the years we've been together, not once have one of them hoes gotten out of line with us. A few, I saw around town while I was with him. Hell, one does my nails, and one served us food one time.

"The point is, none of them hoes even remotely got out of line with us. They did their job and kept their heads down because they know if they even breathe my way, he'll body their asses. Shit, I think he tells them bitches up front if y'all tell Jackie, y'all dead. Hell, he knows either he gone kill them bitches, or I will, but they not living. Besides, his ass knows if he don't kill them, he gone catch a bullet as well," she said, dropping some knowledge on me.

"So what exactly should I do about Trina? Make Ja get rid of her?"

"Hell no, and don't tell him no shit like that because he crazy enough to do it. With her turned snitch, the number-one suspect would be him."

"So I just let her make our lives a living hell?" I asked.

"I never said that. It's time for Mrs. Carter to earn her stripes and title. You think I became Jackie Carter because I cried or worried Maxx about each time I had an issue?"

"Earn my stripes how? We already fought," I said.

"Yeah, and your first mistake was letting her live to tell the story," she said as Camille came back from the bathroom washing her hands.

"No, GiGi, these are for me," Camille had the audacity to say because I had started eating one of the rolls off of her plate.

"Your GiGi needs to eat for the baby," Momma Jackie said. Ever since we told her that I was pregnant, she had been hell-bent on feeding me any and everything in sight.

"Glam-ma, will the baby be my little sister since GiGi is my big sister?" Camille asked her.

I shook my head each time I hear her call her Glam-ma. She had told Camille when she first met her to call her Glam-ma instead of grandma. Thinking over Camille's question, I didn't know how to explain to her that this would be her niece and not her little sister. This was not my area of expertise, and I realized it was a lot of things I would be struggling to explain to her that I just wasn't prepared nor ready for.

How am I expected to raise a baby, if I couldn't even answer simple parenting questions? I thought to myself panicking.

"Yes, she will be," Momma Jackie spoke up winking at me.

"Camille, I have a very important job for you. Do you think you can handle it?" she asked her.

Camille quickly nodded her head up and down.

"I need somebody to help cook in the back. You think you can go assist Jessica in the kitchen?"

"Yess!" Camille said, jumping down and running back in the direction she had just come from.

As soon as she was gone, Momma Jackie spoke up, "Chile, you won't have all of the answers today, but don't stress it. You will make a good mother," she said as if reading my mind. Since I met her, she has always been like a mother to me.

"I don't know if I can do this. All of this is to much—" I started until she cut me off.

"Uh uh, baby. You know I don't do that weak shit. You better stop that shit right now. With everything my son has on his plate, he don't need to be worrying about you and your state of mind either. You gotta tighten up and play your part. A wife is her husband's backbone in these streets. He can't function out here properly if he think something is wrong with you.

"You know with shit getting hot the way it is, Ja will be out here tearing shit up. He don't need to be off his square. One thing I won't do is bury my fucking son. I'll shut this whole fucking city down and turn this bitch into a ghost town before that happens," she said, flipping her hair so effortlessly.

Something told me she was no stranger to shooting someone.

"This baby has me so emotional, then with everything's that's happened, including with my mother, it's just so much," I said.

"What mother? Chile, please that's a mammy because the bitch most definitely wasn't a mother. Ja better find her before I do because I'm stomping a hole in her ass if I ever see her. I hate an ain't-shit bitch. Girl, she got my blood pressure up. Let me to check on my food before Jessica burn my shit. You know she can halfway cook."

"Why do you still let her cook then?" I asked, laughing because Jessica really could not cook.

"You left. Stacy left. Shit, Jessica the only one I can deal with. You know I'll be done bat one of these hoes in they mouth, especially how they be looking at my husband," she said.

This lady was a trip, but Pops was one handsome, old man.

"I got Camille tonight, get some rest," she said like she was helping me out. Really, in such a short amount of time, she had grown attached to Camille and loved her like she were her own grandchild.

"Aight now. Don't you and Pops get to spoiling her," I said.

"You need to be talking to him not me. You need to see the room full of toys he went out and got her," she said, and I just shook my head as I went back to eating my food trying to finish so I could have Roy, the bodyguard I can't go anywhere without now, to take me by the grocery store.

This would be the first time me and Ja would be alone in the house in a while, and I wanted to do something nice for him. Besides, he rarely says two words to me these days, so I want to pick his brain to see what's wrong with him and lay everything out on the table.

* * *

AT THREE MONTHS PREGNANT, I barely had a belly, so I still could get away with wearing sexy lingerie. I sprayed behind my ears and on my wrists with my current favorite perfume, Gucci Guilty for women. Ever since I smelled it it on Ja and fell in love with it, he had went out and bought me the female version of it.. After giving myself the once-over in the mirror, admiring how my body fit the sexy, nude, Victoria's

Secret lace-plunge teddy. I grabbed the matching robe and walked out of the room and down the stairs to the kitchen to take everything out of the oven, and set the table.

Even though I had eaten all of that food earlier, my stomach still growled as I got a whiff of the garlic potatoes and pork chops. Setting everything up, I lit a few candles and grabbed a Heineken out of the refrigerator for Jakeem. Hearing the door open as I was grabbing plates out of the cabinet, I smiled widely as tingles went through my body. I was so excited to be preparing this meal for Ja and spending a little one-on-one time with him.

Lord knows I missed my husband and needed these stolen moments more than he would fully understand.

"It's smelling good as fuck in here, baby," he said, walking into the kitchen removing his shoes as he kissed me on the cheek.

I was hoping for a better kiss because he's been giving me forehead or cheek kisses these last few days. I needed a real kiss, a real tongue, and real emotions. Walking off, he headed to shower and changed as I began fixing our plates and whipping up some Glory Foods Greens in a can. Miss Mary turned me onto these greens from a can, and they are super good, and it only takes just a few moments to warm up since you don't have to cook them.

By the time the greens were finished and plated, Ja was walking by down the stairs wearing basketball shorts, looking good enough to eat. Walking up and placing my arms around his sexy body, it was my intention to get a real kiss, but he took my arms and moved them as he side stepped me, sat down, and dove into his food. My feelings were kind of hurt by his actions, but I held it in as I also sat down as picked up my fork.

After about five minutes of silence, I decided to speak up.

"We said we would always lay everything out on the table and not jump to conclusions anymore. So what's your problem with me? You've been giving me the cold shoulder for days, and it's really stressing me and your baby out," I said emotionally as I dropped my fork, feeling the tears coming.

I hated being pregnant because I was already an emotional person, but now I cried at the drop of a dime, and it honestly annoyed the hell out of me.

"Well, stop stressing my damn child out because we good," he said.

"You don't act like it. You don't treat me like it either. You won't even touch me," I said, getting up and walking off headed back to our room.

Here I was all dressed up in this sexy outfit with my hair and makeup done, and not once has he mentioned it. Throwing myself on the bed all dramatically, I just laid there until I heard Ja come into the room.

"Take that shit off," he said.

Sitting up, I asked, "What?"

"You said I haven't touched you, so that must mean you want some dick. Take that shit off," he said again.

"I don't want it like that! You telling me to take my clothes off! I want to know what's your problem with me!" I yelled.

Looking at me, he smirked and said, "I didn't want to get into this. I was just going to let the shit go, but fuck it let's do it," he said walking over to his phone, unlocking it.

Finding what he was looking for, he said, "Explain this picture to me," he said, thrusting his phone in my face.

Taking the phone, the color drained from my face as I came face-to-face with a picture I had prayed I would never see.

"I-I-I can explain," I stuttered.

"Shit ain't that what the fuck I just asked your ass to do?" Ja said.

"It's-I—" I said, lost for words on where to begin.

"Just tell me the person who said they was a virgin when we fucked, wasn't really at college sucking and fuckin?"

"No, I didn't willingly have sex with him! I mean, I planned on it because I'd had a crush on him for four years, and though I was being forced to marry a stranger and—"

"That's the same excuse you told me. You fucked me because you thought you was marrying a stranger," he said, cutting me off.

"It's true though," I said defensively.

"So you was just gone use that logic for every nigga, huh?"

"No, only Kyle. I had no intentions on coming here that weekend, and when I did, I couldn't resist you," I said to him.

"OK, but what about ole boy? You couldn't resist him either, huh? When you suck his dick? Before or after I fucked?" he asked harshly.

"After, but in my defense, I didn't plan on ever seeing you again, and thought I would never see Kyle again either. Four years of college, and my nerves only allowed me to tutor him, and that's it. After my encounter with you, doing something I would have never done normally, that gave me confidence to talk to him in a different light than schoolwork.

"He invited me to a pre-graduation party, and I went with every intention on having sex with him. He pulled me into his friend's room, and even though it felt fishy, I still allowed everything that happened to happen. The camera flash is what ruined everything because then he tried to rape me," I said, knowing it sounded crazy but it was the truth.

"He tried to rape you? You didn't look like you were being forced to put your mouth on his dick to me," Ja said.

"I wasn't at that point, but—" I was saying until he interrupted me laughing. It wasn't a funny hearty laugh but more so a sinister laugh.

"So let me get this straight, you telling me you was about to fuck him, you sucked his dick, heard a camera flash and then he tried to rape you? Man, get the fuck out of here," he said, walking toward the door.

Panicking, I ran and jumped in front of him.

"No, you gone listen to me, dammit!" I screamed, not believing what happened to me was coming back to really ruin my life.

It was only so much I can take at this point. I kept taking losses, and I was fed the fuck up. I've lost my best friend and my mother. I couldn't lose Ja too.

"Gon' 'head, Giovania before I hurt you. You foul as fuck, bruh. Get the fuck out my face before I forget you carrying my seed," Ja said.

"Didn't we just go through this with the bitch you fucked and who jumped on me in a parking lot, and the whole 'I put a hit on you' thing! What did we say? Didn't we agree we would talk everything out from now on out! What the fuck, Jakeem! You just gone assume some shit without talking to me? When have I ever fuckin' lied to you!" I screamed as tears ran down my face uncontrollably.

The look of disgust on his face right now caused my heart to feel as if someone had stabbed me repeatedly.

"That was before you failed to mention you tried to give my pussy away and was about to fuck another nigga. If you didn't know somebody was taking a picture, you would have sucked his dick and let him beat my pussy up, huh?" he asked, instantly shutting me up because I really would have fucked him had it not been for that.

"Yeah, cat got your tongue now. Watch out, bruh," he said again, trying to go around me. Still, I wouldn't move.

"No, you gone stay here. Yes, I would have, but I fucking didn't! Did you miss the part where I said he tried to fucking rape me? He punched me like a whole guy when I resisted him and slapped me a few times. I had to fight my way up out of that room and run home naked. Naked, Ja, because he ripped my dress.

"Then to add insult to injury, he lied on me and told the entire school I ran out of his room crying because he fucked me and told me he didn't like me like that! You don't know how that shit hurts or feels, so don't sit up in my face, mad about some shit I almost did with a nigga when bitches probably hopped on your dick the very next day after you fucked me!" I screamed as I hauled off and slapped the shit out of him for making me feel bad for some shit that happened to me. My hands had barely touched his face before he quickly reached out and grabbed me by my neck.

"You done lost your damn mind, bruh," he said, getting that dangerous look in his eyes—the one he gets before shit about to get real.

I should have been alarmed when he choked me, but being that it's been a few days since we had sex and this baby had me literally craving sex all day every day, the feeling of him squeezing my neck instantly caused my juices to flow as my breathing became erratic, and my eyes rolled into the back of my head.

Seeing my reaction to his anger, caused him to choke me harder as a moan escaped my lips.

"Ahh," I moaned, trying to focus on him, but losing the battle as the harder he choked me, the wetter I became. It felt like I was having an out-of-body experience, and I knew any moment now, I would explode.

"Yo' freaky ass is turned on by this shit. You tore up, bruh," he said, smirking as he dropped his shorts and roughly slammed me against the wall.

Shit, even that turned me on. I don't know what the hell has gotten into me, but the more he was rough with me, the more I enjoyed the shit—welcoming the pain and anger. With his hands still wrapped about my throat, he positioned himself at my opening, and roughly pushed inside of me, causing me to gasp.

"Fawwk! This pussy so fucking good," Ja said as he leaned up and latched his mouth onto my neck removing his hand as he sucked passionately on my neck, moving to my collarbone before locking down to my nipple, sucking on it as he kept pumping into me.

"You gone do that shit again?" he asked me, taking my leg and placing it on his shoulder allowing for a deeper penetration.

"Oh God, baby, nooo!" I screamed.

Whereas a few seconds ago I welcomed all the pain, that move caused him to damn near touch my spine, and I quickly realized these were not the problems I wanted. Scooting up the wall, I didn't get far as he pulled me back down onto that monster he called a penis.

"Naw, don't run now. Take all of this dick. What was the shit you was just saying?" he asked as he grabbed a hold on my leg on his shoulder and licked up and down the spots within his reach as he kept giving me stroke after stroke.

"I'm sorry, baby. I was wrong," I said with my eyes closed, lost in bliss.

I was in between telling him to stop because he was too deep and wanting him to keep going because the pain hurt so good. Without warning, he picked my other leg up sitting it on his shoulder as he pulled out of me, lifting me high as he dove face first into my happy place, causing my eyes to roll into the back of my head.

Grabbing the back of his head, I rode his face into ecstasy as I felt myself explode into his mouth. Walking with me from the wall to the bed, he tossed me down before reaching down and slapping me hard as hell on my ass.

"I'ma teach your ass to stop fucking playing with me. I don't give a fuck if we wasn't together back then or if we break up tomorrow, this my pussy forever. Since you wanna play, I'ma about to punish that ass, and you bet not tap out because I'll tie your ass up and still continue fucking the shit out of you," he growled, making my body tingle.

"Assume the fucking position, and you better make sure that arch on point," he growled at me.

This was about to be a long ass night, but technically, this is how I had planned on ending our night in the first place.

Ashanti

It had been a few hours since I talked to Yari, and I was going crazy. Last time I spoke to him, he told me the flight was delayed for a few hours but to try and get some sleep. I couldn't sleep even if I wanted to. I was going crazy in this quiet ass apartment.

Each time a car passed by, I thought it was the police coming to get me. I can't believe I killed my father and Crystal. Shit, I can't believe they were fuckin', or that my father had killed my mother and sisters! This was all too damn much for one person to take in.

Feeling another pain hit my side, I doubled over, trying to control my breathing until the pain subsided. I had been hurting since I left my father's house but refused to go to the hospital. With how bad the pain felt, and how frequent it was coming,, I was scared for my life and my child's life. But,Yari said stay put, and I wasn't moving. I've been around this life my entire life, so I know how it works. He needs to do damage control, and clean up the mess, so that meant stay where I was until he took care of things.. If I checked into a hospital, detectives would be on my ass like white on rice, and I wasn't mentally stable to face them right now.

Ring! Ring!

Hearing my cell phone ringing, I jumped up, despite the pain in my side, and ran to get it. Not bothering to check the caller ID, I slid my finger across the screen to answer it.

"Hello?" I asked as another wave of pain hit me, this time worse than the others, causing me to scream out as my knees buckled.

"Ahhh," I said, dropping down.

"Hello? Ashanti?" I heard my name being yelled over and over again, but that last pain had taken my voice box completely out. I couldn't even speak as the pain became unbearable.

A life for a life, karma had come back knocking and wanted my child for the two lives I had taken. Silent tears ran down my face as I hugged my stomach tightly wounded on the inside at the thought of living without Tariq. He was the one that was supposed to love me and never leave me, and even he was being ripped away from me like a thief in the night.

It felt like I was laying on the floor for hours when really it was only about thirty minutes or so when I heard banging on my door. My entire body felt paralyzed as all I could do was shift my eyes toward the door because of the pain I was in.

Hearing the continued knocking followed by my name being called, I fought to find my voice as I mustered up everything and yelled out, "I'm here!"

I yelled, but I think it didn't come out as loud as I wanted. Before I could pull myself up, my door was kicked in, and the person rushed through the door full force. Through half-closed eyes, I saw figures running into my house with guns drawn, and right before I passed out, I knew it was the SWAT team coming to take me away.

Beep! Beeep!

The sound of beeping woke me up as I looked around the unfamiliar room that I found myself waking up in. Raising my hand to my forehead, I noticed an IV drip as I struggled to sit up at the same time as the door to the room opened, and in walked the last person I expected to see, Lexx.

"W-What are you doing here? And how did I get here?" I asked, looking around the room, realizing although it had hospital equipment, it wasn't exactly a hospital.

"A thank you would be nice, and your ass here because after I kicked the door to your apartment down, I found you halfway passed out. I don't do police or hospitals, so I brought you to my crib. I had this part of my house converted into a hospital wing years ago. Thankfully, I haven't had to use the shit in a while," he said.

"I never told you where I stayed, so how did I get from my place to here? Damn, you didn't follow me home did you?" I asked, not needing anymore crazy shit in my life because all those positions were currently filled.

"Followed you? Shit, you fine, but you ain't all that, bruh. You left your debit card at the shop. My aunt called and told me. I was meaning to call you about it earlier, but I got caught up. Then when I called you, your ass answered, then started screaming like you was being murdered. I had my lil' podna that work in IT to track your cell phone number, and that's how I found your address." He struggled like it was normal as he sat a tray of food in front of me.

"Wait, you kicked my door in as well? You need to replace that shit today, and I'm not playing. My baby daddy will think something happened to me, and the last thing I need is for his crazy ass to go on a rampage killing people," I said as I looked down at the tray.

All logical thinking and questioning went out of the window as soon as I saw the same sandwich I was eating when I met him—roast beef and pastrami.

Grabbing the sandwich, I quickly bit into it as my eyes rolled to the back of my head. It was good as hell and had the exact toppings on it that I loved so much.

"Damn, ma. You attacked that shit," Lexx said, laughing as I tore into the sandwich. "And I'm not worried about your bitch-boy baby daddy, and I'm not about to keep repeating that. Besides, I already took care of the door. Type of nigga you take me for? I know what type of suspicion that would have created, and I don't need them problems."

"I'm not asking you to be worried about him. I'm saying regardless of what we have going on, I know how he can get, and I don't need those problems right now. And don't laugh at me, I'm hungry," I said, laughing at myself as I took another big bite of my food.

If I didn't need anything else, I most definitely needed to eat. The more bites I took, the better I began to feel. It felt as if I hadn't eaten in days, when really it's only been a couple of hours.

"He be popping up at your place or some?"

"He doesn't even live in the same state as me, so no, he doesn't pop up at my place."

"Well, how he gone see your door if he don't pop up at your spot?" he asked, looking at me like *yeah right*.

"Look, I don't even know you to be lying while you looking at me like that. He was supposed to come by or should be at my place by now. Where is my phone? I need to see if I have any missed called from him," I said, looking around.

"It's on the dresser, and it hasn't rung, so maybe he stood you up."

"Naw, he wouldn't, not with this. This is important. Last time I spoke with him, his flight had gotten delayed, but he was on his way. He has to come," I said, sensing my emotions getting the best of me.

There was silence in the room for a few minutes until Lexx spoke up.

"So you gone tell me why you was passed out on the floor? Why didn't you call an ambulance?" he asked me.

"You just said you don't like hospitals, so how you gone get mad at the fact I didn't go?"

"I said me. That ain't had shit to do with you. You pregnant and live alone. You should have went. Your blood pressure was crazy high, and you were dehydrated. You also had Braxton's Hicks," he said, reading off a clipboard. "That was reckless and stupid of you."

"Well, damn, tell me how you really feel," I said.

"All bullshit aside, talk to me, ma. What made your shit shoot up like that? I know you ain't stressing yourself out about that fuck nigga not showing up like he said."

Rolling my eyes, I said, "Damn, for the last time, this has nothing to do with Yari. Geez, he is coming, but as far as future tense goes, I'm done caring about him and his new bitch. Me and Tariq are better than good," I said, rubbing my belly.

"Ain't that right, momma's big boy? You scared momma for a second. I thought they tried to take you away from me. My mistakes will never affect you, I promise," I said, forgetting for a second Lexx was even in the room with me.

Looking up, I noticed him staring at me intensively before asking, "Who tried to take him away from you?"

Putting my head down, my hands clammed up as the machine started going crazy. Just thinking about what I did made my blood pressure shoot back up.

"Doc!" Lexx yelled, going and banging on another door in the room that I had just noticed.

Less than a few seconds later, a white doctor rushed out of the room and over to my bed.

"Listen to me, I'm going to need you to calm down. It's not good for your son. You hurting your baby," the doctor said to me as Lexx stood before me looking genuinely concerned.

"What's got your blood pressure up? Who tried to take Tariq?" Lexx repeated.

"I-I—" I said.

"If it ain't the fuck nigga, who it is, Ashanti? I ain't about to ask you again," he said in a stern yet authoritative tone. He seemed like he was really concerned, but I was nervous as to how he would view me once I confessed.

"I can't tell you," I said.

"Why not?" he asked me before looking at the doctor telling him to leave out.

Once the door closed behind him, he kicked his shoes off and climbed onto the bed with me before saying, "Ashanti, you can't tell me shit I ain't already heard, seen, or been through before. You not leaving this room until you talk, and my schedule is cleared for the day, so I ain't got shit but time," he said.

Realizing he was serious, I took a deep breath and begin telling him about Giovania. How I thought she was a bad friend to me, but she really was my best friend in the whole wide world, and I had lost her forever. I told him about how I didn't give it a second thought when she left, and I found her phone. How I assumed she went home, but I didn't care one way or the other, and if I'm honest with myself, I knew something seemed suspicious because only some of her clothes were gone, not all. How I loved Yari, but I played so many games with him, but he wasn't up my ass like everybody else was and didn't care about my father's status in the streets like other niggas. Finally, I got to my father, and I told him about how he has the root of all my problems, and the reason my blood pressure sky high.

"What he do? Was he touching you or something?"

"Hell no!" I yelled, cutting my eyes at him.

Throwing his hands up, he said, "I had to ask. Well, shit, how he the root?"

"Just listen, Lexx, damn," I said before I started back talking.

"My father not only was responsible for kidnapping Giovania, but he was also sleeping with my friend, Crystal. On top of that, I found out he killed my mother and sisters," I choked out.

Regardless of the relationship I had with my mother and sisters, they were my family, and everyone at one point in life doesn't like their family. That doesn't mean I wished death on them though.

"That's fucked up. Is your home girl alright? And how you know he killed your family? Those some serious accusations. You need to be certain about that first before you step to him. Who is dude?"

"Big John," I said as I watched his jaw clench. "What? You know him?"

"Know him? I got beef with that fool, and no offense baby girl, but take it however you want. I like you and wouldn't mind seeing where this could lead, but I got a few bullets with his name on it, and he gotta see me as soon I catch up to his bitch ass. I actually left you yesterday because I got word from my peoples that they spotted him, but he slipped away," he said calmly, not cracking a smile.

"Well, you don't have to worry about him anymore, and those not accusations. I heard him yesterday out of his own mouth saying he killed my mother and sisters. He was arguing about it with Crystal, my own damn friend, and before I knew it, the gun was in my hands, and I-I shot both of them repeatedly until there were no more bullets left!" I cried as fresh tears fell down my face. I was happy to have gotten that off my chest but scared about the fact that I had gotten that off my chest.

"Damn," was all he said at first until he reached out and pulled me into his arms.

"Calm down, baby girl, all of that crying isn't good for lil' man. Listen, I know killing your pops and his side bitch, who happened to be your homegirl, wasn't easy for you, especially you finding out they killed your family, but it's gone be alright. I'm sorry this happened, regardless of my beef with the nigga, but I wouldn't have wanted the shit to go down like that for you to body your own pops. Damn, remind me never to piss you off. You a fool with that trigger. Let me find out you realer then a lot of these niggas," he said, trying to lighten the mood. It worked because I started to laugh.

"But listen, I know it's hard because you have to be really built Ford tough to actually take a life. Niggas talk about the shit all the time on the streets and in these rap songs, and all that shit is just what it sounds life, talking. Your mental gotta be right to play God and kill someone. I'm gone get you through this, I mean, I know I just met you, and I ain't the type to be attached to a girl, but I'm here to stay, and I got you every step of the way making sure you straight for yourself and baby boy.

"I can't offer you much now because neither of us are in a position to give the other what they need, but I can offer you something better —a friend in me. I'm the nigga you want on your side that's gone ride for life. From here on out, won't a soul bring tears to those eyes again, and I put that on my parents who I also lost a long time ago," he said with a far-off look in his eyes.

I don't know what happened to his mom and dad, but it doesn't seem to have been of natural causes. Laying my head of his chest, it wasn't my intentions to fall asleep, but as soon as he begin stroking my hair, that's exactly what I did—fell straight to sleep.

Yari

Stepping off the plane in New York, I stopped and purchased a charging pack in the airport as I hooked it up and powered my phone back on. Noticing I had a few missed calls from Danielle, and a missed call and text from Ja, I decided to only answer Ja and deal with Danielle later. I knew I should have confided in her about everything that had happened and let her know I was headed to New York, but the fact of the matter was I was single and didn't have to explain shit to anybody. My baby momma needed me, and I was here, that's all that mattered, the rest was irrelevant.

"What's up, nigga? Your Captain Save a Hoe ass good?" Ja asked me as soon as he answered the phone.

"Fuck you, bitch. Save these nuts," I said, laughing. "But yeah, I'm straight. My damn plane had a damn near six-hour layover, and my phone was dead, and it wasn't no damn where to charge my shit at in my terminal," I said. "I just got your text, you good man?"

"Yeah, I'm straight. Them niggas ain't have shit on me, and they knew it, but check this out. You know how momma cook been missing in action? Come to find out, we saw her ass working with our competition store across town," he said, speaking in code letting me know they found Trina, and she working with the police.

"Word? They must be paying her more over there," I said.

"Shit, I don't know, but I think her ass violating and telling all of our cooking recipes in specific word-for-word detail that's been in the family for years," he said, letting me know the bitch was violating in the worst way running her mouth.

I wasn't too worried about her saying anything about me because I been switched shit up, but you never really know what all she said or what evidence she got. From here on out, we gotta move carefully, but that rat ass hoe not stopping my money. Business been booming since we became the plug.

"Damn she doing it like that bruh? Oh, hell naw! She gotta be sued. That's in direct violation of the code of ethics," I replied.

"Right, that's the same shit I told Ma Dukes to do. You know how she be stressing about the small shit, stressing pops out and shit," he said.

"Bet. Well, I won't be out this way too long. After I check and make sure baby momma straight, I'm more than likely bringing her back to New Orleans with me until she have my son. It's too dangerous for her to be living alone and so far along. Anything to can happen to her."

"You digging your own grave, my nigga, bringing her back, knowing the shit you and D got going on; and shit, Giovania and Shanti ain't exactly on the best of terms right now."

"What me and Danielle got going on will never effect my kid, and sis and Shanti ain't gotta work it out, but my child gone be with me. On the plane, I was thinking long and hard, and I think I'ma give my family a shot. Shit, nigga never had that growing up," I said.

"My nigga, if that's what you wanna do, handle your business, but when that shit blow up in your face, yo' ass better not find your way to my couch," he said.

"Why would I be on your couch when I got a room?"

"Had a room—baby took that," he said.

"Shit it's three extra rooms in your house nigga."

"Yeah, and my wife is turning one into a playroom and one into my son's room," he said, still believing he was having a son.

Shit, I hope he did so we both can groom our juniors to be a beast in these streets just like us. A bunch of hard hittas.

"OK, nigga, that leaves one room, my shit."

"Naw, baby girl got that one."

"Who?"

"Giovania's baby sister," he said.

"Damn, nigga. You got a house full and shit, but I don't appreciate their asses taking my shit," I said laughing. "But check it, I'ma run it with you later on. I need to gone head out to Shanti crib. She texted me the address yesterday, so I ain't gone bother waking her ass up," I said, ending my call with him.

After I ordered an Uber, I went got some food while I thought about how I would get rid of the bodies and clean up the house so that no evidence that Shanti was ever there existed. It's crazy how a couple days ago I didn't give a fuck about her, but now here I was thinking of making plans to bring her back to New Orleans.

I found between a rock and a hard place. I think I loved Danielle, and I wanted to see where this could go, but at the same time, shit like this that happened with Shanti would never have happened if she were with me. Besides, I'm sure that's what Shanti ass wanted anyway. To have a nigga all to herself.

Hopping into the Uber, I headed to Ashanti's house first, and from there, I would have her show me where the bodies were after a nigga caught a quick nap. I was tired as hell. I really needed to invest in me a private plane like Ja's because the seats, even in first class, still were not comfortable at all.

About an hour later, we pulled up in front of Ashanti's apartment, and I got out and headed up the stairs to her place. Knocking on the door a few times with no answer, on a whim, I twisted the lock and the door came open.

"This damn girl gone make me hurt her ass. Got the door open and shit," I mumbled as I walked inside the small but nicely-decorated apartment.

"Damn you should have kept your damn condo. This place small as fuck!" I yelled out, dropping my bag in the living as I walked in search of her.

I mean, the apartment was every bit of about 900 square feet, so it wasn't far I had to walk to find her. When I didn't see her anywhere in the apartment, I figured she had stepped out for a second, and had left the door open for me.

Making sure the door was locked, i walked into her room and grabbed a pillow off of her bed before I reached into my Gucci carry-on bag and grabbed the black briefcase I had placed in there. Walking back into the living room. I opened the case revealing my gun that I had taken apart so that it wouldn't be detected. It was no way I was traveling to another state naked as fuck. Quickly and skillfully putting it together, something Maxx had taught me and Ja to do, I made sure it was assembled properly before I placed it under the pillow then laid down to catch me a much-needed nap.

When she got back, I would get on her ass about leaving the door open; she could have waited on me. She needs to know she can't try that shit in New Orleans, no matter what part of town you in. You leaving your door unlocked is just saying "Yeah, nigga, you can run up in my shit. It's cool my dude take whatever you like."

Like I don't know what she used to in New York, but she gone have to tighten the fuck up in the boot because them a whole different breed of niggas.

* * *

IN THE LINE of work I was in, being a hard sleeper could very well cost you your life of a nigga caught you slipping, so when I heard voices walking into the house, my hand went to my gun quick as hell as I had it cocked and ready to let loose in a matter of minutes.

As my eyes adjusted to the darkness and people standing in front of me, I noticed Shanti standing there with some fuck nigga, who had also pulled his shit out.

"Yari!" she yelled out through the darkness. To be raised around this life, she wasn't the brightest apple on the bunch.

"Yeah," I said as I heard movement, followed by a light being switched on, giving me a clearer view of the nigga in front of me who moved to stand protectively in front of my baby momma, never taking his eyes nor his gun off of me.

Shit, he was acting like that was his bitch, and I was an intruder or some shit. When her hands went to her stomach and one of his hands reached out and rubbed her belly as well but still didn't take his gun or eyes off me, I lost it.

"Who the fuck is this, Ashanti? This the shit you on when you knew I was coming up here? This why I don't fuck with your hoe ass," I said angrily.

"Hold up, playboy. Don't be talking to her like that. What the fuck wrong with you? I don't know what the fuck you used to do, but that shit ain't flying this way no more. It's a new sheriff in town, and he ain't taking no bullshit," he said.

"Check this out, playboy. Nigga don't give a fuck about all that hot shit you poppin', ya dig? I said what the fuck I said, and that's what it's gone be," I said, looking him up and down with a scowl on my face.

"Ole bitch ass nigga, I don't know what fuck niggas you used to, but I ain't the fucking one. I'll put this gun down and beat you bitch ass up. Hoe ass nigga," he said.

Quickly tucking my gun in the back of my pants, I pulled my jeans up and hauled up and caught his ass with a clean left hook before we both started fucking each other up. I can admit, I was much bigger than him, so I expected him to go down after that first lick, but the nigga surprised me when he came back with a punch of his own.

"Stop it Yari! Lexx!" I heard Shanti yelling, but I wasn't stopping shit. That nigga just tried to hoe me, talking about he'll beat my ass. Nigga musta thought I was a soft ass nigga or some shit, and that's why he made that off-the-wall comment. Nigga like me been coming from the shoulders. Fuck he thought this was.

"Ole bitch ass nigga," I said, stepping back and catching him with a nice ass two-piece combo. He stumbled back, shook the shit off, and came back with a lick of his own that damn near paused my ass.

"Fuck you, nigga I ain't never been pussy," he said, still hanging in there with my ass. I was tired as hell because we was going lick for lick in this bitch, but I refused to stop fighting. A nigga gon' have to give me about my respect. Like Gates said, *I'ma die about that shit.*

"Stop! Stop! Stop!" Shanti again yelled as she walked over to us trying to pull us apart at the same time as she hit both of our asses.

I made a mental note to fuck her ass up as well when I was done. Wasn't nobody exempt at this point. I don't know how it happened, but in the midst of us fighting, somehow Ashanti was pushed down to the ground.

"Ahhh!" she cried out as she doubled over in pain.

That instantly paused both of us as we each looked at her on the ground and ran to her. He reached her first, but I pushed his ass out of the way as I bent down and picked her up bridal style, like her big ass weighed five pounds, and sat her down on the couch.

"Put me down!" she yelled, kicking her legs as I placed her on the couch.

"Shawty, you good?" the nigga she had called Lexx asked her.

"No, I'm not good. Both of y'all selfish asses in here fucking my shit up like this is about either of you when my ass the one pregnant, stressed, and possibly going to jail. I'ma have my baby in jail and have to fight a big bitch named Baby Dee every night so she won't try and take the pussy," she said as I burst out laughing. His ass tried to hold his shit in, but after a few seconds, he started laughing as well.

"I don't find shit funny," she said, rolling her eyes.

"My clean-up crew already handled that, baby girl, so you won't be in jail fighting no bitch named Baby Dee in this lifetime, so quit letting that shit stress you. You be done fucked around and snitched on your damn self. Real talk, you gotta tighten up, because sooner or later, them boys gone come looking for you asking questions. You gotta be prepared to answer and on your square," he said.

I didn't like this nigga, but what he was spitting was all facts. Her ass needed to tighten up or else she would be in jail.

"Oh you handled that issue?" I asked him with a smirk.

"Naw. A boss doesn't do a worker's job, but my crew took care of it," he said.

"I wouldn't know shit about being a worker. Shanti should have told you that shit since y'all seem comfortable enough to share everything else," I said, referring to her telling dude about the bodies.

This the shit I'm talking about. I told her simple ass to sit put, don't leave out the house, and don't tell nobody shit. She can't even follow simple directions. I was already regretting my decision to try and make it work with her childish ass. She wasn't ready for these adult problems I came with. Bitch a have a nigga doing life quick as fuck how she moved.

"Naw she ain't mention you. I told her don't talk about fuck boys to me," he said.

"Make me beat yo' ass again," I said.

"Again? My nigga you ain't beat my ass the first time. Yeah you bigger than me, but you felt them bitches connecting," his cocky ass said. "And any nigga that leave their pregnant girlfriend alone is real bitch made. I had to break this door down to get to her, and she was passed out on the floor, damn near unconscious. Blood pressure was too high, and she was dehydrated. No matter what beef y'all got going on, she was posed to be in your care at all times until she dropped ya seed. So naw, I can't respect that hoe ass shit," he said looking at me like he really wanted to charge my ass again.

I done caught my wind now, and I was ready for round two. As soon as his ass think about swinging, I'm diving on his ass.

"You don't know me or our situation, so don't speak on me my nigga. I don't know how they do that shit up here, but niggas get bodied for less in the boot. Play them fuck games if you want, and find yaself toe tagged and body bagged."

"Is that a threat?" he asked me.

"Naw them facts playboy," I said, making a gun with my fingers.

Smirking, he said, "That's cute. You obviously don't know who the fuck I am, and that's why you throwing out them idle threats. I'd watch that if I were you Yari," he said my name like he knew exactly who the fuck I was. Not wasting anytime, I pulled my gun at the same time as he pulled his.

"Both of y'all stop it, and one of y'all idiots take me to a hospital.

Clearly, I fell on the fucking ground, and my side is killing me," Ashanti said.

"You know how I feel about hospitals so I'm out.Call me when you get there, and keep me informed on everything," Lexx said

"Naw, she good. She got me, so your services are no longer required," I said.

"We'll let her decide that," he said.

"You heard what the fuck—" I started until Ashanti interrupt me,

"Yari, you can't tell me who I can and cannot talk to. Don't you got a girlfriend that you told me you happy with? I ain't fucked up about it either, so if I can respect that, respect my friends. Lexx, I'll call you tomorrow," she said as he winked and walked off.

I had told her a while ago that Danielle was my girlfriend when she had called me one time going off and Danielle had answered the phone since I had damn near moved in with her.

"I know what the fuck I said. What that got to do with that nigga?" I asked.

"Everything. You don't want me, and that's fine, but step your blocking ass out my way so the next nigga can catch this glow," she said, rolling her eyes at me, looking cute as hell in her T-shirt dress she had on.

"Roll them again." I smiled as I bent down and kissed her on the forehead. "And you taking this shit off before we go to the hospital. I don't care how much pain you in, that dress showing entirely too much ass, and I'd hate to have to give them doctors what I just gave your little boyfriend," I said, slapping her on her exposed thigh.

"Let me find out you're jealous," she said.

"Naw, I ain't jealous of shit that's mine already," I said.

"Boy, bye," she said, rolling her eyes.

"Roll them bitches again. I'll pop them hoes out and have them staring back at you," I said.

"You make me sick, Yari. Help me up so we can go because my fat ass is not changing, and I really am in pain," she said.

"Where yo' truck keys at?"

"Why?" she asked with attitude.

"Man dead that fucking attitude, you know a nigga ain't drive my car here, so yo' ass either want me to drive you or not," I said.

"They in my purse on the counter," she said.

Walking over to the counter, I grabbed her purse and brought it to her.

"What you giving me this for?"

"So you can get the damn keys, bruh," I said.

"Really, Yari? You couldn't reach in there and grab the keys?"

"Hell naw. Now hurry the fuck up."

"Rude ass, stupid ass nigga," she mumbled.

"Dick good though," I said as a smile she tried real hard to stop spread across her face.

"Whatever. It's barely that," she said.

"Aight, don't fucking play them type of games with me if you really in pain as you say cuz I'll snatch them panties off you and beat that lil' pussy out the frame," I said, looking at her lustfully.

I've always heard it's something about pregnant pussy that will make a grown man cry it's so good. And pregnancy looked good as hell on her. Even though her eyes looked so sad, my son had her glowing and growing. Her breasts were damn near spilling over the top of the dress she had on, them juicy ass thighs made me want to put my face between them, and I just know it tasted like water.

"Don't play yourself. You could never touch me again," she said, rolling her eyes.

"Bet," I said, taking the keys out of her hands as I once again lifted her up like she weighed five pounds, carrying her out to the car. Popping the locks, I opened the door, placing her into her backseat as I hopped in the front, pushing the car to start and setting the GPS to the hospital she gave me in my phone as I took off down the street headed that way.

* * *

"WELP, mommy, we ran a few test on you, and so far everything came back fine. The fall you took more than likely just upset little man, and that's why you felt discomfort. He more than likely shifted around a bit. You both are fine though. I'm waiting on your bloodwork to come back, and if everything is OK, you'll be good to get on out of here," the doctor said to us before checking the machines that Ashanti was hooked up to again before leaving out of the room.

"Now can you stop stressing my baby out because y'all both good?" I asked her.

She didn't respond to me, but instead turned her head the opposite way and got comfortable on the bed with her eyes closed. Climbing onto the bed with her, she didn't protest as I pulled the blanket down until it revealed her stomach and laid my head on her belly.

Rubbing her stomach, I kissed it a few times before I slid my hands lower until I found what I was looking for. She pretended she didn't know what I was doing until my fingers touched that pussy, then she wanted to place her hand on top of mine trying to pause my movements. It was too late by then though. Once I felt how tight she was letting me know nobody had been inside of my pussy, I refused to stop.

"No, Yari," she moaned.

"Shhhh," I said to her, inserting another finger as she arched her back into my fingers.

That fuck nigga might have her attention right now, but he'll never have her like I got her. I got her heart, and got the power to do this, so I'm not fucked up off that conversation he be getting. It's just the principle of how he tried to play me. Fuck nigga. Jealous that my fingers were having all of the fun, I removed my fingers, as I just blow on her sweet spot for a few seconds before placing my entire mouth over her.

"Fuckkk, Yari... OMG, no... we... can't... no," she moaned louder than before.

"Shit, we can if you quiet down before the nurses come in here thinking something wrong. You stressed out, so let me make you feel better. I know you wanna feel better. Let me do this," I said to her, licking on the outside of those pretty lips, yet never taking my eyes off of her.

I watched the will to fight or give in to me play out in her eyes. When she finally nodded her head yes, I dove back in like I was a professional deep-sea diver. I know what I was doing right now was wrong, considering I did like Danielle—hell, loved Danielle—but I couldn't help the feelings that came rushing to me the moment I heard Shanti on the phone in that panicked voice.

Was it possible to move two different women at the same time and not hurt either one of them?

Jakeem "Ja" Carter

"So I subpoenaed the body cams off the arresting officers, and they have been placed on administrative leave, pending a thorough investigation. Seeing as though you never resisted, nor were you read your Miranda Rights, I expect the charges to be dropped on that case. However, the prosecution is moving forward with charges against you, Yari, and Maxx Carter for drug trafficking, distribution, prostitution, and a slew of other charges. I hate to say this, and I'm sure they have no solid evidence, or they would have picked you up by now, but the deciding factor will ultimately be Ms. Hill's testimony, who I know I specifically told you to stay away from," Stan said.

"My nigga, I tell you what to do. You don't tell me shit, and don't you forget it. Don't piss me off, Stan. I'm trying to have a good day," I told him with my penny loafers resting across my left leg as I sat back in my seat like a boss.

"I'm not telling you what to do like a damn worker. I'm telling you what to do as your lawyer," he said.

"How you expect for me to stay away from a bitch that pops up wherever I am hell-bent on causing a scene?" I asked him, because not only did she pop up at the mall, but she also popped up on me on the block, and it took everything in me not to choke the hoe to death. What I can't understand is how the fuck did Stan know this.

"How you know she been around me?" I asked him, giving him the side eye.

"The day of your mall incident, I got a call from Detective Morris, informing me that my client was slowly sinking himself further and further into a hole. He said you verbally threatened her in a room full of people," he said.

"I didn't threaten the hoe. I told that bitch facts. It's a difference," I said.

"Facts, threatened, they are all the same when dealing with a situation as sensitive as this one."

"Man hold all of that noise. I don't give a fuck what that hoe testify to. The fact of the matter is I ain't never said shit incriminating in front of the before, during, or after she was swallowing all of a nigga's kids. I'll holla at my niggas, but I don't think they that dumb either. You keep saying this whole case depends on her testimony but won't let me kill the hoe. What type of shit is that?" I asked.

"No you can't kill her, but you can hit her where it hurts. What's something you know that will hurt her?"

"Her kid she think I didn't know about. She more than likely moved him by now," I said.

"Find him. You need her to say detective Morris made her lie, kill two birds with one stone. From there, I'll bring up his brother's murder, and that will destroy any credibility he ever had. Bingo!" he said.

"Fuck his credibility. I want his life."

* * *

"WHERE YO' bitch ass been hiding?" Sade asked me as I walked into the warehouse.

"Damn, you must missed a nigga, ole ugly ass lil boy." I shot back.

"Hell naw. Sage ass kept asking me about your ass and shit. I told him your ass was straight. Giovania just got you on a curfew. Yo' ass gotta be home when the street lights come on," he said.

"Bitch, don't lie on me, ole 'behind the bus' looking ass," Sage said.

"Bitch if you don't get your *Bonnie and Clyde* looking ass. Ole 'happy birthday, thank you' looking ass," Sade said.

"'You funny as fuck Bri Bri' looking ass," Sage shot back.

"Nappy neck ass bitch you fucked last night looked like 'all my life I had to fight.' Two-for-twenty tracks wearing ass. Ole 'this that wet and wavy' looking ass," Sade said.

"I know you ain't getting on girlfriends with Melinda ole *Tales from the Crypt* looking ass. Trade-looking ass, 'meeting in my bedroom' looking ass. Shorty pussy got more miles on it than a 1999 box Chevy with her expired-pussy having ass. Shorty Lo-looking ass," Sage said.

"That's not my bitch," was all Sade said.

"Since when, nigga? She broke up with your ass again? Don't start begging again like Keith Sweat and shit," I said.

"Nigga, I know you ain't talking. Giovania—" He started until Sage cut him off.

"Don't do it," Sage said, shaking his head vigorously.

"Ain't nobody scared of Ja ass. You might be scared to roast sis, but me, I'm the twin that's gone step. With her 'hurry up and bye' looking ass," Sade said.

"You think you funny, huh? *Hustle and Flow* looking ass. Little ass shirt on, that Polo screaming Sade I don't fit you, *Eight Mile* looking ass. Fake ass body builder. Bob the Builder-looking ass," I said.

"Damn, he said fake ass body builder. That shirt is too lil' though, bro. I just ain't want to be the one to tell you," Sage said.

"Fuck Ja his dreads tighter than my shirt, SpongeBob SquarePants-looking ass nigga," Sade said.

"Ahhhaaaaa! He said your shirt screaming I don't fit you. You can't shake back from that one, nigga." Sage said, doubled over laughing.

"Now let's get down to business though. Real talk, this important," I said.

"What's up?" Sade asked, putting his serious face on.

"Who body we gotta drop?" Sage asked.

That's why I loved they ass, they went from playing to serious as fuck.

"Long story short, Trina working with Detective Morris now, and she talking. She can't speak on shit on my end, but she can place y'all at traps and shit," I said.

"I don't recall saying shit incriminating in front of her, and you know we don't even make sales no more. The workers do," Sade said, looking deep in thought.

"I can't lie. I don't remember what I have or haven't said in front of her, but I did cook up at her house a few times when I needed product right then, and nobody was around to cook," Sage said.

"Fuck," Sade said, hitting his fist of the table. "My brother ain't going down for that snake ass bitch. I'll kill the entire police squad before I let that shit happen," Sade said sitting there looking like he had fucked up.

"Man," Sage said, running his hands over his face.

"We gone fix this, bro," I said to him.

This shit was fucking me up. Fucking with my family is something I don't play around with. Fuck what Stan talking about. If push comes to shove, I'll kill Trina, the prosecution, and everybody on the jury.

"How?" Sage said.

"Her son," I said.

* * *

I RUN SHIT, no effort, walk by faith, I'm careless
No weapon formed shall prosper, I'm a god, nigga, be careful
Nigga slapped you, you ain't that 'bout it
So pussy nigga, whatever

RIDING down the street listening to Kevin Gates "Luca Brasi Intro", my mind went back to them pictures of Giovania. I know what she told me, but the shit still wasn't sitting well with me, so I had sent the shit to Danielle last night. Her ass ain't got back to a nigga yet, so I was doing a pop up on that ass later on, because I needed answers, and this wasn't like her to take this long for some information.

I needed to know who the fuck was behind this shit to have my personal number. The only ones who could have did it were supposedly dead, the only person that left that could have did it was Ashanti. I pray for her sake that she ain't do no fuck shit like this, because I don't give a fuck who baby momma the hoe was, I don't tolerate disrespect from a bitch or nigga.

Playing with me is like gambling with your life, and anyway you spin it, the end results are always the same—you gone wind up six feet under. I am not the nigga to be fucked with on no damn level.

Ring! Ring!

"Hello?" I said, answering the phone for my pops.

"Come get this cock-blocking ass child from my house," he said.

"Don't do my lil' homie like that," I said.

"All ya momma wanna do is sleep with her ass in our bed and show her all the attention. That's why we only had one child. I couldn't deal with that shit. Giovania baby not allowed over here, hell, because next your momma will be asking for another baby," he said as I took the exit headed toward their house since I wasn't far from it anyway.

"Man, my T-lady don't want another a baby. You bugging. This coming from the same lady who tell everybody not to even bring their kids to her house if they not old enough to take care of themselves because Jackie Carter don't do diapers. Ma too fly to be worried with a kid. She might just be lonely and trying to tell you to spend more time with her," I said, repeating some shit I read in one of those Cosmo magazines Giovania's ass always has laying around. Knowing that shit was really rubbing off on me had me feeling gay as fuck and soft as hell.

"That shit sounded fruity as fuck. You better tighten the fuck up son. I taught you to whip pussy not to let pussy whip you. You over there sounding like a whole Lifetime movie and shit, talking about some she might be lonely and trying to tell you," he said, laughing.

"Ain't no pussy ever whip me," I said, lying through my teeth. I was whipped, sprung, and a sucker for dat pussy, but I would never verbally admit it for this very reason.

"You over there sounding like Sade's sucker-for-love ass. I told you about hanging out with his ass. He'll have you out here being faithful and acting committed and shit," he said.

"Man, gon' 'head, old man. Who the hell you think you talking to?" I asked, but truthfully, my ass had really straightened up and got my shit together because my body and heart had betrayed my ass anyway.

It don't matter how much shit I talked about Giovania, evenwhen I thought she tried to kill me, my heart still wanted her. And each time I tried to slide into something new, my mans wouldn't even get on hard. She had my heart and dick, but my mind was still my own.

Pulling up to the gate, I looked into the circle as it scanned my eyes before the gates swung open, and I drove up the winding driveway to the front. Although I wasn't worried about a bitch nigga doing shit to me, I had been thinking about moving into a crib like this for Giovania and my son.

We still didn't know what she was having, but I was claiming a son, and for her sake, her ass better be pregnant with one. If not, fuck what the doctor was talking about with that six weeks shit. The day she pushed that baby out, we would be back at it, making another one. She gone give a nigga a junior by choice or by force, so she better have a pep talk with her eggs.

I don't care how many kids she gotta push out until she gets it right. I'll have seven girls and one boy and be cool with that. Only problem with that would be, it'll be a lot of dead muthafuckas in the world. Even though I wanna raise my junior just like me, my daughters bet not ever run into a nigga like daddy because I'll chop the heads off them niggas right in front of them.

Naw, I want my girls to talk to a square ass nigga. One of the 401(k) plan having ass, *Harry Potter*-watching ass, bow tie wearing niggas. This not the life I want them living. Although I will make sure they are made aware of everything and teach them how to shoot and kill, I still want them to live a simple life.

"Baby," my T-lady said as soon as I walked through the door.

"Hey, pretty lady," I said, walking up to her and kissing her on the cheek.

"Boy, I don't know where them lips been today. Don't be kissing all on my skin," she said, playfully wiping my kiss away.

"I ain't ate on Giovania today, so you good. I ate the soul out of her ass last night though," I said to her.

Shit, niggas probably wondering like did this fool just say that to his mother? It's book three, bitch. Shut up and keep reading. Y'all know by now a nigga ain't got no filter, and this just the type of relationship me and my dukes had with one another. I told y'all this was legit my best fucking friend. Me and Pops was close, mainly because of all my extracurricular activities, but Ma Dukes was my dawg. We ran it about any and everything.

"Nasty bastard just like your father," she said.

"Naw, I'm nothing like his old ass," I said just as he walked up.

"What I tell you about that damn old word. I can take any bitch you ever had," he said

"Take their asses straight to the morgue. Don't fuckin' play with me, Maxx Carter," my T-lady said, hitting his ass quick.

I don't know what's wrong with these New Orleans chicks. It don't matter how old they are, all they asses crazy as hell and will fight a nigga quick.

"Damn, Jackie. I was playing, bruh. Chill out before I hem your ass up in here. Don't show out in front of my son like you running shit. I already taught him who runs shit in the household," he said.

"And who the hell running shit, Maxx?" she asked with her hands on her hips.

"Abort," I said, being messy.

If your woman puts her hands on her hips and does that little neck roll, fellas, y'all ass better go dumb and catch amnesia quick as fuck. I'm telling you. You don't want them problems.

Pops too old not to know this though, because instead of catching amnesia, this bold ass nigga gone say, "Dick runs this household. Don't act like you don't be screaming, talking about it's—"

"Whoa, bruh! Y'all asses too damn old to be talking like that," I said as she blushed as her face softened. That shit made my stomach hurt just thinking about it.

"Man where Camille at so I can leave, because y'all asses give me nightmares. I don't need them type of images in my head," I said seriously.

"Nigga of all the shit you've done in life with that sick ass fetish with swords that you have and all the people you've killed, that's the thing that will give you nightmares?" my mother asked with her head cocked at me.

"Yeah," I said, not giving it a second thought.

"That's your crazy ass child," she said to Pops.

"I told you when you dropped him to go get his ass examined, but you didn't listen," he said, laughing.

"Y'all just ain't about to talk about me like a nigga ain't standing right here though," I said.

"Jakeem!" Camille said, running into the living room, coming straight to me.

I still had to get used to her ass calling me Jakeem, but when Giovania introduced us, that's what she told her my name was. I still wasn't used to the hugs and affection though, so I didn't hug her back when she hugged me, but I did offer a smile. That was the best a nigga could do shit. That was the homie though.

"What's up, homie," I said dapping her up.

What else a nigga was supposed to do? I wasn't too good with kids obviously, but that don't mean I didn't like kids. I had a back-to-school bash, toy drive, and lots of other shit for the kids yearly that I always made time for.

"Nothing. Glam-ma and me played dress up and got our nails did," she said.

"What the hell is a Glam-ma?" I asked in confusion.

"Me. I'm too young and fly to be called grandma. That sounds like an old lady with tired ass church wigs on, Madea-looking dresses with dentures, and them orthopedic shoes. I stay slayed with some inches, fresh to death, and I can still drop it like it's hot and pick that shit back up," she said, busting out in a nasty ass swiggle mixed with a little bounce.

"Alright now," Pops said, joining her.

That's another thing about our culture, it doesn't matter how old you were, what color you were, or what you did for a living, everybody danced. It's just the New Orleans way. If you from here and don't know how to do the bounce or swiggle, bitch, you a fraud ass mutha-fucka tryna lie to kick it.

Tapping me on my leg, I noticed Camille motioning for me to lean down to her as she whispered in my ear, well tried to whisper any damn way.

"I don't like this stuff on my nails Jakeem," she said.

Pops burst out laughing before he said, "That's what her ass gets."

"Come on, Camille. Say bye," I said, quickly grabbing her hand trying to get my homie out of there before my T-lady went slap off on her.

One thing with Jackie Carter, age wasn't a factor when she got to going off. Nobody was exempt. Hell, not even my black ass.

* * *

"SAFARI, stay where I can see you. You know better." Danielle scolded as the girls ran ahead of us headed to the Cajun Seafood downtown. Giovania had Camille's ass hooked on seafood because that's all she craved during her pregnancy; seafood and wings from Who Dat Chicken and Shrimp.

Since the parking is always crazy downtown, I had parked my car, and we were walking the few blocks to the restaurant. As soon as we got close to Cajun Seafood, we saw a crowd of people with a jukebox on the ground as girls were bent over with little ass booty shorts on, ass cheeks hanging out, bouncing to "Give Me My Gots" by Shardaysa Jones.

You wanna ram it in my cat

Or Slash
Gimme them gots
No Slash gimme my gots
Eat it from the
Eat it from the
Eat it
Eat it
Eat it
Eat from the back

THIS WAS JUST another typical day in the city, ratchet shit like this; but a nigga loved this ratchet ass shit no lie. There's no place in the world I would rather live than my city. I'ma 504 baby until I die.

"Ayyeee," Danielle said, bending over joining in on the ratchet festivities.

I told you it don't matter who the hell you are or where the hell you at, when you hear music, you gone start dancing.

Wearing her signature sweat pants and tank, D bent over, throwing that big ass like she had a point to prove and I'ma say this again, if she wasn't a beast at her job, and I didn't want to cause confusion with our business relationship, I would have been gave her fine ass the business.

Turning around and looking at Danielle, Camille tried to mock her by putting her hands on her knees, trying to dance. Kids too damn impressionable these days.

"Nah, homie, that ain't for you," I said, quickly making it over to her, lifting her ass up. My ass went into father mode quick as fuck when this wasn't even my child. Maybe I was gone be OK at the parenting thing after all.

Laughing her ass off at me, Danielle caught up to us as we all walked inside the restaurant.

"That shit ain't funny," I said.

"Yes it is. Yo' ass was serious as fuck. Not Ja though. This shit crazy to witness," she said. "Look at you growing and shit," she said.

"Man, you tweakin," I said, laughing as I ordered our food.

After we got the girls settled with the food at one table, we sat directly behind them so that I could have a line of sight to them but also get down to what I really wanted to talk to Danielle about.

"So D, what's up, bruh? It ain't never took me this long to get back to me on some shit," I said as I tore the head of the crawfish off and squeezed the head at the same time as I bit it and sucked the juices out of it. Nigga be fucking over some crawfish, especially if they seasoned properly.

"My bad, I just have a lot on my plate, Bull blowing my phone up. I think he stalking me, then Yari missing in action," she said, letting me know this was really about Yari all along.

This why I ain't want him fuckin' with her from jump, because I didn't want exactly what was happening to happen. Speaking of the devil, at that exact moment, my phone rang, and it was this nigga calling me.

"Hello?" I said.

"Bruh, tell me why I had to beat a nigga ass yesterday at Shanti house, the nigga is supposed to be her friend," he said all hype.

"Yo' soft ass sound hurt she got a friend. Get out your feelings crying and shit. You said you ain't even want shawty anyway so what's the problem? Butshit, that nigga still want smoke? I can hop the plane and be there in no time," I said serious as hell. Yari was like my brother, and any problem he had, I had because I made that shit my problem.

"I ain't fucked up about that weak ass nigga. It's the principle he came at me spitting that hot boy shit, then said he would beat my bitch ass up. Shit, you know me. I wasn't for the talking. Bitch you gone have to live that life with me, and that's what happened. But naw, you ain't gotta come. That nigga lightweight with his bitch ass. I can't lie though, he stood under them bitches ten toes. I can give his bitch ass that," he said.

"Fuck that. I got some hot for that bitch to stand under," I said.

"I guess your ugly ass good for something since you stay on go, old *Alien Vs. Predator* looking ass nigga," Yari said.

"Oh no you didn't just try it, you upside-down popsicle-looking ass nigga, 'big, I can't believe it's not butter' looking ass boy. 'Keke, do you love me' face ass," I said as we both burst out laughing.

"But check it, I forgot to ask you the other day, but ask Shanti some shit for me. She with you or with ole boy?" I said, sliding that in there just to fuck with him.

As much as he rode me about Giovania, he know just fucked up telling me about this shit. I was on his ass.

"Don't fucking play with me. She know what it's hitting for, her ass right here."

"Nigga you ain't gotta front for me, Craig. If a nigga took your bitch, he just took your bitch. It's cool. It happens to the best of us. Well, ain't no nigga ever took shit from me, but I'm the exception to that," I said laughing.

"Fuck you, Ja. What the fuck you want?"

"You called me, ole bitch ass nigga, fuck you mean?" I asked.

"You just asked was Ashanti by me. What you want me to ask her ole slow ass nigga? Yo' ass need a slow check for real," Yari said.

"Whatever, bitch, but ask her about a pre-graduation party. I need details on what happened with Kyle and Giovania," I said, not bothering to tell her Giovania's version.

I wasn't altogether sure I could trust a bitch whose best friend went missing for weeks, and she didn't bat an eyelash. But I needed to make sure their stories matched up just in case she did tell the truth.

"Hold on, let me ask her," he said.

While he paused, I continued fuckin' my plate up. I had crawfish, boiled shrimp, mussels, crab legs, corn, and potatoes.

"Ay, she said Kyle was somebody she had a crush on for years. They finally got ready to smash for the first time ever, and he tried to do some foul shit to her, then lied and tried to play her out in front of the whole school. She ain't say what he tried to do, but she said he a bitch-made ass nigga," he said.

That let me know Shanti didn't want to talk about the almost rape with us but let me know exactly what I needed by her choice in words.

"Bet that up. Tell her a nigga appreciate that. Good looking out, though. What you wanted anyway, because you hit me up?"

"How my business running?"

"Bitch, do I look like your secretary or some shit? Hell, your business running the same way it does when you go out of town or don't show up for days. Niggas know not to play with our money. We done made an example out of enough them niggas for everybody to get the point by now," I said.

"Aight, well, I'ma check ya later and finish running it," he said, hanging up not even bothering to ask about Danielle.

He needed to get his shit together, because one minute, he confessing his feelings for D, and the next, he ready to body a nigga about his baby momma. I mean, I can't talk because Trina jumped Giovania, but in my defense, that hoe knew where I stood with her ass. I wasn't telling them both one thing. This nigga playing a dangerous game, and he know how crazy these damn New Orleans women can be. I ain't helping his ass if they all jump him either.

"So I guess that was Yari. At least that means his ass is OK. I thought about tracking his phone, but I was trying to give him his privacy just in case it was a business-related reason that he was missing in action," she said as her voice cracked a little.

"Look, bruh, I ain't the nigga to lie or sugarcoat shit to spare ya feelings. I barely do that shit with Giovania, and she got a nigga heart, so I'ma keep it a buck. Yeah, that was Yari, and he is taking care of business, and if he didn't want you to know about it, then it's for a good cause," I said.

"Taking care of business, but Ashanti around him? Get the fuck out of here with that bullshit, Jakeem," she said.

She never called me that, so her little ass must really be mad, but what she want my ass to do? Dime my boy out? Fuck no. You can catch that nigga deep up in the pussy, and I'ma have a story about he was really with me, and you was set trippin because that wasn't him. Shit, bros before hoes his ass better not even tell Giovania no shit, even though it'll never be shit for him to tell because I'm trying to change.

"Yeah, if you was doing your job, I wouldn't have to send Yari on these damn duck missions blind. I sent you them pictures to see who the fuck sent me that shit, then Ashanti revealed some shit to me the other day that had me thinking whoever sent that shit from New York. I can't afford to leave my baby right now, so I sent Yari. You expect him not to check on his baby moms while he there? So you want him to be like Bull and disown his seed? That's fucked up, ma, I ain't take you to be the type of female to a make a nigga choose between his seed and his girl," I said, laying it on her ass thick.

I half hoped she would see through my bullshit and make me call the nigga back. I always considered Danielle to be a strong woman though so I doubt she would.

Shit, to my surprise, she nodded her head and said,

"You right. I'm tripping, I just been had a lot going on with threats from Bull. I feel like somebody always watching my every move, and withYari just up and leaving me, it didn't make my paranoia any better. I just want him here is all," she said.

That nigga must sucked her damn toes or some shit. Instead of speaking on it, I did like Webbie when he said *before I get in another nigga business, I'ma mind my own.*

"As far as Bull goes, just say the word, and he'll become a distant memory. What the fuck he threatening to do to you?"

"Sue me for full custody," she said. I figured she was about to say the nigga threatening to kill her or some shit.

"Just let the man see Safari one time at a very public place, and maybe he'll go away, or tell his wife on his ass," I said.

"The mall was very public, and I remember his ass chasing me out of it last time," she said, rolling her eyes and neck at me.

"Shit, son. I don't know what to tell you. But I do know you gotta figure all that shit out on your own time. You on the clock now, and time is money. Back to me and what I asked you to do," I said as I resumed eating.

I needed to find Trina's son Antwon so we could get this ball rolling. Shit, I also needed to find out who the fuck sent me these texts. I had a strong feeling it was this bitch ass nigga Kyle, but I just know from the way he sounds that his balls ain't big enough to fix his fingers and write me.

Pulling out her laptop from her bag she had already her shoulder, she began typing away on it reminding me of that chick Penelope from *Criminal Minds*. It's still crazy how Danielle so damn hood but nerdy at the same damn time.

"Yeah I actually ran it through the database, and the number that texted you was from a burner phone, so it's gone take time for me to get that one traced back if it's traceable at all. Now I did have luck finding Antwon and Ms. Wanda. She had dropped off the map, stopped using her credit cards, and cell phones, but she slipped up when she has her prescription sent from Texas to an apartment in Mississippi, and I'm sending you the address now," she said.

"Bet," I said, feeling the pocket of my burner phone vibrating.

"Stay on those text messages. It's some type of way they can be traced, and another thing, get me the address to a Kyle from New York who went to school with Giovania," I said.

I made my mind up that I was gone holla at the nigga. I hadn't decided if I would kill his ass or kick his ass, but I do know about my wife, I was most definitely gone see about that.

"What's important about him?" she asked.

"Just get it, and what's the status on Byron's wife?"

"Still searching for her. She must not be new to this because she's never slipped up once. She didn't even attend her parents' funerals. I sent Justin and Boobie, and she never showed. I think you underestimated ole girl," she said.

"Fuck. That bitch gone slip up. They always do. I won't stop looking for her ass, but for now, she pushed to the back of the list."

"You have jobs piling up, waiting to be accepted. Some people willing to pay three times the amount just to get the job done," she said in a quiet yet rushed tone.

"Naw I ain't doing shit else until I get my home front straight."

"Somebody offering $500,000," She said.

"I said I'm good, D. They gotta wait, and that's all there is to it. My pockets long as fuck, so I ain't hurting for no amount of money they offer me," I said.

After we finished eating, I dropped Danielle and Safari back off to their car as me and Camille hit up the mall and fucked off a few commas. I hated to admit it, but her ass was really growing on a nigga.

* * *

"BABY, CAN I HAVE A RANGE ROVER?" Giovania asked me as soon as I walked inside of the room.

"Hell no. What you need a Range Rover for when you have a G-Wagon?"

"Because I don't think a G-Wagon is a mommy car like a Range Rover is. I need to have something safe for me and Isabella."

"Who the hell is Isabella?" I asked her.

"Our daughter." she said.

"We having a son, and his name is Jakeem Javarious Carter Jr.," I said, naming my name after me and only changing his middle name.

"That's cute for when we have a son, but this is a girl. Everyone says so," she said.

"Well they asses don't know what the fuck they talking about, so tell them to shut their nappy-headed asses up discussing my son," I told her as I took my shirt off and walked into the bathroom where I got undressed and got in the shower letting the hot water run down on me.

I was in the middle of lathering my body up when Giovania stepped in the shower fully clothed as she stood in front of me and tongued kissed me for a few minutes before dropping to her knees. Ever since I taught her the proper way to give head, she been sucking a nigga go like a pro.

Placing her hands on my knees as not my dick, I glided myself intoher waiting warm mouth as she effortlessly took me down her throat with no hands.

"Fuck, this exactly what I needed," I groaned as I wrapped my hands around her hair gently fucking her face, trying my best not to be as rough since she was pregnant.

Taking my dick out of her mouth and slapping it across her face a few times, she raised my shit up as she licked under it and gently put my balls in her mouth, sucking gently. When she placed just the tip of her finger in the space between my ass and dick at the same time as she deep throated it that shit felt so good. I instantly shot my kids down her throat.

"Arghhhhhh!" I said as I emptied damn near a football field of nut into her mouth.

When she opened her mouth to show me the nut on her tongue before swallowing, that did it for me. After I had got everything out, I had to sit on the bench to catch my breath because she had literally just sucked damn near all of my energy out of me.

"Damn girl," I said, breathing heavily as I looked at her like she was an alien. My wife just sucked my dick so good I almost got mad at the nigga who taught her ass how to do that until I realized I'm the one that taught her ass.

"Say give me five minutes to get dressed, and we'll go pick out the truck," I said as her goofy ass smiled widely as she walked out of the shower.

* * *

"I WANT THAT ONE BABY," Giovania said, pointing at a cocaine-white Range Rover.

"Excellent choice, Miss. If you guys want, we can step into the office to run your credit to see what down payment you guys qualify for," the car salesman said.

"Nigga, did I ask you to see what I qualified for?" I asked him.

"I don't understand, you said you wanted the truck. I'm trying to get you the truck. That's the steps I have to—" He started until I pulled out my wallet and slid him my black card.

"It's hot as fuck out here, and my wife pregnant. I don't have her outside like this for very long, so you got twenty minutes to get her all the paperwork and pay for that shit, or I'll find another salesperson," I said to him.

He acted like somebody had lit fire to his ass how he took off running. Shit, he knew like I knew that that would be a big as commission check for him because I was paying for the shit in cash. It didn't even take him ten minutes before he was running full speed back toward us.

"Say, you ran track or some dude?" I asked him, laughing.

"No, sir," he said with a big grin on his face.

After he gave us our paperwork and keys, I dismissed him out of my face.

"Roy, drive my shit," I said to Roy, Giovania's security guard. He usually only is needed when I'm not around her, but since he was at the house when I got there, I had him come with us to drive my shit home.

"Yeah!" Giovania said as she ran to the truck and jumped in the driver's seat.

"Naw, you can drive when you in your truck solo. Your wild-driving ass can't drive me nowhere anymore," I said as she stuck her tongue out as me and hopped down. When I got in the driver's seat, I couldn't deny the truck was nice as hell.

"Thank you, baby. I love you so much," she said, leaning over and kissing me as I pulled off heading toward the highway.

"Show me that you love me. You only gave me some head. Where my pussy at?"

"Say no more," she said.

Without saying another word, she smiled as she reached over and unbuckled my pants. Leaning the seat back a little, I spread my legs and got comfortable as she freed the beast, spit on my dick, and went to work.

"Show daddy you like your new truck," I said to her with one hand on her head, and the other hand on the steering wheel.

With both of her hands, she massaged my dick in a circular motion as she went up and down on my shit. Each time she came up, she put more in her mouth when she went back down. What did it for me when she started humming on my shit, making my shit touch her tonsils.

"Fuckkkk! I'm about to nut," I said as I felt her suck that nut right out of me.

Hiking her dress up, I already knew what time it was when she climbed on top of me reverse-cowgirl style and sat directly on top of my waiting dick. At the rate that we were fucking, if she wasn't already pregnant, she would be pregnant with twins right now. I couldn't get enough of this pregnant pussy.

"You gotta steer, bae. Try and keep your eyes open and focus on the road," I said to her, because although we've done car sex before, we never had sex while the car was actually moving.

"I'ma focus, baby. I won't wreck my own shit," she moaned out, moving her hips in a back and forth motion on my dick.

Letting go of the steering wheel, I wrapped one hand around her waist as I reached around her and put another hand inside that dripping wet pussy.

"Oh my God! Fuck, Ja," she said, throwing her head back on me.

"Sit up, bruh. You gotta focus. See? We ain't doing this shit no more," I said, laughing because I knew this was gon' happen.

"It's so good… You so deep… Ahhh!" she screamed as she gripped the steering wheel extra tight.

I started rubbing and massaging her pussy as I pumped into her at the same time getting a good rhythm going.

"You missed the exit," I said as I pumped into her from the bottom as I looked around, noticing we were no were near where we was supposed to be.

Focusing my attention on the road, I directed her where to go to get us back going the right way to get home. The entire time I was directing her, I was still giving her slow strokes as she rotated her hips in sync with mine. Licking up and down her neck, I latched onto it, biting and then sucking trying to brand my mark onto her.

Removing my hand from her clit but leaving my other hand around her throat, I grabbed ahold to my arm rest for balance as I slightly lifted up and plunged deeper inside of her at a more rapid pace. I kept moving faster and deeper, not letting up, even when she began screaming louder than the music playing.

"Don't try and run now. Didn't you say you wanted it deeper? Take all of this dick Giovania," I said, feeling myself on the brink of a massive nut but not wanting to let the shit go yet.

"Fuck, Ja. Ohhhweee I'm about to cum!" she screamed.

"Let that shit go, I'm right behind you," I said to her as I relentlessly and ruthlessly pumped into her, hell-bent on getting this release.

"I'm right behind you, let that shit go," I said, giving her a few more pumps before I nutted everywhere—some inside of her, some on the seats.

"Aye, pull over so I can gone get us home before I go to jail fucking around with you," I said laughing.

One thing I can say is a nigga was enjoying the married life.

Sade

It's about time Carmen came to her senses and gave a real nigga a chapter, fuck. Ja knock-off Prince-looking ass thought he was the only one people was checking for, but I told that nigga, ain't nobody come to see you, Otis. "Is there a heart in the house" looking ass. Finally, I get to tell my shit and let y'all step into my life for a change. I don't want to hear y'all questioning shit either. Just shut the hell up and read the book, hell. Now let's get back to the book, bruh. I'm done interrupting, but aye, real nigga shit, don't a nigga make a good commentator?

* * *

I HAVE NEVER STRESSED over a girl harder than I did Kosher. She was stressing me out. I know I wasn't even supposed to love her, but I did. Everybody thought I was always up Melinda's ass, and people thought I was a sucker-for-love ass nigga behind her, but that was far from the truth.

At first she started off as just a joce, but then I started fuckin with her tough only because she was the only chick who ever listened to me and took into account what I was saying. I know that shit sounded gay, but it felt like with Melinda, she saw the real me, not the Sade everybodyelse saw that cracked jokes all the time and was always smiling.

Not the Sage that has a crazy ass twin that was equally as funny and just as lovable. Melinda saw the Sage who felt like he had to laugh all of the time to keep from letting the pain consume him.

She used to be the only chick texting me asking how I was doing and didn't mean how my day was going, but how I was mentally doing. Each day I felt like it was a struggle to get out the bed and be happy, because I had a lot of internal issues I have yet to fully bring to the light and address head on.

My childhood really fucked a nigga up on some real shit. Growing up without a father and a mother who struggled to take care of two twin boys wasn't an easy life to live. My T-lady made sure happen for us the best way she knew how. I still remember everything like it was yesterday.

She dropped us off to our uncle Maxx's house because she had a job interview to go to. We were eight at the time. When she didn't get us that night, I felt in my soul something was wrong because it just wasn't like her to leave us somewhere for that long.

That's another thing about my T-lady, she never left her kids off on anybody like that, not even relatives. She worked during the day so she could be home with us at nighttime.

So when I woke up the next day still in the same place I went to sleep at, I got a scary feeling in the pit of my stomach that I couldn't shake. Sage being my twin felt the same shit because he came and gave me a hug. He didn't say anything, just hugged me.

Since he was born first, he considers himself the older brother and takes that job really seriously. So in that moment, even though he felt the pain as well, to him, it was still his job to make sure his little brother was straight. A couple hours later when Unc Maxx started to worry as well, we all went in search of her starting at the house.

We was only at home a good five minutes before we got a knock on the door, opening it to see police officers standing there. They told us it was a drive-by shooting outside of the gas station located next to the hospital our mom was interviewing at. Apparently she had simply stopped for gas and became the victim of another senseless killing in New Orleans. That's the first and last time a nigga cried.

Back when I actually did care for Melinda, I had opened up to her and told her about my mother, a topic I never discuss, and that's what ever brought us closer. Now it's fuck that hoe. She caused me to lose something I could never get back, my seed.

I know it's fucked up to love Kosher, but I do. It's crazy how you can know someone your whole life, but see them one day, and it's like you're seeing they ass for the first time. That's what the fuck happened with me and Kosher. She's Ja's cousin on his mom's side—that's her brother's child, and I've know her my whole life, but it's like I didn't truly notice her until the night of Ja's wedding in Dubai.

It wasn't unusual for us to chill together because we used to match one all the time, so when she showed up at my room bored, talking about put her on, I didn't think twice about letting her in.

Knock! Knock!

"Damn, it better be Miss America knocking on my shit at this time of night," I said, getting up to go open the door.

I had just scored some fire ass Dubai weed, and the shit was putting me on my ass. The shit was fire as hell, and I planned on buying the shit by the boatload and taking it back to the States and trying it out at a few traps to see if they bit off it.

Knock! Knock!

"Fuck, I'm coming," I said, finally opening the door to see Kosher standing there in a Truth pullover hoodie and some Tweetybird pajama shorts.

"What's up?" I asked her.

"I'm bored, and I ain't got shit to smoke. Match some," she said, pushing past me into my shit like she was an invited guest.

"Damn, how you ain't know I ain't have a bitch in here or some?" I asked, laughing as I closed the door behind her.

"I don't give a fuck about that bitch. Just give me the weed, and I'll sit out here. You can go hit that hoe, then y'all can come smoke with me. My room boring. Kemari ass snuck off with one of these Dubai

niggas, I don't know where Danielle went, and you know Giovania with Ja," she said, taking the blunt I offered her.

Shaking my head at her ass because she was serious about waiting in the living room, I grabbed the bottle of Hennessy off the counter and put my phone on the iPhone charging dock.

"Gone in there with your company. I'm good," she said, hitting the blunt again before passing it back to me and grabbing the bottle out my hand turning it up.

Of the two, me and Kosher were closer than me and Kemari because even though she didn't act like it, Kemari ass was nineteen years old, whereas me and Kosher were both twenty-one. Age never stopped Kemari from doing the same shit we did though, but me and Kosher just vibed better. That was the homie for real.

"Man, gon' 'head. I ain't got no damn company. If I did, I would put your ass out because I wouldn't want you uncomfortable with all that screaming."

"I didn't take you for the screaming type." She shot back, taking another shot out the alcohol.

"You funny as fuck, ole rockhead ass girl," I said, hitting the blunt again.

"Don't get to ribbin', nigga, because we can do this, spider monkey-looking ass." Kosher shot back.

"Naw I don't want no smoke, Ms. Celie. I just want to smoke and drink in peace," I said, taking a few more pulls of the weed before I passed it back to her while snatching my bottle back.

"Damn, don't find your whole family in my shit. Just like a black person to invite their own damn self over, eat and drink all your shit up, and dip. Tell yo' ass straight from New Orleans," I said, laughing.

"Put some music on. It's quiet as fuck in here. Yo' ass in here getting lit in the quiet and shit. Who does that?" she asked, getting up and stumbling to my phone to put some music on.

Her ass was feeling them shots, and this weed will put you on your ass quick as fuck bruh. That's why I couldn't leave here without a few pounds. Shit kicked in instantly. I was so damn high that I felt like I was floating and shit. Like my body was on the couch, but I couldn't even feel the damn couch. Shaking my head, I tried to shake back as I focused on what Kosher was doing.

"You got the wackest songs on your playlist, dude. Like this shit poo," she said.

"Hook your shit up then," I said as she took my phone off and replaced it with hers.

"And none of that girly shit either, ole ugly ass lil' girl," I said, leaning my head back on the couch closing my eyes. I was officially more fucked up than I've ever been. This shit was the truth real talk.

"Shut yo' ass up, boy, while you done laid up dea' and got fucked up."

"Nigga higher than the muthafuckin' sky, ya heard me, but don't act like that shit ain't put you on yo ass either," I said, laughing lifting my head up looking at her.

"Hell yeah that shit legit," she said. As a song came on.

"Ayyeee!" she said, turning around and throwing her ass to the beat.

Bitch I'm from Louisiana
I'm from Louisiana
bitch I'm from Louisiana
we call it that boot
bit... bit... bitch I'm from Louisiana
you we go down
this where niggas 'bout that action
we don't really fuck around

"Cut up, cut up," I said, bucking her up as she bent all the way over making one ass cheek bounce than the other.

Here our asses was all the way in another country still turning that bitch out New Orleans style. You really couldn't take us no damn where.

Ring! Ring!

The ringing of her phone temporarily paused the music as she got up to press ignore and resumed dancing. A few incoming texts came after that, pausing the song between each text.

"Hold up. You ain't ready for this one," she said as she stopped

dancing and walked back to her phone, typing away as she switched songs.

Laughing and shaking my head, I said, "Shii! Put the shit on then," as I sat fully up at this point. As soon as I heard the best drop, I jumped up and starting dancing, that was my shit.

I do it, I stick it

I stick it, I do it

I do it, I stick it

I stick it, I do it

I do it, I stick it

I stick it, baby, do it

"Oh, you bucked up! Oh, you bucked up!" Kosher said as she ran over to me and grabbing me lightly be the tops of my shirt, jigging to the beat with me.

We was all into it until her phone started ringing yet again, this time killing' my vibe, so I stopped dancing and went sat down.

"Damn, you got the hotline tonight, huh?" I asked laughing.

"Man this stupid ass nigga won't stop calling and texting me. Can't give good pussy to everybody because they don't be knowing how to act," she said, texting rapidly on her phone as she put it down and once again switched songs.

When Plies "Real Hitta" came on, I simply laid there and vibed to the beat before I said, "Girl, good pussy? Yo' shit probably poo as fuck. Don't let these niggas lie to you, sis."

"Poo? Naw your dick poo. Bitches probably gotta fake it till they make it with your ass, then finish themselves off in the shower, ole quick-pumper ass." She shot back.

Laughing, I asked, "Quick pumper, huh? That's how you feel, maw? Quick pumper be done put this dick on ya and have ya mind gone. I got enough bitches stalking me. I'on need no more," I said, laying my head back on the couch.

"You wouldn't even know what to do with the pussy if I put it in your face," she said.

"That's what you tell them fuck niggas and lil' boys, but I'm a grown ass man. You put some pussy in my face, and I'ma show you

what you 'posed to do with it. Don't act like you ain't heard these hoes call me the pussy monsta, ya heard me," I said laughing.

This was normal for us to throw around sex talk mixed with our conversation. Like I said, that was the homie. Shit got real quiet, and I was on the verge of falling asleep until I felt her climb into my lap, then stand up on both sides of me.

Opening my eyes, I sat up to a very naked Kosher with that thang sitting up and poking out, looking at me. I looked into her eyes with the intention of telling her crazy ass to gon' 'head, but when our eyes locked, it's like, on some real shit, I was seeing shorty for the first time ever. Had to been the weed because she was beautiful as hell.

"Quit playing with me, Kosher," I said low as hell.

"Who said I was playing?" she asked me before she moved her body closer to my face.

I took a split second to process how wrong this was before I pushed the shit to the back of my mind and pulled her ass down until she was sitting directly on my face. Locking my arms around both of her legs, I licked up and down her thigh on both sides, biting and sucking on them bitches like they had a taste to them. I was really just fuckin' with her letting her know all that shit talking and bossy attitude worked on other folks, but in my world, I ran shit.

"You gone eat it, or you gone play with it, bruh?" She hissed as I continued teasing her, this time licking on the outside of her juicy lips before French kissing the pussy, still not opening it up diving straight in.

The lips on her shit were closed tighter then a bitch tracks sewn down, so I literally had to pull them apart with my fingers as I decided to stop playing with her ass and gone show her with this mouth do.

"Fuckk!" she said, throwing her head back as I went in for the kill slurpin', lickin', and suckin', trying to imprint my name in that pussy.

"Ohh shit, Sade! What you trying to do to me!" she screamed as I latched onto her clit, refusing to let up.

"Snatch your soul, and I need you to come up off that muthafucka tonight," I said, standing up and flipping her over before I dove back in head first as she wrapped her legs around my head.

Taking a finger and inserting it deep inside of her, I fingered her at the same time as I delivered waves of pleasure to her body. Feeling her legs beginning to shake, I sucked that orgasm right on out of her body but refused to stop until she came four more times.

"Oh my God! No, I can't take anymore. Hmmm," Kosher moaned.

"Give me four more, and I'll let up," I said.

"I can't. I only ever came once," she said, thrusting her hips up toward my face.

Her mouth was telling me she couldn't cum anymore, but her body was telling me she was on the verge of another orgasm. Taking my hand and placing it directly above her pretty pussy, I massaged it as I made love to her with my mouth.

"Sadeee!" she screamed as the floodgates opened up and blessed me once again.

Being the greedy ass nigga that I am, I caught all that shit using my mouth as a suction cup catching all of that shit. I felt her body got limp as I kept licking.

"No, I don't have two more in me," she said, pushing at my head.

"I said you give me four, and that's what I meant," I told her as I raised up, pulled a condom out of my pocket, dropped my pants, rolled it on, and roughly entered her, long stroking that pussy like I had a point to prove.

"Fuck," I said, not expecting the shit to be this damn good.

"BITCH, you ready to go, or nah?" Sage asked as he burst into my room, interrupting my thoughts.

We did everything together growing up, and even in our adult life. We lived together and got this money together.

"Damn, fuck boy. Knock next time," I said.

"Why? You must was in here beating ya shit off," he said, laughing as I tossed a pillow at him.

"Fuck you, bitch boy, but yeah I'm ready. Let me grab my keys and shit," I said, getting up as I grabbed my phone, keys, and checked to make sure I was strapped before I walked out my room.

Regardless of the respect we had in these streets, a nigga will still try and run up on you, looking for a come up and to try and get some clout. We might just be twenty-one, but since we been out in these streets for so long, we was OGs to a lot of these niggas.

* * *

"WHAT THE FUCK we gone do about this lil' bitch Trina?" Sage asked after we got in his black-on-black Range Rover.

"Shit, the hoe gotta go. We just can't kill her ass without it coming back on Ja. We can pay some lil' niggas to run up on that hoe," I said.

"What if they ass fuck up and get to running they fucking mouth though?" I asked.

"Shit, you right cuz niggas ain't built for the life they try and live. I guess we gotta try Ja route and snatch her kid up," he said, firing up a blunt as we headed out to our first stop.

We was collecting money today to take to the warehouse, count up, then separate Unc cut out and take it to him. This was a normal routine for us, and the shit a nigga lived for.

A few hours after we had picked all the money up and dropped it off at the warehouse, we went to get some food, before we came back to count it up.

"Go to Popeyes. A nigga want some of that good ole chicken, ya heard me," I said, passing him back the blunt as he headed that way.

We had been getting blowed all day and had the munchies and shit. I normally didn't entertain smoke so much throughout the day, but Kosher real life had a nigga stressed the fuck out. After we came back to the States, we was fucking around strong, but I wanted to keep it under wraps until I talked to the family about it. She took that as me trying to downplay her and our situation and still fuck with Miranda.

When she killed my baby, I was crushed, so I tried to hurt her like she hurt me by throwing Miranda in her face at every family function, hang-out spot, and club that I knew she'd be at and see us. Melinda already knew how I felt about Kosher because I got drunk one night and told her that Kosh had my heart.

A hoe like Melinda, that always has ulterior motives, didn't give a fuck one way or another. She claimed she wanted me, but she really wanted the hype and bragging rights that came with me. I do believe at one point she did love a nigga, but now it's all about my clout in these streets and showing out for these raggedy ass hoes.

Half the shit dealing with her is my fault because I allowed the shit to go on rather than putting a stop to it. People assumed I was a sucker for love behind her ass. I just didn't have time to deal with the shit. If I was dealing with a bitch and she allowed Melinda's crazy antics to run her away, then that wasn't the woman for me. Any woman dealing with me gon' bat the fuck out of Melinda each time she come around with that dumb shit—a woman like Kosher. Melinda ass ain't never and will never try Kosher.

Pulling around through the drive-through, the lady on the intercom asked, "How may I help you?"

, "What you want?"Sage asked me.

"Aye, see if they got that lil' five dollar box shit still. I saw it on TV," I said.

"May I help you?" the cashier repeated, this time with a slight attitude just like a bald-headed ass drive-through bitch.

"Damn girl hold up right fast, bruh," Sagesaid. That nigga went from zero to one hundred quick.

"Well let me know when you ready to order." She shot back, throwing that same attitude back at his ass.

"Aye, saylove, I had seen a lil' commercial, ya heard me, and shit say y'all got a lil' box of chicken for like $5 and some change or some shit like that, maw, ya dig? Nigga need two of them shits, ya heard me," this rude ass nigga said. I don't know why I even let his ass order the food.

"Man, that bitch gone spit in our shit fuckin' around with you," I said, laughing.

"Bitch better not," Sage said.

"We ain't got the chicken box no more. That was just a special going on," she said.

"Damn, why y'all show it to a nigga on TV then, ya dig?" Sagesaid.

"Boy, I don't know. I don't even watch TV," she said with much attitude.

"Man, fuck no. Nigga don't want this shit no more. I ain't got time to be killin' this bitch for spittin' in my shit. Let's just go to We Dat Chicken and Shrimp," I said, but the nigga ignored me.

"Well, when them bitches coming back though, ya dig, cuz a nigga want one?" he asked.

"Sir, I don't know. I just work here," she said.

"Say, maw, how you look though? You sounding cute over the lil' intercom. I'ma pull up and give you my number so you can let a nigga know when y'all getting them boxes back," Sage said, shooting his shot.

"Boy, you so funny. I'm aight though," she said, laughing.

Bitch went from an attitude to a smile. I could hear the smile in her voice.

"This nigga think he on *Love Connection* and shit," I said as we pulled around.

I expected shawty to be bald headed with thin ass edges and a nappy Duby bob. I didn't expect her to have the nerve to be bad a lil' chocolate broad.

"I ain't gone hold up your line ya heard me, but this my number. I'ma joce you while you at work ya dig. Call my shit right now before I leave," Sagesaid to her.

"I can't pull my phone out on the clock," she said.

"Man, fuck them people, ya dig? Call me right now so I can lock ya number in. Them hoes hating cuz they want a nigga to talk to them," he said as she blushed and pulled her phone out ignoring the stares from her coworkers.

Shit at this point she ain't have a no choice. It's hard to tell a New Orleans nigga no once we set our sights on you. After Sage got her number, we pulled off, heading to get some food before going to count up all this bread.

* * *

"'PRECIATE IT, NEPHEW," Unc Maxx said as he took the bag of money I handed him containing $750,000, which was his cut for the week.

"Can I run it with you real quick?" I asked him.

"What's on your mind?" he asked me as I followed him through the house to his man cave.

He waited until he had fixed both of us a drink, and we sat down before he said anything.

"What's up?" he asked me.

Taking a sip of my drink, I meant to start talking, but that shit burned like hell as it slide down my throat. Patting my chest a few times, I had to take some deep breaths to recover.

"This that grown man drink," he said, laughing.

"Hell naw. That shit taste like some damn motor oil," I said.

"Make your chest hair stands up. That separates the boys from the men, but what you wanna talk about?"

"I need some advice on a situation that I'm in," I said.

"What type of situation?" he asked, immediately turning serious. Since we were his sister's only kids, he was as protective of us as he was of Ja.

"Nothing we gotta see about, but something that..." I said, pausing my conversation.

"Damn Melinda's ass done gave you something, huh? Shii, just go to the health unit on the outskirts of town," he said.

"Why the fuck is that people first thought?" I asked, laughing because that's along the lines of the same shit Yari said to me.

"Now, son, you know that girl gets passed around more than a football during the playoffs," he said. Taking a deep breath, I tried to get my nerves under control as I prepared myself to tell him about me fucking Kosher. I wasn't sure how he would react to me fucking his wife's niece though but I was prepared for whatever.

"OK, look, man, I'ma just throw it out there, me and Kosher fuckin', and I love her ass," I said, picking up the cup downing the burning alcohol.

"About time you admitted the shit. Nobody knew why y'all asses was trying to hide it. The plan ride home, y'all couldn't get any more obvious. But I will say this, you my nephew, and that's my niece, and I love both like my own children, but if you still fuckin with Melinda, either tighten up and get the hoe in check, or leave Kosher alone. I'm telling you now, crazy runs in their blood. She will fuck around and kill you and Melinda's ass. The women in that family crazy as fuck," he said, laughing as I joined in.

I felt like a weight had been lifted off my shoulder after I talked to Unc, and now that I know it's not a secret, I'm about to go full force in getting my girl back. She got me fucked up if she thinks she gone move on.

* * *

NOTICING KOSHER PULLING up in the driveway, I got out the car with the intention of having a peaceful conversation until I noticed her car door opened, and some nigga hopped out the driver side. *This bitch got me all the way fucked up,* I thought as my hands went to my gun.

"Say, my man, call you an Uber to get home. I gotta holla at my ole lady," I said walking up on them.

"Boy, I know you fucking lying. Gon' 'head with that stupid shit, Sade," she said, rolling her eyes.

"Naw, playboy. I'ma go in here and eat that crawfish, then we gone chill, fuck, and then she'll drop me back off to my shit," he said.

"Wait, pause, nigga. I never said you was getting no pussy. I said Netflix and chill, fuck."

"Damn, it's like that? Some pussy, huh, my boy," I asked him.

"Kosh, you passing my pussy out?" I asked her.

"Hell no. We was just going to Netflix and chill," she said.

"Netflix and chill does mean fuck," dude said.

"You can't be serious, bruh? Really, Kosher? This clown ass nigga is who you tryna front of me for? This nigga paid $6 for some crawfish and want some ass," I said.

"He thought," she said.

"Say, bruh, I don't give a fuck what y'all got going on ya dig, but it —" He was saying until I pulled my gun out on him. It was taking everything in me not to shoot his ass, but we was catching enough heat lately, and I didn't want to add to it in a sloppy way.

"Man, this hoe ain't all that. I'ma dip, but I'm taking my crawfish with me," his broke ass said, walking off down the street.

"Why you come over here starting shit? Where yo hoe Melinda at? Go bother her and run her dates away shit," she said, walking into her house as I followed behind her.

"I don't remember inviting you in, Sade," she said, trying to act mad, but I knew she wanted a nigga here.

"Shit, you didn't have to because I was gone invite myself in, regardless of that fuck shit you was talking about, ole ugly ass girl," I said.

"You and Sade always talking about somebody with y'all 'Thing 1 and Thing 2' looking asses," she said, laughing at her own stale ass joke.

"Baby I love you, but yo, ribbin' ain't for you. Leave it to your man to fire somebody ass up," I said, not even realizing for the first time ever, I had confessed my love to her.

"What did you say?"

"I said leave the jokes to me," I said, trying to backtrack."

"Before that nigga."

"Shit, I smoke so much my mind bad," I lied.

"You said you loved me," she repeated. It was silent for a moment before she said, "I love your stupid ass too, but I won't let you hurt me. I'll you and that bitch and cry at your funeral before I let you hurt me again," she said.

"Look, a nigga gone quit frontin'. I love you, and I'm in love with you," I said.

"Continue," she said.

"Shit, that's it. I can't give no long ass, romantic speech because I'm not that nigga. That's all I got. I love you and I'm in love with you," I said. "You gotta take that shit or leave it ya heard me."

"I'll take it for now, but you and that hoe know that's up with me.

People in relationships talk about they problems and shit with each other, not floss another hoe around in they girl face."

"Shit same for you. They don't abort babies just because they mad. That's some foul ass shit that's still fucking with me. But fuck it. I already talked to Unc, and he ran it to me like everybody knew about us and was just waiting for us to address that shit, so fuck, we played ourselves tryna keep it under wraps and both did fucked-up shit," I said, pulling her in my arms.

"You missed me?" I asked her.

"Naw, but I missed what that mouth do though," she said, laughing.

With my woman back on my side, I was ready to tackle these problems in the street.

Giovania

"Bitch, I wish I would have been there. I would have decked them hoes right in the mouth for playing with you. They know you pregnant, and that's why they keep trying you," Danielle said, walking out of the kitchen.

It had been awhile since I saw her, so I popped up on her for a playdate with Serenity and some girl time because I missed my friend.

"If Ja would have let me, I was gone beat both of their asses," I said half confident, half just talking because it was the heat of the moment, and I was buckled up.

"They're constantly harassing Ja because they know he's not about to risk going to jail, but you should have seen how mad Ja was. I thought for sure he was going to shoot both one of them," I said.

We had ran into Trina yet again, and she had pushed my buttons for the last time. Momma Jackie had told me it was up to me to do a job my husband couldn't do but make sure it didn't come back to my husband if I did it. I had thought long and hard about it, and I was sick of this bitch, so she has to go. I was finally ready to step up to the plate and be the ride or die my husband needed me to be. It was time to take this hoe out, and fast before I got further alone in my pregnancy.

Yesterday when she put Ja tires on flat outside of one of his hangout spots,that was the last straw. She knew he couldn't touch her without going to jail, so she was doing everything in her power to provoke him to attempt to hurt her so he could go jail for life.

I'm sure that detective put her up to this since Ja already told me they had no real evidence. His lawyer had already filed a motion to view their evidence, and so far, they haven't turned any over because it wasn't anything to show. His family needed him, and I'd be damned if I let this bitch take the father of my child away from me all because she's upset about some dick.

If I would have known she would be this much of a pain in the ass, I would have allowed Jakeem to continue to pay for that raggedy ass apartment and old ass car she was driving. She should have shit while she still had the option to and stayed in hiding.

"I know I don't want to shoot her or anything like that, besides I don't think anyone can even get close enough to her to do something like that. We have to catch her someplace where she knows she can't go with the police," I said.

"They havin' a party at House of Blues in two weeks. Some up-and-coming rapper performing," Danielle said.

"But how we know she going?" I asked.

"Because bitches like that put their entire life in on Facebook," Danielle said, laughing.

"Idiot. These people will eventually learn that posting your every move can be dangerous. Her fuck-up is good for us though because that's the only time I have to strike. I can't miss this window of opportunity, I don't know what I'ma do or how I'ma do it, but that's the perfect scene to do everything quickly, effectively, and undetected," I said.

"Bitch you been reading too many books and watching entirely too much TV, talking about some damn quickly, effectively, and undetected," Danielle said, laughing. "Don't fuck around and go to jail shit trying to mimic some shit you seen on TV and fuck it up."

"No, I know what I'm going to do, and I won't even have to touch her to kill her. I'll only need a few minutes tops to complete it," I said with a devilish look in my eyes.

"Yeah you been around Jakeem Carter far too damn long," she said. "Both of y'all crazy ass deserve each other."

"Speaking of crazy, what's going on with the Bull situation? He went from chasing you through the mall to wanting custody of Safari? What the hell type of games he playing?"

"I don't know, but I do know I'll never play about my baby. I'm dying behind that one. Whatever fuck games he tryna play with me, he needs to leave that shit between us and leave my child out of this. In one breath, he lie like he want see ha, but then you following me on the highway, playing chase and shit. You leaving threatening messages on my phone and shit. Bitch, which one you want? You wanna be a father? Or you wanna beat my ass? Like pick one, hoe," she said.

I understood completely where she was coming from because I had already bonded with my child and was over protective already.

"That's crazy, what does Yari say about the situation? Why hasn't he stepped in and done something?"

"Fuck him. That bitch better not come around me," Danielle said angrily.

"What's going on now?"

"Oh, Ja ain't tell you Yari came back from New York with a new houseguest?" she asked me.

I had heard Ja mention Yari brought Ashanti back with him to get her away from everything that transpired.

"Yes, but I didn't know she was his houseguest," I said.

"OK, so boom, I go over there because the nigga ain't been answering the phone, and bitch, you ain't about to play on my top, hoe. So I goes over there to get some answers, like why you been playing me like some groupie or some shit. She answered the door and told me he wasn't there, and I 'bout lost my muthafuckin' mind and burnt that bitch down.

"I ain't got smoke with her. My thing is this bitch I was fine with getting the dick here and there and being cool. You made me, forced me, to give you a chance to see where this shit could go, then switched it up on a bitch. That's what pissed me off. Like if you knew this wasn't what you wanted, or you wanted to do your own thing and be cool, fuck nigga, say that!

"Got me stressed out, edges falling out and shit because you wanna play games. I don't have no beef with his baby momma, but I do feel like he doing this shit because of her and won't fuck with me because of her. Maybe to protect her feelings, but what about my feelings? It's fuck Danielle, huh? So how I feel, fuck both of them. I'll step on both of their asses," she said, releasing all the pent-up anger she had been holding on to.

I hope for his sake, Yari got his shit together.

* * *

LAYING down in bed while Ja laid his head on my stomach, we watched his favorite movie, *Life*. This are the moments I lived for—him home with me at a decent time of night, cuddled up in bed watching this corny movie. Even though I've seen it plenty of times, it still wasn't funny to me, but I liked it because my man liked it.

"You gone eat yo cornbread," Ja said, laughing hard as hell.

His laugh was so contagious, I started laughing as well until I passed gas. Lately I had been so gassy, and it was becoming embarrassing because I couldn't control it. I was gone mention it to my doctor tomorrow at our appointment.

"I know yo' ass didn't just fart on me?" Ja said, lifting his head up staring at me with an angry expression on his face.

The way he was looking was so cute to me even though he was mad, and it caused me to laugh enough harder.

"I'm sorry, babe," I said, passing gas again. It had to be the pasta I ate for dinner.

"Man, get your shitty-booty ass on," he said. "You need to get up and check your panties to make sure yo ass ain't shit on yourself," he said with a serious expression on his face.

"My panties are fine. I wouldn't be gassy if it wasn't for your darn child," I said.

Leaning down and rubbing my belly, he said, "It's alright, baby boy. I know it's already hot as fuck in there, now yo' momma shitty-booty ass got it hot and funky in there," he said, placing his head on my belly.

Boom!

"What the fuck!" Ja said, jumping back to examine my stomach. "Damn, bruh, you got the bubble guts or some shit? What the hell going on in your stomach?"

"No, your baby kicked me," I said just as surprised as he was because I had yet to feel my baby move. My doctor told me it usually happens between thirteen and fifteen weeks, and I was now going on fifteen weeks.

"Oh my God, Ja," I said, sitting up in bed as I felt all over my stomach trying to get this stubborn baby to kick me again, but nothing happened.

"Do what you just did it again," I said to him as I grabbed a hold of his head with both of my hands, pulling him toward me to lay his head on me. I wanted to feel my baby kicking again.

"Damn, girl if you want me to munch on that lil' pussy, just say that," he said, laughing as he laid on my stomach. Again my baby kicked the spot Ja's head was at.

"Ahhh!," I squealed, clapping my hands. "My angel kicked me. Did you feel that?" I asked excitedly.

"Yes, I did. Damn, lil' dude. What you in there doing? Trying out for soccer or some shit? We ain't doing none of that lame shit. You get that from yo' momma. You need to be practicing basketball," he said.

"What's wrong with soccer? I think that's a good sport," I said.

"Bruh, get the fuck out of here. My son ain't playing no damn soccer," he said serious as hell as we began to debate back and forth about everything from possible baby names, to what his or her favorite hobby would be, school they would attend, and even friends they would have.

Ring! Ring

His ringing phone interrupted us in the middle of me telling him my child was not going to hit someone in kindergarten if they got their crayons taken away by another kid. I think he should inform the teacher while Ja wants our baby to punch the kid in the mouth.

As he got up, I got up behind him to go take a shower. I didn't want to tell Ja, but the last time I laughed really hard, I peed a little on myself. This baby was turning me gross and disgusting.

Looking down at the bed, I breathed a sigh of relief as I noticed none had gotten on the bed. Half an hour later, I returned to see Ja fully dressed, getting ready to leave.

"That was Yari. We gotta go handle some business. He don't want to leave Shanti at home alone, so he bringing her over here," Ja said.

"Wait, what? No," I said alarmed.

Two weeks ago, Yari had returned home with Ashanti until she had their baby. He told Ja that some guy name Lexx had convinced her that this was good for her until the baby came. I had been avoiding her like the plague since then, ignoring text messages and phone calls.

"Naw. I'm fuckin with you, but you are meeting her for lunch in two days, and I don't want to hear it," he said.

"But why, baby," I said pouting.

"Don't poke them lips out. You meeting with her to hash all this shit out. Don't act like I haven't noticed how sad you get when anything pertaining to the baby shower is mentioned. You want your family there as well, and Ashanti is your family. Let the last go and hear your best friend out," he said, kissing me on my lips.

When he tried to pull away, I wrapped my arms around his neck depended the kiss.

"Let me go before I be done gave you the best two minutes of your life. Keep that thang wet for me," he said, before adding, "Don't wait up," and walking out of the room as I laid back in bed lost in thought.

Was I ready to finally hear Shanti out?"

* * *

Keke, do you love me? Are you riding?
Say you'll never ever leave from beside me

'Cause I want ya, and I need ya And I'm down for you always
KB, do you love me? Are you riding?
Say you'll never ever leave from beside me
'Cause I want ya, and I need ya And I'm down for you always

As Drake's "In My Feelings" played, I tried to do the dance with Camille, so we could upload it to Facebook. When the part of Magnolia Shorty came on and Camille started doing the swiggle, I was in shock.

"Mille, who taught you that?" I asked her.

"My glam-ma," she said, which caused me to shake my head at Momma Jackie's ass teaching her to do that dance.

"GiGi, why didn't God give me another father when he took mine?"

"What do you mean baby?" I asked her.

"You told me my daddy was in heaven with God because he needed him back. Why didn't he give me another daddy if he needed my daddy back?" she asked.

I was literally lost for words and couldn't even form a full sentence.

"I-I umm, well, it doesn't exactly work like that."

"Well, can Ja be my new daddy since God took my daddy and didn't give me a new one?" she asked.

She was hitting me with back-to-back questions that I wish I was prepared in advance for. I would have googled them. I found myself doing that a lot with Camille. It's like I see her in an entirely different light since she's been in my care.

My little sister transformed into my little daughter before my eyes. I was expected to play parent as well as big sister, and pretty soon I would have a new baby, and an eight-year-old, and I was only twenty-one.

I wish Ja were here to help me out, he was so good with Camille and her questions. Him and Momma Jackie answered them without a second thought.

"Listen, Camille, it doesn't work like that in life. We all get one mommy and one daddy. When they are gone, we do not get a new one —" I was saying until she interrupted me.

"It's not fair! The baby gets to have a daddy and not me!"

"If you let me finish, I was saying there are people who come into your lives you take on the roles as ours parents but aren't exactly our parents. Those are the relationships we cherish the most. Momma Jackie isn't my mom, but I value our relationship and her motherly advise. Jakeem isn't your father, but he spends time with you like a father does, and you guys have a good father-daughter bond. He can be your godfather," I said.

"OK," she said with a huge smile on her face.

"Now let's upload our videos to Facebook so Tommy can take you to therapy. I'll pick you up," I said.

Tommy was her bodyguard who always accompanied her everywhere even if she was with me and my bodyguard was with us, Tommy wasn't far behind in her own car.

"OK, let's send it to Daddy Ja first!"

* * *

SINCE JA WANTED me to finally hear Shanti out, I decided to meet with her thirty minutes before Kosher and Kemari were to meet me for brunch to discuss the baby shower. Danielle was also supposed to come, but she said she had something to do with her baby daddy. She had been distant ever since Yari came back in town with Shanti. I don't know what the status of their relationship was, but I did know Yari needed to make up his mind about what and who he wanted before he lost both women trying to have his cake and eat it too.

Looking up, I saw a very pregnant Ashanti wobbling toward me. My eyes grew big as saucers at the sight of her. The last time I saw her, she was barely showing and that was about two months ago.

"I know, I know," she said as she sat down.

"Girl, what the hell," I asked her.

"Bitch, I don't know. I just know one day I went from barely showing to big as a fucking house, and I'm sick of it," she said, rolling her eyes.

"You are huge. Like your belly is really round," I said, getting up to touch it before my brain even registered what I was doing.

Whatever I was feeling, or ill feelings I was harboring melted away when laid eyes on my best friend. I wanted to hate her, but truth be told, even when I was mad at her, I still loved her. She was the big sister I never had.

"Bitch, get away from me with the cute baby bump you're sporting. Meanwhile, I look like the blog from Dragon Ball Z," she said.

Going back to sit down, I laughed at her for a second until silence fell between us and it got very awkward.

"Listen, Shanti—"

"No, let me explain," she said, interrupting me.

"You don't have to explain anything. Ja already told me how you honestly didn't know what your father was up to, and by his own admission to me, you really didn't know. He and Crystal told me their plan for you and her to go off while Big John kidnapped me," I said as tears slid down her face.

"I was mad at the longest time for nothing really when I really should have been comforting my sister. You lost your entire family in a matter of minutes, and I should have accepted your phone calls, and I'm sorry. I was just angry because it felt like everyone I loved I had lost, and I was angry with the world, with you, and with God for taking me through all of this," I said as tears poured down my face.

The more I talked, getting everything out, the better I felt. This was the healing I needed. Yes, Ashanti might have been petty not reaching out to check on me, but ultimately, she wasn't the one behind the act, and she had lost far more than I did. She lost both parents and her siblings. My parents were still alive—for now.

"No, I'm sorry. I should have reached out and checked on you when I saw your phone and clothes. I was being petty and selfish, and because of me, my father hurt you.

"That wasn't your fault, and this the last time we crying over his evil ass," I said, wiping my face.

"Agreed," she said, dabbing at her eyes.

"A bitch mascara all fucked up," she said as we burst out laughing.

It felt good to have my friend back as we spent the next few minutes catching one another up on the happening in each other's lives. I loved Kosher, Kemari, Momma Jackie, and Danielle. To me, they me were Ja's family. I now felt like I had someone important to me here with me to enjoy the moment, and that's all I ever wanted.

"Oh, bitch before I forget, I heard Yari and your boo had a fight. Spill all the tea," I was saying as Kosher and Kemari finally arrived.

"Hey cousin," they both said in unison.

"Hey, y'all. This is my best friend, Ashanti."

"Hey, cousin friend," Kosher said.

"What's up girl," Kemari said.

"Hey," Shanti said.

"Don't avoid the question," I said to Shanti.

"Lexx is not my boo. We are, however, getting to know one another," she said, cheesing extra hard.

"Baby, you smiling too hard for that to be a lil' joce, yeah," Kosher said.

"Right, sista. She smiling like she getting to know that dick, yeah," Kemari said.

"I wish I was," Shanti shot back.

"Ohhhweee hoe," I said.

"How he look?" Kosher asked as Shanti pulled up a picture of him.

"Yeah, you better than me, cuz I'd a been done busted it open for a real nigga," Kemari said, laughing.

"What about Yari?" I asked her.

"Girl, bye. I already told him we strictly co-parenting. I only came to New Orleans because Lexx felt after everything happened, how I was acting, and after he found me dehydrated and passed out in my apartment, it was best to come here with Yari and you. I explained to him aboutyou, and what what happened with us. Hehad faith we'd reconcile," she said with a huge smile.

"What you gone do when you have yo' baby?" Kemari asked.

"Go home," Shanti said.

"You gone still be alone, whether you pregnant or not," Kosher said.

"Yeah, but for the time being, I needed to get away," Shanti said.

I know Kosher and Kemari didn't know what she was talking about, but I know she meant she needed to get away after she killed Big John and Crystal. I loved having Ashanti back, and we even made plans to chill again soon, and she was even excited to meet Camille after hearing about her for so many years. I just didn't know how Danielle would take our renewed friendship since her and Yari's relationship was strained right now.

I know one thing; I didn't want to lose Ashanti again.

* * *

AFTER LEAVING from lunch with my girls, picking Camille up from therapy, and dropping her off to Momma Jackie house, somewhere she always wanted to be lately, I walked into the house, stopping in the kitchen to grab a snack. I noticed that Ja was home. The house just appeared to be strangely quiet. Flipping the light switch to turn the lights on, nothing happened.

"Ja?" I said, calling out his name.

"The lights not working," I said.

"Did we not pay our bill?" I said, thinking out loud.

"Miss Mary?" I said.

No one answered me.

Abandoning my snack, I slipped my shoes off, and slipped on the fur house slippers I kept downstairs. Heart beating fast, I used the flashlight on my phone for light as I reached into my purse and grabbed my mace as I called out to my husband again.

"Ja?" I said with again no answer.

Thoughts of my kidnapping crept in my mind as I slowly walked up the stairs. Stopping in front of my door, I noticed an envelope taped to it with my name on it. Grabbing it and opening it, I pulled out a note with a message that said, *pleasure is in the heart of those with no limits.*

Not really sure what that meant, I opened the door and the room is lit with candles burning everywhere as rose petals littered the floor and bed. Smiling brightly, I walked further into the room, grabbing a sticky note off my vanity mirror that said *strip.* Slowly taking off my clothes, I was still slightly scared, but turned on all at the same time as I turned to the bed to grab a sticky note off the headboard.

"Head to the bathroom." I read out loud as I walked into our bathroom where I found a bubble bath drawn with a bottle and glass of my favorite apple juice.

Attached to the mirror was another sticky note that said, *get in shitty booty.* I laughed so hard when I read this because only Ja could have something so romantic set up, then say something like this.

Stepping into our huge Jacuzzi-sized tub, I grabbed the wine glass, and bottle of apple juice chillin' on ice and took a sip, and I let the bubbles and bath salts relax my body. After the long day I've had, this was the perfect end to my day.

Laying my bead back on the tub, and closing my eyes, I was in complete bliss when I heard the door creak open. I opened my eyes to see my sexy ass husband walking up to the tub fully naked and dick just swinging, looking like breakfast, lunch, and dinner all wrapped into one.

"Where were you?" I asked.

"I was here the entire time, scary ass," he said, laughing as he leaned down and kissed me.

"Baby, where did all of this come from?" I asked him.

"Damn, a nigga can't be romantic with his ole lady though?" he asked.

"I never said that. I love it. Get in with me," I said.

"Naw, get out with me," he said, pulling on my arm as I stood up.

Without warning, he picked me up and sat me onto our bathroom counter, kissing and biting my neck attacking me without warning.

"Baby, mmm," I moaned.

"Relax, and let your man cater to you, Mrs. Carter," he said.

Although I loved rough-around-the-edges, shit-talking, crazy Jakeem, I also loved this new side he was showing me as well. He was taking his time with me making love to every part of my mind, body, and soul. Licking and sucking my breasts, he slid down to my inner thighs, making sure to tease my pussy as well.

"Ahh," I moaned in pure torture because I wanted him to put me out of my misery.

"You ready for daddy to taste that pussy?" he huskily asked.

"Yess, please," I damn near screamed.

"Say, daddy I'm ready for you to taste this pussy," he said.

"No, just do it," I said as he quickly let go of me, taking the wonderful feeling with him.

"Say it," he said.

"Daddy, I'm ready for you to feast on this pussy. Put your face in it, and eat it like this your last meal on earth," I said, surprising both of us because that's so out of the usual for me to say.

"Your wish is my command, Mrs. Carter," he said, coming back to me, wasting no time dropping fully to his knees, and diving straight into me pulling me to his mouth so that his mouth was full, and his tongue was on the prowl sucking, slurping, and licking my orgasm out of me.

I was so turned on that in two seconds, I was literally squirting all over the place. Not bothering to let me catch my breath, Ja slid me down off the counter into his waiting dick, bouncing me up and down at a rapid pace.

"Fuck," he moaned out, leaning up and latching onto a nipple.

"You so deep, baby," I said with my head thrown back.

"Fuck me back, girl," he said, slapping me hard on my ass before giving one of my cheeks a huge squeeze.

"You so deep! Fuck!" I screamed.

"A nigga know that. I want you to feel me," he said, squeezing my hips tightly, and he slammed me down into his waiting dick over and over again.

"Do you feel me, girl?"

"Ohh, yess, baby! I feel you! I feel all of you in my stomach!" I screamed out, feeling my legs shaking as I came once again.

"I feel you cumming. Nut all on this dick, girl," he said.

"We ain't done," Ja said as he placed his hand around my throat and began to fuck me harder and harder until I exploded again, and my knees became weak as I feel backward onto the counter.

Leaning forward dick still hard and inside of me, he whispered in my ear, "It's not over yet."

Danielle

Who came to make sweet love? Not me
Who came to kiss and hug? Not me
Who came to beat it up? Rocky
And don't use those hands to put up that gate and
stop me.

Tank's "When We" blasted through the surround sound as I found myself with my legs spread open into a split. My hands were holding each of my feet by the tips of my toes as Yari sprayed whipped cream all over my body before bending down and feasting on the snack he had prepared for myself.

I know, I know. I had talked all of that shit about fuck Yari, and now here I was about to actually fuck Yari. It never was my intention to sleep with this man. It just happened. He showed up at my house with flowers and weak ass apology, and instead of hitting his ass with those flowers slamming the door in his face, I had let him in to hear him out.

I don't know how we ended up in the bedroom, or how I wound up in the current situation that I was in. But here I was about to let him eat my pussy like he had been lost in the jungle for some months, and this was his first meal since finally finding his way home.

Starting with my breasts, he licked whipped cream off of both of them, toying with my nipples a bit before he put his entire mouth on my breast, alternating between licking my nipple and sucking on my breast.

Every now and then when his teeth grazed one of my nipples, the pain caused me to moan out in ecstasy. It was a very pleasurable pain. I moaned out in pleasure as well as pain.

"Yari," I moaned as he still took his time with me.

We usually got straight to fucking and skipped foreplay, so I was confused and extremely turned on by this change in things.

"This pussy leaking for daddy," he said, slipping a finger into my sloppy-wet, throbbing pussy as he dove fast-first into my center, skillfully bringing me double pleasure as he fucked me with his finger and tongue as I exploded all in his mouth. Spent, I dropped my legs and laid there breathing heavily.

"We not done yet," he said slapping me on my ass. "Turn that ass over and assume the position."

Even though I was drained, I eagerly flipped over, anxious to receive the dick. What I felt instead, causing me to jump as I felt a vibrator being stuffed inside of me and turned up to max level.

"Fuckk, Yari!" I screamed as I felt him bending down and licking up and down my back before he removed the vibrator and pushed inside of me.

* * *

"WHERE YOU GOING?" I asked Yari as I saw him roll over to grab his clothes.

"My baby momma just texted me and asked if I could bring her some food."

"Her legs don't look broke to me," I said.

"Don't start this shit, Danielle. I already explained to you earlier what it as with Ashanti."

"Naw, nigga, you didn't explain shit. Was this before or after you ate the soul out my body or fucked me into a coma. Was your intention to fuck me so good I would be OK with the bullshit you spitting? You say you want to build something with me, yet immediately after you have sex with me, you leave because your baby momma texted you to bring her some food? She get around to everywhere else, so why she can't go get food? You busy with me," I said.

"Because I want to feed my baby. Damn, is that so hard to understand?"

"Feed yo' baby what? Dickor food?"

"Man, as much shit as I got going on, I either need you to be my calm or lose my number. I thought you would be my safe haven from everything else and be a real woman and hold your man down. Naw, all your ass wanna do is argue and trip about shit that you made an issue. My baby momma lost her entire family, and she doesn't have friends; well, her and Giovania made up," he said.

"What," I asked, trying to make sure I heard him correctly.

No he didn't say Giovania and Ashanti back friends. Like that's some foul shit, and I can't respect it. I can't fuck with people who fuck with people I don't fuck with. She either gotta pick a side or stay the fuck from round me, but she couldn't have both.

"Yeah, they cool again while you the only one still on this bullshit," he said.

"Maybe if you stop sticking your community dick inside of me, I wouldn't be on no bullshit," I said.

"I ain't force you to keep hopping on it either. You could have stopped me at any time," he said.

"I like you, but you need to calm down, becool, and let shit continue falling into place," he said as I burst out laughing.

"Let shit continue falling into place, huh? You know what I take that back, I can't be mad at Giovania about being cool with her old friend. I ain't even mad at your bitch. It's your ass that's the problem. But I'm good on you from now on, so I'ma answer your question and take option B for $200 Alex; I'll lose your number.

"I can't focus on my work for Ja for dealing with your lying ass. You talking about some being a damn calm, but for the last month that's all I wanted your ass to be—my calm. I'm dealing with a lot of shit from my child father's and other shit. I just wanted you to be the same calm you seek, but I guess neither of us could do that.

"I refuse to lose my sanity behind this. Don't call me, don't text me, and stay yo' ass ten feet away from me at all times. You know your way to the door," I said, walking inside of the bathroom and closing the door behind me.

I didn't want him to see the tears that couldn't wait a second longer to fall. I've loved Yari since I was fourteen. Even when he didn't notice me, I still loved him from a distance. It hurts to have finally gotten what I've waited my whole life for, only for it to be taken away before it's fully had a fighting chance.

I can't fight for him. I won't fight for him. If he wants me, his actions gone have to show it. Other than that, I'm officially done.

Picking up the pregnancy test I had taken earlier, I just stared down at it, wondering how I had once again found myself in a situation like this.

* * *

AFTER GOING BACK and forth all morning, I decided I would go see Bull once and for all to see what he really wanted and make him leave me alone. After that high-speed chase through the mall, I would never have him around my baby again. She was still shaken up from that incident.

Just in case Bull was up to bullshit, I dropped Safari off to the safest place I know, Momma Jackie and Maxx Carter's house. If he killed me, I know they would never let him have my baby. I don't trust himas far as I can throw him which wasn't far at all. I was taking every precaution possible becauseI'd be damned if this wasanother trick or ploy to harm my child. The day I became a mother was the day I met someone worth dying for. I would risk it all for my baby, even staring the devil himself in the face.

Pulling up at the park, I was ready with my wheat Timberlands on, biker shorts, and sports bra. I had some mace in my bra, and a box cutter.

"Where Safari?" Bull asked as I walked up to him.

Ja suggested we meet in a public place, so I figured a park full of kids and adults would be best. Especially if he tried the same shit he tried at the mall that day. This wasn't the park or the side of town he wanted to pull a gun out on me at. These were Yari's streets, and these niggas over here wouldn't care if it was their beef or not—they pulling out their guns shooting just because they see a gun and a nigga in the wrong part of town.

"I didn't bring her," I said.

"What type of games are you fuckin' playing?" he asked me.

"I'm not playing no games at all. I never went outside to recess in school because I wasn't one to play games. You the one with the bullshit. What type of games are you playing? You don't even want my daughter, asked me to abort her, and I'm guessing your wife doesn't know about her. So those idle threats on getting full custody, you can miss me with, because you and I both know wifey not having it. Whatever problem you have with me, don't involve my child in it, because I'll die behind my baby," I said.

"That's cute," he said.

"I'm not scared of you, Bull, so if today was supposed to be an intimidation factor, you failing."

"I don't recall saying you supposed to been scared. Shit, I still don't know why you ran that day in the mall, I have no intention to do you bodily harm," he said.

"Cut the bullshit and let's get down to why am I here."

"Because you've been avoiding me, and we have important business to discuss."

"Only important business we have to discuss would be Safari, and she's not here. So therefore, I'm leaving as well," I said.

I was preparing to walk away until he said, "I'm sure your secret with the body and bloody knife are still buried in the same spot with that same bloody rag," pausing me as all the blood drained from my face.

"Do I got your undivided attention now?" He smirked as he straightened his tie.

"What do you really want, Bull?"

"I'm back for an extended amount of time trying to reclaim my throne but there's something standing in my way. Yari, I need his operation because it can only be one sheriff in town.

Giovania

"Did I tell you that Camille asked me the other day about you being her daddy since God took her dad away?" I asked Ja as I took a bite of my wings.

"Naw what you tell her?"

"I told her that it doesn't work that way, and you can't replace your father, but you can have someone step up to the plate. Then she said it wasn't fair the new baby got to have a daddy, and she didn't," I said, feeling myself getting emotional. Each time I thought about the hurt and pain my selfish ass mother caused my sister, it just broke me to the core.

"Don't start that crying shit, stressing out my damn child. I've been thinking about it for a while now, and I think I wanna adopt her," he said.

"No, Ja, you can be her godfather. That's some weird, VH1 ratchet TV show drama. If you adopt her, that will be your daughter and sister-in-law, and our baby's auntie and sister. That's just too much for me. I told Camille you could be her godfather," I said.

I wanted nothing more than to give Camille the father she longed for, but signing a birth certificate and giving birth to a baby doesn't make a man a father. It's the love, time, effort, and consistency he puts into that child. Ja doesn't need a paper to validate that. We don't need any more crazy antics added to our already dysfunctional family.

"She can be my goddaughter if you feel that strongly about me not adopting her," he said.

"Because that's just crazy. Your sister-in-law and daughter? That's some incest, *Jerry Springer*, *Oprah* type of drama," I said, laughing.

"When you say that shit out loud it sound chap as fuck," he said.

"Right, that's what I was trying to tell you. Sounding all kinda of crazy," I said, dipping my fries into honey mustard and my ice cream before I put it into my mouth.

My cravings were so off the wall with this child that the other day while walking around the store, I had the urge to eat baby power. It tasted like heaven for some reason, which disturbed me a lot especially because I couldn't stop eating it.

"I do want to change her name. Everyone in the house will be a Carter except her. That won't be too awkward or crazy," he said.

I thought it over for a minute, and he was right. We were all Carters while Millie was a Santiago. However, it was her father's name, and one day, it's my hope for her to connect with her other family. I really liked her father, and he was a good dad, and I think she should honor him and keep his legacy.

"I don't think I will change it. Her dad was a good man, and that's all she has left to remember him by because we never knew any of his relatives or much about him," I said.

"Yo' pink starburst-looking ass always try and be right. You do have valid points though," he said.

"Don't talk about me, baby. But speaking of talk, you really need to talk to your friend," I said, referring to Yari.

"What friend?"

"Yari," I said.

"Nope," he immediately said.

"You didn't even ask me what about."

"Shit because a nigga already know what about. That ain't my business or your business."

"But both of them are my friends, and he is not being fair to them," I said, pouting.

"You can poke that lip right back in because again everything you just named was still somebody else's damn business. I don't get in another grown man's business unless it involves a nigga that want some smoke. If they ain't tryna step, I mind my own business. That's exactly what yo' ass gone do, and let me find out you didn't do that," he said.

"Is that an order?"

"Naw, I ain't order you to do shit. I just know what you not gone do. Dick run this household and don't you forget it," he said.

I chose not to respond to that because a few months ago when he made that statement "dick runs this relationship," and I argued that the statement was a lie, he withheld sex from me for a few days. Back then, that wasn't so bad, but now, I would die. I'm not sure if it's this baby or the vitamins that I'm taking, but I want sex all day, every day. I can't go a few hours, let alone a few days. So I knew when to shut my mouth.

"That ass stopped talking quick. You know what time it was about to be. No dick for you," he said.

"Fuck you, Ja," I said, laughing.

Checking his phone, he said, "We won't make it all the way back home and back this way for your doctor's appointment, so we can do car sex again, or I'll book us a room right beside the hospital," he said, sticking his tongue out at me and flicking it up and down. My juices instantly soaked my panties as I got all hot and bothered.

"Since my back been hurting lately, I'll choose the hotel," I said, eagerly flagging down a waitress to get a to-go box.

* * *

"WHAT UP, MY MAN," Ja said dappin' Dr. Palager up as we walked into the room.

Today I was nervous because I still had not been able to see the sex of my baby. We had decided against a gender reveal because this baby was acting stubborn just like Ja's ass. He was already rubbing off on our child.

"So how have our parents to be been doing? Any pains or discomforts since our last visit, mommy?" he asked.

"No, I—" I started until Ja's ass interrupted me.

Each time he opened his mouth at my doctor's appointment, he embarrassed me. I already knew what was about to happen, so I just put my head down.

"Yeah, I got a question," he said.

"I would have been surprised if you didn't," Dr. Palager said, laughing.

"No it's nothing crazy this time, doc, this shit important. You said last time the size of my dick wouldn't hurt Giovania, but what about my baby? Oh, check it, the other day I got on my fifty shades of freak shit, and I swear for God I was pushing on my son's head, giving him brain damage and shit. Do he feel that?" he asked. His delivery was always terrible, but he really meant well.

"Jakeem!" I said.

"It's OK, Mrs. Carter. That's a perfectly OK question to ask. Mr. Carter, I can assure you that you cannot touch the baby's head."

"See, I don't know about that, doc. How deep in the pussy I always be, I couldn't even go that deep this time because I felt like I was pushing on a wall. I think that was the baby's head. And even Giovania was sore as hell for a few days, so I think that was the baby disagreeing with all that extracurricular activity and shit," Ja said.

"Please, don't answer that, doctor, and Ja stop talking," I said with my head in my hands.

"These questions I need to know, bruh, because I don't want to traumatize my seed," he said really dead ass serious.

"To answer your question—" the doctor started before I cut him off.

"No, doctor, we don't want to hear. You answered it the first time. Can we please finish our doctor's visit?" I asked, but his ass looked to Ja for confirmation before he continued.

"Yeah, I'll just book own damn appointment to ask all these questions by myself," Ja said.

"Yeah, you do that," I said, rolling my eyes.

"Well, parents, are we ready to see the gender of your little one?"

"Yes," I squealed, laying back on the bed.

After he squeezed some type of lube shit onto my stomach, he used this suction cup type thing to rub it all around my stomach. This wasn't the first time I've been through this, but I still got amazed each time I had an ultrasound performed.

Come on, momma's baby. Show yourself, I thought to myself with my eyes squeezed tightly shut.

"Finally, the little lady opens her legs," he said.

"It's a girl," Ja said.

"Daddy's princess."

"And his prince," the doctor said.

"His what?" I asked, sitting up.

"We could never get an accurate reading because one was really two, but the girl has been cuddled up next to her brother this entire time. They both just rolled over today," the doctor said as I felt like I was about to pass out. Ja on the other hand was happy as hell.

"Hell yeah that's what the fuck I'm talking about," he said before he looked down and grabbed this manhood, and said, "That's what the fuck we do. That's what the hell I'm talking about my nigga. We did that, ya dig," he said.

This has to be such a bad dream, two babies? Three kids.

* * *

"HELLO?" I said, answering my phone that wouldn't stop ringing.

"Giovania, how are you?" the caller on the other end of the phone said. The last person I thought would ever call me again.

"You don't care how I am, so why the fuck are you calling me, Mateo?" I asked.

"Is Camille OK?" he asked as if he were genuinely concerned.

"After you tried to kill her, now you want to know if she's OK? You sick son of a bitch, don't call my phone anymore. If I were you, I'd keep running and keep hiding. I would hate to be you whenever Ja catches up to you," I said.

"Everything you think you know, is not what it appears to be. And the first lie you think you know is I'm hiding from anybody. I'm in plain sight if Jakeem Carter wants to find me."

"If you were in plain sight, you would have turned up when they came looking for you. Don't call my phone any more. Dead men can't make phone calls anyway," I said, hanging up in his face.

I had no desire to hear anything he was talking about at this point. I didn't give a fuck who the mastermind behind everything was or whose real idea it was. He went along with everything; therefore, he was just as responsible as my mother was in my eyes. Both of them can die together.

* * *

WALKING down the stairs in nothing but lingerie with a robe on, I tried to steady my nerves. What I was about to go could potentially get somebody killed; me included. Picking up my phone, I pressed 3, signaling my bodyguard to come inside the house.

In less than two seconds, he raced in, gun drawn and ready for war.

"Giovania, Mrs. Carter!" Roy yelled out.

"I'm in the kitchen, Roy," I said.

I timed it just perfectly so that as soon he walked into the kitchen, I let my robe drop. I had never been this exposed to a man other than my husband. Kyle doesn't count.

"Whoa, what the hell," Roy said, quickly turning around.

"It's too late now. You saw me in this black lace panty and bra set," I said.

"It was green," he said then said, "Fuck, Ja gone kill me."

Smiling brightly, I put my robe back on.

"You can turn around now," I said.

"Hell no, bruh. I don't know what type of shit you on, but I got two kids to think about. You need to take your ass back upstairs with that shit you on," he said.

"I put my robe back on" I said.

"If that's all, I'ma dip back to my post," he said.

"I'm going out tonight, and you not coming with me," I said before I thought about it and changed my mind.

Ja told me he was doing an overnight job, Camille was with Safari at Momma Jackie's house, so that left me in the clear to attend this party tonight at the House of Blues.

"No, you are coming with me, but you not telling Ja. If you do tell him, you'll have to tell him you saw me in my underwear, and how you think he gone react, even if it was an accident?" I said as he slowly turned around and looked at me with death in his eyes.

"You would gamble with my life knowing I got kids to make it home to? You know Ja ain't the type of nigga to be fucked with, and he knows everything. I wouldn't be surprised if it ain't cameras all around this house. I'm not doing that shit," Roy said.

"If I go by myself, and I get hurt, what you think gon' happen then?" I asked him.

He knew I was right, and that's why it took him a while to respond.

"Whatever. We going, but we only staying two hours tops," he said.

"That's fine. I don't even need that much time. Oh, after I finish getting dressed, we need to stop by and get Shanti," I said.

This original mission was supposed to be with Danielle, but I switched to Ashanti because she isn't from here, so it looks less suspicious. Everybody knows Danielle and Ja cool.

* * *

> I-n-d-e-p-e-n-d-e-n-t do you know what that mean
> mayne?
> I-n-d-e-p-e-n-d-e-n-t do you know what that mean?
> She got her own house
> She got her own car
> Two jobs, work hard, you a bad broad

"BITCH, we been here an hour, what's the plan because I don't know if you forgot or not, but my ass is damn near ready to pop. My ass sitting over here looking like an uncomfortable Miss Piggy," Ashanti said.

That's all she's really been doing—complaining since we got here. I was waiting for the right time to strike. Everything had to be calculated. Trina was in her section turning up and popping bottles, and I wanted sis to enjoy her last party.

In order for it not to appear suspicious, and to look like an overdose, I needed everything to line up. While she thought a baller was sending bottles to their table, I had really slipped the bartender ten thousand dollars to keep sending them bottles.

Being that she couldn't get away from Instagram and social media in the past, I thanked my lucky stars that she was on Facebook live right now as she turned a bottle up taking a long drink from it. Making sure to screen record the live video just in case somebody tried to delete it, I figured we had enough proof to rule it an accidental death. Catching the eye of the same bartender that I slipped money to, I discreetly nodded my head as she started making the shots I had also paid for.

For this last job, I had paid her twenty thousand. It's amazing what people would do for money. Making the drinks, she passed them off to the bottle girls as they made their way to Trina's section. Making sure to sit Trina's shot down in front of her, the bottle girls gave everyone their shots as they did a toast and threw the shots back.

About five minutes later, I saw Trina's fanning herself as she grabbed a bottle of water drinking it. A couple minutes about that, she made her way out of the section, through the crowd, and toward the restroom.

Looking at my phone, I said, "In about three minutes, we going to the bathroom, then we leaving. Make sure you have all of your stuff together," I said.

When it was time to make our move, I calmly stood up and headed toward the bathroom with Ashanti wobbling behind me. Pushing inside the women's restroom, I saw Trina bent over the sink splashing water on her face.

"Damn, I'm fucked up, yeah," she said, bouncing her ass as she heard music when we opened the door.

Looking up, she saw us and immediately started laughing.

"Well well, well. If it isn't Molly the Maid and her new sidekick," she said, laughing slurring her words.

"Bitch, I got your sidekick. Don't let the belly fool you hoe," Ashanti said.

I calmly grabbed her arm.

"It's OK best friend. We letting God deal with these demons in 2018. I wish you nothing but the best in life, Trina. You are a miserable, jealous, and depressed troubled soul who needs to get right with the Lord before it's too late. All that hate in your heart for a man who has never nor will ever love you in this lifestyle or next is preventing you from living your best life. If me and him divorced, I would still live every day like this my last," I said.

As I was talking I had slowly started walking toward her because I had something else to say. Everything I just said was only for the wire she always wears, but I was gone cut the water on and use the transmitter jammer that discreetly clicked on in my purse. I wanted them to hear the first part, that's why I didn't immediately turn it on. After everything was in place, I cut the water on and turned to her.

"My, my, my, how those tables have turned. You wanted to let Detective Morris allow you to gamble with your life each time you popped up on Jakeem, and now, it has cost you your life," I said.

"Bitch, what the fuck are you talking about?" she asked, her words becoming more slurred by the minute.

"I slipped more than enough Cyanide in that shot you took to kill you."

"Hahahaha, bitch, you bluffing. You ain't got the balls to kill me, bitch."

"Without the antidote, you'll be dead within the next few minutes by my calculations. Give or take a minute," I said.

"Bitch, you not about the life you try and live with that nigga. You a square ass bitch. You wanna be down. As many times as I fucked Ja shit up, and you ain't get off. Bitch, bye. The only time you wanted to fight was when you had Kosher and Kemari for back up. Get yo' ass on, acting like the big bad wolf. But you an all bark and no bite ass hoe," she said as snatched the choker off her neck, running to the sink to dash water on her face.

"Airway restrictions is one of the first symptoms. Shortness of breath, dizziness, slurred speech, and chest pains—also all symptoms. You'll eventually go into full cardiac arrest," I said to her.

I watched her for a few more minutes as her lungs almost closed completely up on her before me and Ashanti made our escape. By the time someone finds her, she'll more than likely be foaming at the mouth. The poison will be long gone before she reaches the hospital. This was the perfect murder that was executed to perfection, it was only one problem, Jakeem. I could only hope he never found out what I had done.

"Oh, shit," Ashanti said.

"What?" I asked her.

"Yari asked where I went dressed up," she said.

"Girl, just say you came to my house or something," I said.

"That's the *oh shit* part," she said, looking at me with bucked eyes.

"What is?"

"Yari said he'll know if I was at Ja house or not because Ja has cameras all throughout the house, and he'll have them run the cameras back," she said as I felt all the blood drain from my face.

He has cameras? Fuck!

Jakeem "Ja" Carter

"Let me get two custom baby chains that say *daddy's prince* and *daddy's princess*," I said to my jeweler.

Ever since I found out I was having twins, I been buying the mall out and stacking up for my kids. It's crazy how we both got what we wanted on the first try. I never expected Giovania to be carrying twins, but that was the best thing I've ever heard aside from when Giovania said "I do." It's strange how so ready I am to become a dad.

"Damn, nigga. You going overboard," Yari said after I gave Jacob the $250,000 for the pieces I just asked him to make.

"Nigga, I ain't bought shit but what the kids need," I said, lying.

"You worse than these females, bruh. Shanti don't even shop for Tariq like that.

"I just told you, nigga. I only got shit they needed," I said.

"Shit they need? What is your daughter gone do with a pandora bracelet? And you got lil' man a diamond-studded pinky ring," he said.

"Nigga, fuck you. Worry about your own damn kids," I said, laughing because I didn't even have a comeback.

"Naw. Don't say kids, nigga. I only got one kid, and that's how it's gone stay. Nigga not having another one, Hell, Shanti got the weird ass cravings and always got my black ass up in the middle of the night running from store to store. She only likes fruit from this store, water from that store, shit is crazy."

"It is, but see, I already know all of Giovania favorite snacks, and I rack up on them and anything else I hear her talking about throughout the day. If she mention it, I go get it," I said.

"Nigga, you don't do no damn shopping. You mean Ms.Mary goes and gets it," he said, laughing.

"Shit, me, Miss Mary, it's all coming from my pocket," I said.

"That's what you need to invest in," I said.

"You right. Hell, I need a nanny for my situation to fuck," he said, laughing

"Speaking of your situation, you need to tighten up and get your shit together. If my lady yells at me one more time because you playing both of her friends, I'm kicking your ass," I said to him.

"I'm stuck between a rock and a hard place," he said, running his hands down his face.

"Nigga, I ain't tryna stand here and run it with you about your feelings on some bitch shit. I'm just saying tighten up." I said.

"Nigga, how you lost your damn mind when Giovania left you. I know damn well you not talking about nobody and their damn feelings, ole crying ass nigga. You was running around this bitch looking like you had lost your best friend," Yari said.

"That's different," I said.

"Naw, bitch. It's the same shit," Yari said, laughing.

"It's different because I'm a handsome ass nigga, and I can do that," I said.

* * *

We got him. Sage texted me.

Bet. I texted him back.

At the last minute, I had let the twins and Yari go and get Antwon for me and bring him back to the warehouse. I had more pressing matters to tend to. I had been actively searching for the $400,000 truck that Nancy, Giovania's mom, took from her. I wasn't fucked up about the truck. I had purchased my wife another one truck the next day, and she has a Range Rover. I wanted to catch up with the truck, so it could lead me to Nancy and possibly Mateo and his sons.

Giovania told me he called her the other day talking about some shit wasn't what it seemed, and he wasn't hiding at all. Niggas always talk real greasy when they not in front of you. Keyboard, cellphone thugs. I had something special planned for them when I got up both of their asses. That's the real reason I haven't accepted anymore jobs yet and was stressed the hell out.

To some people, a stress reliever would be sex or exercising. To a nigga like me, I relieved all of my stress when I killed a nigga. I haven't killed a nigga in at least a few weeks, and that was a long as time for me. I tried to stop bodying niggas in my city because my lawyer advised me to cool off with everything until he gets this case taken care of, and even though Giovania has a high sex drive right now due to the baby, she can't handle super rough sex, but I still try and take my problems out on that lil' pussy every chance I get. It's only a temporary fix, until I'm back stressed.

Shit, I been walking around the last few weeks like I'm OK, but deep down inside, a nigga just wanna chop somebody head off and watch their body drop. Killing is such a natural high for me. Afterward, nigga be walking around smiling hard as fuck like I just got my dick sucked from the back by two big-booty freaks. When Lil' Wayne said he needed pussy to survive, I felt that shit because I needed to body a nigga to survive as well.

Pulling up on the run-down block that I had finally tracked the truck to since they disabled the tracking device on it, I parked at an abandoned house and walked down the block to the house. These niggas either gotta be the boldest niggas alive or the dumbest niggas alive.

There, parked in the driveway, was the G-Wagon. They could have at least took it to a chop shop, got it painted, or some shit. The only thing them niggas did was take the plates off.

Creeping around back, I looked around at the empty backyard

before I picked the lock and went into the house. The shit was filthy as hell and smelled like stale ass mixed with funk and dirty ass clothes.

I wanted to kill Nancy's ass so fuckin' bad I could taste it. My shit rocked up at the thought of slicing this bitch nipples off one nipple at a time and gutting her like a fish. She fucked up when she pulled a gun on Giovania Carter and fucked with Camille Carter. I don't give a fuck what Giovania says, Camille is a Carter.

Disrespect of any kind toward me family is an automatic death sentence. I know Giovania has expressed lots of time that she wants to kill her mother, but let's face it, my baby ain't no killer, and I'm OK with that. She talks shit because she feels like she has to stand up for herself, but she is a gentle soul. Maybe every now and then I wouldn't mind her chopping a bitch head off and playing basketball with that hoe, but while she carrying my twins, her ass not doing shit but sitting around eating and feeding daddy's babies.

Walking slowly to the back room, I had to hold my breath to keep from breathing in the funk because the shit for worse the further I walked. Of all the situations I've been in, including getting shot at, this felt like it would be the one thing to take a nigga out—this fucking odor.

Finally stopping at the room I heard noise coming out of, I kicked the door in to see a crackhead ass naked giving a nigga some head.

"What the fuck," he said jumping up looking embarrassed that he had been caught with this *Tale from the Crypt*-looking bitch.

"For an extra $200, I'll do both of you at the same damn time," she said.

"Bitch, I hope that's not your pussy smelling like that. Got the whole fucking house smelling rotten. You need to check and make sure ain't shit dead inside that trash-can pussy," I said to her.

"Nigga, fuck you. This some of the best pussy you'll ever receive in your life," she said, getting off the bed licking her lips while looking me up and down as if I were a T-bone steak.

"Don't act like you don't want a taste of this. I see how you looking at me," she said.

The second she started advancing towards me, I lither ass up with bullets, I didn't want it getting to close to me looking like some shit off *Wrong Turn* and smelling like seafood that's been sitting out.

"You can have whatever you want," the nigga had the audacity to say.

"That gotta be a joke right? Whatever I want? Nigga, ain't shit in this bitch that nobody fuckin' want. The only thing of value is that $400,000 truck sitting in the yard."

"You can have that. I don't have the keys to it though, that's why it's sitting there," he said.

"Where Nancy at with the keys?" I asked him.

Hearing movement behind me, I crept behind the door a bit as two niggas appeared in the doorway.

"Bruh, what we tell you about bringing these dirty ass crackhead hoes to this spot. You need to be focusing on how you gone snatch the kid and her sister," one of the men said.

No this nigga didn't call nobody dirty when this entire house was filthy I thought to myself. Lining the scope of my gun up with the nigga that was behind him not talking, I shot his ass in his dick as blood exploded in his pants, and he dropped to his knees.

"Arghhhhhh!" he yelled out.

Before the talking ass nigga could make a move, I slammed the door into his face. I quickly moved from behind it and knocked his out with the butt of my gun. Looking back to the bitch ass nigga sitting on the bed damn near 'bout to pee on hisself, I decided I was gone have to suck it up and torture their asses here because I would have had to burn my whole car had their asses gotten inside of it; that's how bad the smell was. Shit, I still might burn my shit or give it away because that smell might get on me.

Taking my book bag off my back, I pulled out duct tape, rope, and zip ties. I came prepared.

"I swear I'll tell you whatever you want to know. Please don't kill me. I never wanted to be involved in any of this shit to begin with. My cousin put me on because I needed the money," dude said, running his mouth as I busied myself tying the nigga up I knocked out.

The nigga I shot in the dick was already going into shock from blood loss, so I was gone let his ass bleed out awhile.

"Damn, you ain't got no damn heart do you? This a grown-man business; this not the Girl's Scouts," I said to him, shaking my head at how quick the nigga folded.

"I want my son to have heart like me. Like I couldn't imagine his ass folding like you. This some real bitch shit, nigga. But shit since you ruining the fun of torturing, your ass gone tell me what you know before I wake this nigga on the floor up. I got a feeling he knows more than you," I said just as the nigga started coughing. He shook back quicker than I had expected.

"Fuck this nigga, Shayne. Don't say shit to him. He gone kill you regardless of what you say," he spat.

Looking at me, Shayne said, "I'll tell you whatever you want if I can walk up out of here," he said.

"Bet. Get to talking. Where is Nancy, and what is she up to? Also, where is Mateo?" I said.

"Go!" I told him.

"Nancy at her boyfriend or whoever the nigga is to her house. She got the keys with her because she feels like we would drive the truck if she left us with the keys, and she didn't want us ruining it," he said.

"Ruining what?" I asked him.

"I don't know," he said.

"Nigga, shut your soft ass up. Running yo' mouth like a bitch," the nigga still on the floor said.

Without even looking down, I shit his ass, not sure where the bullet landed. I just know from his screams that it connected.

"Where Mateo live?" I asked him.

"Who?" he asked.

"Nigga, you said she was at her boyfriend house, so where the fuck Mateo live at?"

"I don't know no damn Mateo," he said.

"Well, who her dude then?" I asked him.

Looking at his face, I knew that's all the information that he knew. Pulling my butterfly knives out of my bag, I walked over to him and with precision, sliced both of his ankles right about where his ankle and his foot met.

"Fuck, that was all I know! You said you was gone let me talk out of here!" he screamed.

"I told you he wasn't, stupid ass nigga," dude said.

"Don't listen to him. You are free to go," I said, barely getting the words out before his ass jumped up, and the minute he put pressure on his ankles, they damn near split in half.

Still, he attempted to leave out of the room determined to get away. I let him get entirely out of the room before I shot him in the back of the head. I said he could walk out this room alive, but I never said he could keep his life.

Laughing, the nigga I shot spit blood out of his mouth that landed by my feet—the ultimate form of disrespect.

"Nigga, you better be glad it stank worse than a rotten sewage tank in this bitch, or you would have died slowly," I said as I shot him in the face five times.

Walking over to the nigga with I had initially shot, I saw that, surprisingly, he was still alive.

"I can put you out your misery if you answer one question, or I'll let your ass lay here and bleed out. It could be days before you die of blood loss," I said.

"OK," he said barely above a whisper because he was in so much pain.

"Why is my truck here? Where is Nancy and her nigga? What's her nigga's name?" I asked.

"Nancy showed up one day with the truck, and it's been here ever since. We didn't know where it came from. She is with her boyfriend, and they are actively plotting against you," he said, not coming as a surprise to me.

"So you know me? How you know me?" I asked him.

"Was shown a picture of you before," he said barely above a whisper, his life slowly slipping away from him.

"What was y'all supposed to do when y'all found me?" I asked him.

He didn't respond, so I kicked him.

"Aye, what was y'all supposed to do when y'all found me?" I asked him as his eyes popped open.

Licking his lips he said, "Bring you to Nancy's boyfriend. He said you know too much, and he has to get rid of you. He's tried a few times and failed," he said.

Now I was really confused because I don't know what Mateo was getting at with that one? Did he mean I knew his ass was broke? Or that I knew he was in the United States?

"Where is Mateo right now?' I asked him as he eyes rolled to the back of his head.

"I don't know a Mateo," he said.

Just when I was about to get pissed off because if it wasn't Mateo, who else I knew too much of and was Nancy's nigga?

I didn't have to wait too long because he said, "Her boyfriend name... her boyfriend name..." he said fading in and out.

Shaking him I said, "What's the nigga name?"

"Her boyfriend is Judge Thomas—the judge whose wife you killed."

Giovania

"Fuck, how did you miss the fact his crazy ass had cameras?" Ashanti asked, shaking her head.

"I don't know," I said.

"Ohh, bitch, we dead. I mean, you dead. I'll cut Ja crazy ass," she said, laughing.

"I could kick my own ass right about now! But I mean, what was I supposed to do? Ask him when I first moved in if he had cameras in the house so he could kill me? You know he doesn't take any chances if he thinks somebody is moving foul," I said, biting my fingernails.

When the night first started, I was cool, calm, and confident, but now, I was a wreck. I was trying to steady my rapidly-beating heart as I thought about how I would get myself out of this situation with my life and my husband. I wasn't as worried about him knowing I killed Trina as I was about me opening my robe in front of Roy. As soon as I thought about Roy, and what Ja would do to him, I begin to panic. That man had kids and a baby on the way, and I might have just gotten him killed, all for my own gain.

"Maybe Ja doesn't have cameras in the kitchen. I mean, why would he? What he tryna catch somebody doing in there? Stealing bread?" Ashanti said as if reading my mind.

"Y-yeah, you right, and if they ask where we went, we could just say we went to a blues lounge," I said as my confidence slightly returned.

"Bitch, a blues lounge? Really, Gi? Girl, bye! Name me one damn blues song?" she asked, laughing. I knew I couldn't name one, so I began to laugh as well.

"What? It's the first thing that came to my mind," I said.

"Well, bitch, thinking like that is gone get your ass caught up. With a person like Ja, you gone have to be on your toes at all times with your lies," she said.

"I know, man. Dammit, our plan was solid, and we would have never gotten caught if it wasn't for those stupid cameras," I said.

"Bitch, I thought you was about to say if it wasn't for those meddling kids like the niggas off *Scooby Doo* and shit," Ashanti said, laughing.

"This not funny, Shanti. We are in big-time trouble if Ja watches those cameras," I said.

"It's not as bad as you making it sound," she said.

"Not as bad? Not only did I strip in front of Roy, both our pregnant asses went out to a nightclub. Ja gone kill us," I said.

"Again, as I said the first time, I'm not worried about Jakeem Carter," she said, reaching into her purse and pulling out a blade.

"You are not cutting my husband, bitch," I said.

"Keep his crazy ass away from me then," she said.

"Ja not the one you need to be worried about. You must think Yari gone be OK with this as well? You obviously don't know your baby daddy that well," I said as I saw her facial expression change. She knew like I knew Yari acted exactly like Ja when he was mad—shit, maybe worse because he really wasn't wrapped too tight.

"Damn, you right. Fuck, bitch. This what I get for going along with your ass. Who the fuck told you to go G.I. Jane on the hoe anyway? You ain't a killer. We could have just beat that hoe up, pregnant and all. Shit, my hands still work real good. Cut that bitch up or something, but kill her? Where you got that idea from?"

"Momma Jackie said—" I started until she cut me off.

"Shit, that's an old school gangsta. You can't listen to her ass! That lady a born killa. She ain't fooling nobody with that innocent act she be doing. I heard she used to be in a gang back in the day. Shit, she got us into this mess, and we 'bout to go see her ass to see how the fuck we gone get out this mess. Besides, if he don't listen to nobody else, I notice when she say something his ass listens," Ashanti said.

She had a point because Ja didn't play with his momma like he talked shit to everybody else. What Momma Jackie said was final, or she'd go upside his head quick. The first time I saw her do it, I was scared for her until I saw him bite his tongue and do as she said.

"Maybe we can go talk to her tomorrow morning. You can spend the night with me, and we can wake up early and go—" I was saying until she again cut me off.

"Fuck that. Roy, take us to Momma Jackie house," she said as he hit a U-turn on the highway and headed back in the direction of my mother in-law's house.

"What? No. Shanti, its damn near three a.m., we can't show up this late to her house! We'll just go over tomorrow."

"What if they come back before we leave? Naw, all of this is her fault, and she needs to fix it. I don't have time to be arguing and fighting with this nigga for going along with a plan that was her idea from the start. Shit, she should have rode out with you even if she planning shit out," she said.

"The plan of killing her was put into my head by her, yes, but the way it was executed was all my idea," I said.

"Well, bitch, this your fault as well. Getting some dick and suddenly deciding you a killer, ole I'll catch a charge for the dick and shit," she said, laughing. "No matter what you say, we still fucking going. This what you ass get trying to ride out on some Bonnie and Clyde type shit," she said with her mind made up.

"Look, if they come back tonight, we just need to fuck their brains out to take their mind off checking those cameras. You 'bout to drop that baby, but that don't mean you can't still ride that dick on your tiptoes," I said as her eyes got big as saucers. I know I never talked like this in the past, but that's because I wasn't getting broke off every night either.

"OK, who the hell are you and what have you done with my best friend?" Shanti asked.

"It's still me. It's just that a lot has changed in this last year," I said.

"I see. Bitch, look at you out here getting dick on the regular and living your best life. I still can't believe it. I feel like a proud parent. You all glowing and growing and shit. Ms. New New, I'm scare of you! But the new you forgot I ain't fucking with Yari like that, so that plan is out, so we sticking to my plan."

"Bitch, it's not like you haven't slept with him before, so what's the big deal? I mean, the sex had to be good how you was acting," I said, laughing.

"Girl, that dick had me stalking all his social media accounts, ready to knock anybody out who liked his shit, but that's beside the point. That dick is good as fuck, true, but I'm too damn big and pregnant to be dealing with them side effects," She said.

"What side effects?"

"You know on them commercials where they say this pill cures x, y and z, and they make the shit sound really good? Then really fast they tell you the side effects, which supposed to cure one thing, and end up leaving you worse than when you started," she said.

"Yeah, I always thought those type of commercials were funny. Like how you have a headache, but have side effects that include a headache, depression, anxiety, and diarrhea," I said, laughing.

"Feel me, bitch," Shanti said.

"But what does this have to do with Yari?"

"Shit, it has everything to do with Yari. Right now, I'm cool if he fuckin' with Danielle, because I'm still in contact with Lexx. But if I fuck him again, as emotional as this little boy got me, then shit is bound to get ugly. Hell, even talking about the sex got me in my feelings because I'm hot, horny, and hungry. I don't know about you, but this baby got my hormones raging. Anything Yari does makes me want to attack him. He got out the shower the other day, dripping wet, wearing only a towel, and came in my room looking for his lotion I keep stealing. Bitch, I was so jealous of that towel wrapped around his waist that I almost snatched it off of him and deep throated his ass. I know that bitch Danielle catching all them strokes and getting some bomb ass dick. Lucky hoe," she said.

"I want to say you have issues, but after dealing with my husband, I can actually relate. Hell, that's why my plan is better than your plan. My hormones be acting just like that, so gone let Yari tighten you up. It's not like you can give Lexx some sex while you pregnant anyway, so really, you just torturing yourself. You not in a relationship with Lexx, so it's not cheating. Hell, you barely know him. You'll fuck around and get all worked up for some horrible sex."

"You might be right about that because I done hinted around too many times that I wanted a dick pic, but he always dancing around the shit," she said with her hand on her chin.

"See, that's a for sure sign," I said like my ass actually knew what I was talking about.

"We still going to see Momma Jackie, but I might try your idea out as well."

"My idea was so that we wouldn't do your idea," I said.

"Too late we here," she said as we turned on the street.

* * *

"So LET me get this straight, y'all come to my house at this time of morning because y'all went to the club, killed Trina, and scared Jakeem and Yari will find out?" Momma Jackie said, sitting on the couch in a badass lingerie set that had me feeling really self-conscious about my body. It made no sense for someone her age to not only be so gorgeous, but have a body that put women my age to shame. Crazy part was her body was all natural; no plastic surgery of any kind.

"Yeah," I said.

"Girl, I should punch both y'all asses in the face. When y'all showed up on my doorstep, I just knew something had happened to my child," she said, picking up her drink she had fixed herself.

"We never knew it was cameras around the house," Ashanti started.

"And? What he gone do? Get mad because his wife finally bossed up and handled a situation for him? Shit, if his ass gets mad, you go upside his head. I keep telling you I raised my son a certain type of way, and his wife needs to be a reflection of me in order for him to respect her. I see the slow changes in you, Giovania, but you still doing this weak ass shit. It's like you can't be a damn gangsta and a nerd. You the type that would rob a bank, then apologize about doing the shit. Whatever you do, you stand on that shit and then dare his ass to say something" she said.

"That's what the fuck I'm talking about," Ashanti said.

"Don't cosign now when it was your idea to come over here. Shit, y'all both was shaking like crackheads and shit when I opened the door. Like y'all scared Yari rock-headed ass and Ja slow asses can put y'all in time-out or some shit. Hell, it doesn't matter if you did the shit in front of them or not, the job still got done," Momma Jackie said to her.

"You don't think I've dropped a body in front of Maxx? Shit, I didn't hesitate, blink, nor did I pause to think about what the fuck he would say or do. I did that shit and walked away like a boss. Now the real question is, can y'all be tied to the murder? The key is not to move sloppy and create more problems for your man," she said as I took all that she was saying in.

However, all I could think about is me being pregnant with the twins and Ja having a fit. Shaking my head, I slowly pushed those thoughts to the back of my mind because Momma Jackie was right. I did what I did, and I don't regret that. Trina's testimony would have hurt a lot of our family, so I did what I had to do.

"No they can't, I never touched her," I told her, recounting the events of tonight.

"So you let the bartender live?"

"Yes," I said.

"You 'bout as dumb as you look. Lord, I'm glad you got a good education because you gon' need that in life. All that book sense but no damn common sense. No face, no case. You 'posed to have been doubled back and poisoned her ass as well. You don't know that bitch from a can of paint and don't know if she'll fold or not. As a bartender, it's a point where you have to cut customers off from alcohol. If y'all want to say she died from the alcohol, the number one suspect gon' be the bartender. You think that bitch ain't gone throw y'all under the bus first chance she gets? Say she was only doing her job because you was paying her to send bottles to that section?" she asked, dropping some knowledge on me.

"I didn't think about that," I said.

"Exactly, you didn't think. You out here still playing checkers when you need to be playing chess."

"OK, so we get rid of her ass," Ashanti said.

"So the shit could seem suspect now? The bartender who made the drinks suddenly dies?" Momma Jackie said.

"We make her run, so she then becomes the number one suspect. That way, if she comes back and says I paid her, it will still not make sense because she ran," I said.

"Now you using your head, daughter!" Momma Jackie said.

"Bitch, watch too much damn *Criminal Minds* and shit," Ashanti said, laughing.

"Well, now that we solved that, y'all asses gotta go. My man should be on his way back into town, and it's about to be mister nasty time," she said, sticking her tongue out as she stood up twerking.

"Oh, hell no! Y'all need to quit," Ashanti said.

"Girl, I know you fucking lying! Not with both you bitches sitting up here pregnant as hell. Get your life, and get out," she said to Ashanti.

This lady was a trip, but I loved her to death. Times like these made me miss my own mother. Well, the one I had before she became this evil, foul creature.

Once we were back in the car, Ashanti said, "Since I've been in New Orleans, Maxx been back and forth out of town more than Yari and Ja. I couldn't deal with that type of shit." I always thought the same thing, but I never spoke on stuff that didn't concern me.

Jakeem "Ja" Carter

Pow! Pow! Pow!

The moment that nigga told me that Nancy was fucking with Judge Thomas, I damn near emptied my clip into his ass! Of all the people to want to play with me, this the nigga that's been playing these fuck ass games with me knowing a nigga wasn't wrapped too tight. I don't know what the fuck his cracker ass thought this was, but I damn sure ain't give two fucks about him being a judge. I wouldn't hesitate to chop his fat ass up. I didn't hesitate to chop his wife's head off, and his ass could get the same treatment. Fuck he thought this was!

Nigga ain't give no fucks about his damn title; he can get the same treatment. Looking around the room at all the bodies lying around, I shook my head and got mad all over again because this nigga really had me fucked up, and I didn't even know what the fuck his beef with me was. I knew one thing, I wasn't about to be sitting around here racking my brain about the shit either. I was headed straight to the source to get some answers and choke Nancy's ass until her head popped off her body.

Ring! Ring!

Noticing my lawyer calling me, I cursed under my breath as I quickly pressed ignore. It's like every time I found myself doing shit he told me not to do, his ass always magically called a nigga. When he called back, I grew suspicious because it was well after three a.m., and that's never a good sign when your lawyer's hitting your line this late. Not up for anymore fucked-up news, I pressed ignore again as I walked out of the room and out the house the same way I came in. I called Yari to send a cleanup crew to get rid of these bodies, but the nigga sent my shit to voicemail.

"His ass better not be fuckin' a bitch right now," I said to no one in particular.

I wasn't hating on my dawg; we just had shit to handle right now that was more important than some pussy. I needed them to watch Antwon's little ass for me until I there. Until that hoe Trina caught amnesia and retracted her testimony, I planned on sending her son to her ass piece by piece. Women and kids were usually off-limits for me, but when it comes to my family, all bets were off, and anybody could get it.

See, part of the problem was she thought since she turned snitch that, that shit was gone save her. Nigga like me ain't give no fucks about that shit; I only calmed my ass down because of my team. I knew my actions would affect them, especially with this case going on. If she only had shit on me, the hoe would have died the minute she made it out of that precinct—that's how bold I was. But since she going after the twins, Yari, and a few of my other niggas, that was the only reason I had let the hoe slide with all the shit she been doing, but then she started ice skating around this bitch, forgetting who the fuck I was.

Sometimes you gotta go back into beast mode to get a bitch or nigga mind right. After this case was dropped, I didn't give a damn how suspect I looked; I was killing that hoe and not thinking twice about it. Hopping in my car, I made my way to Judge Thompson's crib, not even caring that I was hitting damn near 80 miles on the highway. The more I thought about the shit, the madder I became because this shit wasn't adding up. The real question was, how did Nancy fit into this equation? Last time I checked, Judge Thompson had me body his wife for him so he could move his side bitch and kids into his crib. His old ass cancel bitches quick I see, but what the fuck all this got to do with me, though?

Turning the corner, I hit my headlights as I cruised down the block to his house. Just when I was about to pull into his driveway, I seen a car alarm beep as out walked Detective Morris out the house smiling and shaking hands with the judge. They glanced toward my car, but because of my tint, they couldn't tell who I was.

Quickly cutting their conversation short, Detective Morris hurried toward his car as I sped off down the road. Ain't no reason for them to be talking this late unless the judge was signing off on some shit, and I didn't see no damn paperwork in his hands. It could just be a coincidence that these two happened to be together right when I was coming to check the judge, but a nigga never believed in coincidences. So I knew something else was up. I was damn sure gon' get to the bottom of everything. They can laugh now, but before it's all said and done, I was killing both of their asses.

I don't give a fuck what Pops got to say about the situation either. His biggest mistake was letting Detective Morris and his son breathe all these years, but I wouldn't make the same mistake. Old man Morris was dead, and his son would soon be joining him. Hell, they was gone have one big ass family reunion in hell. Dear ole Judge Thompson just added himself to that reunion as well. It's a damn shame too because I was just starting to like him as a judge. Oh well, guess he not getting re-elected in a few months.

Speeding off toward the warehouse, my phone started going off. Noticing it was Yari hitting me back, I quickly answered.

"Aye, have D ping you the address I just left so you can send a cleanup crew up that way. I'm headed to the warehouse," I said.

"Cleanup crew? What jumped off, and why you ain't hit me up for backup?" Yari asked.

"Backup? Nigga, get the fuck out of here. When the fuck I ever needed backup to body a nigga? You act like I need you to hold my hand or some shit," I said.

"Man, bitch ass nigga, get that bass out of your voice. Shit, if you need a cleanup crew, that means that you ain't body a nigga for a job—you did that shit for something else, and since this my city, yes I want to know what jumped off. Your job is to be an enforcer when I ask you to; my job is to run shit."

"Nigga, don't use that boss role with me, because you quickly forgot this my shit; I'm just letting you run it. I'm not even about to go there with you in your feelings and shit like a bitch. You acting like you about to start having periods or some shit. Hell, nigga, you need a heating pad and some chocolate? Fuck boy, just call the fucking cleanup crew," I said.

"Nigga, call these nuts," he shot back, laughing.

Nobody will ever understand our relationship and the way we talk big shit to each other in one minute and be laughing in the next. Hearing him yelling to the twins, I just shook my head and waited.

"I had Sade hit them niggas up, but check this, I got some shit to tell you when you get here. You won't believe this shit, bro," he said getting serious.

"Damn, man, what the fuck jumped off?" I asked.

"I'll tell you when you get here," he said.

Curiosity got the best of me as I zoomed toward the warehouse.

WALKING INTO THE WAREHOUSE, I dapped few of my men up before I walked into the room they had put Antwon. I wasn't necessarily going in there to check on the lil' nigga. I just wanted to make sure his ass wasn't dead. Lil' niggas his age got a mouthpiece on them, and I know with as low a tolerance as the twins got, they bound to have fucked his little ass up. I couldn't help but laugh when I opened the door and they had hog tired his ass up and had blindfolded him, and duct taped his mouth.

"These niggas wild," I said, laughing as I closed the door and walked into another room to find Sade, Sage, and Charles, a thoroughbred hard hitta, shooting dice.

"Damn, y'all asses just chillin' like this the party spot, huh? And what y'all tie his ass up like that for?" I said, grabbing a pre-rolled blunt out my pocket and sparking it up.

"Man, because his little ass was talking mad shit ever since we snatched his ass up, and even rocked off on Charles for pushing that old ass lady down. I can't lie, his lil' ass got heart, but nigga ain't have time to be dealing with that shit. And hell yeah, we kicked back in the bitch. It ain't like we can leave," Sade said.

"I almost put his little ass out too," Charles said, rolling the dice and bussing Sade's head open.

After he scooped his winning money up, he put it in his pockets before dapping everybody up and dipping out. He knew like I knew that the only people I was gon' tolerate talking shit or slacking from were the people in the room. So leaving was his best bet. Shit, only bet.

"Damn, I was winning until your ass walked in here fuckin' shit up for me, ole bad luck ass nigga," Sade said.

"Fuck all of that, you here now, so we can dip. Shit, you got us in here babysitting and shit when a nigga could be deep in some pussy right now," Sage said.

"Feel me," Sade said, agreeing.

Pops had already hit me up about Sade coming to holler at him about Kosher, so I didn't want to hear his ass cosigning the shit. She was like a sister to me, and him, a brother. So even though I respected their relationship, I still didn't want to think about them having sex.

"Nasty ass nigga, don't agree with him and shit," I said.

"Kosher love this nasty ass nigga, though," he said.

"Bitch ass nigga, I'll fuck you up," I said.

"Black eye and all, she still gone take all these inches." His cocky ass shot back.

"Man, leave Ja dysfunctional ass alone about Kosh before we have to jump his ass in this bitch while he flexing," Sage said.

"Y'all can get off my brother cuz y'all know we nasty from the shoulders so what's up? And fuck you, Sade, ole incest ass nigga. Yo' babies gone come out retarded and shit," Yari said, pulling his pants up and getting in a fighting stance.

Laughing I said, "Man, fuck them niggas, I'll beat both they asses at the same damn time."

"Hell yeah," Yari agreed.

"But what's up, though? You was talking on the damn phone like somebody we knew got popped or something, bruh. What's really good?" I asked him as I took a pull of my blunt and sat in a chair.

"Say, bro, you won't believe the shit I'm 'bout to tell you. On baby, you won't," Yari said.

"Damn, nigga, spit the shit out. Done got us bucked up and shit, meanwhile you bullshitting. It don't even take all of that," Sade said, saying exactly what I was thinking.

"Shut the fuck up, ole ugly ass dude, I'm getting there," Yari said with his no storytelling ass.

"Anyway, one of my bitches I fuck with at the club told me they found Trina dead in the bathroom. Apparently she died from alcohol poisoning.

"All that build up for that? You could have just said that shit," Sage said.

"That's what that hoe gets. She better be glad alcohol got to that ass before I did," Sade said. He was serious when he said he would kill Trina before he let her testimony possibly have Sage locked up.

"Shit, you? She lucky I didn't get to that ass because I had something extra special planned for her ass that was gone make her beg me to kill her," I said with a far-off, crazed look in my eyes. I had already envisioned me killing the hoe, so I was low-key mad I was beat to the punch.

"You one weird ass nigga. They got places for people like you. Yo' ass be doing too much with all them knives and shit. Like what happened to the days where you just shot a nigga and got it over with?" Yari asked.

"Man, you know that nigga ain't all the way there, carrying that damn sword like he a ninja or some shit," Sage said, laughing as Sade and Yari joined in.

"Fuck all y'all. Shit that ain't never been me. Y'all kill niggas how y'all want, and let me chop heads off, slice veins watching them bleed out, or throw rats or some shit on their ass, eating them alive like I want to," I said.

"It's because the nigga was breastfed is the reason he acts like that.

I told Ashanti she ain't giving my baby titty milk. Shit will have you fucked up just like this nigga," Yari said, pointing at me while I just shrugged my shoulders and hit the blunt again before passing it to Sage.

"Fuck all that, how that broke bitch die from alcohol poisoning?" Sage said, accepting the blunt as he took a pull from it.

"That's a good question. Her ass could barely afford a four to four from Wendy's," I said.

"Shit, they pay snitches really well," Sade said.

"My homegirl told me Trina and her crew had a VIP section at the club with bottles in rotation all night long. Not the cheap bottles either. The $500 bottles; the good shit. Say them bitches had about six or seven bottles. But Trina kept getting shot after shot as well and then they all took some shots together," Yari said.

"Damn. I was playing, but I see them damn snitches do get paid good as fuck," Sade said.

"Feel me," Sage said, slapping high fives with his twin.

"Well, least that hoe went out lit," Yari said.

"Shit, I wonder if that's what Stan was calling me about," I said, pulling my phone out, shooting him a text telling him I would come holla at him tomorrow, and I heard about what happened.

"So where does that leave the case, because I been really slowing this money up because of it, even though I switched everything up? That bitch ass detective got a habit of popping up everywhere. Like how the fuck he always know where to find a nigga?" Yari said.

"Wait… he been popping up on you as well? Why I'm just now hearing about this?" I said.

"What I was 'posed to tell you for? You act like I need you to hold my hand or something," he said, throwing my words back at me.

"Everywhere I go, I let my nuts hang, fuck that nigga," Yari said.

"He won't be a problem for long," I said, accepting the blunt from Sage and taking a long pull from it.

"You know Pops ain't gone let you off that nigga. He been a problem for years and still breathing," Yari said.

"Pops can't let me do shit. That nigga Detective Morris's days are numbered, and his ass gone soon find himself on a RIP shirt," I said, pulling out my phone and pulling up my cameras to the crib to check on my baby momma.

"Oh shit. Since you got them cameras out, I need you to rewind and see if Ashanti ass was over there," Yari said.

"What's up?" I asked.

"I checked the camera and saw her ass leaving the house in a short as—" he was saying until Sade cut him off.

"Nigga, you got cameras just to spy on Shanti, ole creepy ass nigga," he said, laughing.

"Fuck you, bitch. I got cameras just to check on my seed," Yari said.

"Nigga, quit lying. You checking on Shanti, ole in love ass nigga. You can't love two chicks, bruh. Keep yo' baby momma; I'ma take Danielle with that ole ghetto booty. Shorty stupid fine and been holding out all these years. Them big, juicy, soup-cooler lips look like they can suck a mean dick," Sage said, slapping five with Sade as Yari's face turned as he got mad as hell.

"Don't play with that, Sage. For real, my nigga. Test me if you want," he said, moving toward Sage.

I jumped up and pushed him back as Sade had his gun pulled out and cocked in a matter of seconds. Even though Sage was older, Sade acted like the older brother because he was bigger and took that role serious as fuck.

"So you gone pull a gun out on me, bitch? Really?" Yari yelled again, trying to charge toward Sade.

"I think he in his feelings, Sade. You max bitch ass nigga," Sage taunted Yari, pointing at him and laughing as Sade begin to do the same thing.

I wanted to laugh so badly, but I knew this crazy ass nigga was deep in his feelings, and shit was bound to go left really quickly. People sometimes forgot, because he rarely shows that side, but Yari's ass may be more throwed off than I am. The way he was flipping out about this nigga speaking on Danielle proved he was in fact in love with her. He could lie to himself all he wanted, but his ass had strong feelings for both Ashanti and Danielle.

"Aye, y'all chill the fuck out everybody before y'all make me mad, and we really turn this bitch up," I said.

"Naw, fuck that what's up," Yari yelled.

"Nigga, is you dead ass right now? What the fuck? I was playing with yo' ass when I pulled my shit out, but you really turning up like that on us over a bitch?" Sade said, shaking his head.

"Man, we out. I was just joking with his ass. Everybody get on everybody fucked-up ass love situation and rag on they ole lady. Nigga wanna take the shit personal and buck like I'ma hoe. I'm gone before he see that savage side that make niggas knees buckle when that smile leaves," Sade said before he and Sage walked off.

Turning back to Yari, who was still mad, I pushed him back hard.

"Nigga, those twins like your fuckin' brothers, and not only that, them your workers. You like to throw the boss card around; well, fuckin' act like a boss. These broads got you in your feelings, and you tripping hard as fuck! I told you before to get your shit together before this shit ends bad. Hell, when Giovania left, I was fucked up, yeah, but you wildin', my nigga," I said to him.

Running his hands down his face, he calmed down. "I know, bruh. Fuck," he said as he sat back down.

"You need to get yourself together, bruh. You fucking up coming at them niggas sideways. You know even after you make shit right, they gone fire yo' ass up every day," I said, looking down at my phone.

"Hell yeah," he said, but I didn't hear him. I had rewinded the cameras back with the intentions of catching a glimpse of his girl, but instead, caught mine with her robe open in front of Roy. My left eye twitched as I felt Grim Reaper slipping to the surface.

"Damn, nigga, why you looking at that screen hard as fuck like that?" Yari said to me.

Instead of answering him, I got up, walked out of the warehouse, and jumped into my car, speeding off. I don't know what's going on, but Giovania better have a damn good explanation or else she was getting the same treatment that nigga Roy was gone get.

* * *

SPARKING ANOTHER BLUNT, I casually strolled on side of the security post beside our house, which wasn't your average post. It was off like one of those big ass Barbie DreamHouses. It came equipped with a bathroom, kitchen, and separate bedroom that he could sleep in on nights I was away.

Roy wasn't the security I had patrolling my crib; I had about eight guards here. He, however, was strictly Giovania's security only. Wherever she went, he went if I wasn't around. They thought they were slick, but I was slicker. I thought about picking the lock, disabling the alarm, and treating this like a real job until I came to my senses. This my damn house, why the fuck would I go through all of that shit. Wiggling the knob, I saw that the door was open, so I let myself in.

Walking inside, I took a long pull of my blunt that I had in one hand while I placed the bag of toys in the other hand down on the counter, and pulled my gun from my waist. Hearing the shower running, I made my way toward the bathroom. Visions of him showering, washing my bitch scent off of him almost made me kick the door in bussing, but I contained myself as I tapped on the door and said,

"Aye, Roy, let me holla at you real quick, my G."

The minute I heard the shower cut off and the door opening, I contemplated hitting his ass immediately or waiting until he got dressed because I wasn't for dicks and balls flying everywhere. I was in luck though 'cause he opened the bathroom door wearing basketball shorts. I smiled to myself excited at my luck as I hit his ass hard as hell across the face with the butt of my gun.

After he dropped, I stomped him out, then hit him with my gun, knocking him out. I wasn't killing him just yet; I needed answers first because too many people as of lately thought they could play with a nigga. Shit it was time I started playing back. Now that the hoe Trina was dead, wasn't shit stopping my alter ego from rising back to the surface to play. It's all fun and games until the rabbit has the gun.

Going back to retrieve the bag I brought in with me, I found the rope and duct tape as I drug Roy into the room, hoisting him into a chair. Then I tied his arms behind the chair and duct taped it for added restraint. I then double tied his feet and legs. By this point, he was starting to regain consciousness. As he slowly looked around, noticing the predicament he found himself in, his eyes grew big as his big ass began to stutter.

"B-Bruh, it's not what it looks like. I can explain," he said, which further pissed a nigga off because that's niggas' number one go-to line, "it's not what it looks like." Meanwhile, it's always exactly what it looked like.

"Nigga, so what you saying? You tripped and fell in my wife pussy? Fuck I look like? Bozo the Clown or some shit? You know exactly how I get down, so you better come better than that before I lose the last bit of mind I do have and start chopping yo' big ass up," I said.

"Man, bruh, please, I got kids—" He started before I cut him off.

"I don't give a fuck about that. I'll body all three of them bitches as well and toss yo' bitch to my niggas. Run that sympathy line by somebody who gives a fuck, because in all my twenty-three years on this earth, I have yet to find one to give." I said, walking out to grab the bag, and coming back into the room where he was.

Taking a smaller black bag out, I unrolled it to reveal my collection of knives, ranging from big ones, to a small butterfly knife. I also pulled out a big ass container of salt and placed it all beside me as I grabbed another chair and sat down directly in front of his ass. If he was gone drop his nuts and lie to me again, I at least wanted him to look me in my eyes like a man and lie to me.

"Come on, man," he said, squirming around, trying to free himself from the restraints, but his ass wasn't going nowhere even if he got out them ropes, that tape was gone hold his ass.

"I'ma ask you one more time," I said, pulling another blunt out and sparking it up as I pulled my phone out and pressed play on the video. I had paused it initially when I first saw it, but now I wanted to watch the show with his ass. When Giovania opened her robe, and he immediately turned around, my face scrunched up because for a second it looked like he wasn't tryna see her like that. However, when he turned back around and held a full conversation with her ass instead of walking away, that sealed both of their fates. I would have liked to know what the fuck they was discussing, but we'll get to that part in a second.

"So you say it's not what it looks like, right? Because it kind of looks like my wife is standing in my kitchen, the one I pay bills at, half naked. Now which part isn't what it looks like? Was that before or after you saw her ass dressed like that and you didn't walk away? Or the part where you still continued to stand there and go with your move?" I asked him, blowing smoke rings his way.

"All of it isn't what it looks like," he said.

Bending down, I grabbed the butterfly knife, and with swiftness and precision, I sliced him across his chest.

"Fuckkkkkk! Ahhhh!" he screamed out in pain.

I waited a few minutes then added the salt to the cut to maximize the pain.

"Let's throw it back old school and play my favorite game, Roy. See the rules of the game go like this. I ask a question, and you answer the question. A right answer earns you a point; a wrong answer earns you a punishment. Three points grants you release," I said, giving him the rules to the game, even though I've never granted anyone a release, but he didn't need to know that. I only ever said that to make people eager to cooperate.

"You already loosing, the score is 1-0. Now, let's try this again, Giovania got damn near naked in front of you, and you didn't immediately call me because?"

"She begged me not to! I swear to God, on my kids' head, I didn't touch her, Ja! I would never do that to you, man! How far back we go, bruh? I wouldn't do that, bruh. I promise I wouldn't. Look at the full video, she did that shit with the robe so she could bribe me into taking her and Ashanti to the club," he said, getting my attention.

"Just the club? She did that shit to go to a club? That's what you telling me?" I asked him as I sliced him again. Again, I waited a few seconds before I put salt on the wound and he again, yelled out in pain.

"Damn, my nigga, did you not understand the rules of the game? Three strikes and you out, off with your head," I said.

"I swear, bruh," he said barely above a whisper. I know that pain was getting to his ass.

"So this just normal for y'all and shit, that's what you saying? She always half fucking naked when you around, and instead of you addressing it to me, like a real nigga, you did what? Hit it?"

"No. This the first time she ever did some shit like that. I told her I got kids and a family that needs me, and she said I just needed to help her because if I didn't and you found out she was at the club solo, I would be dead for letting her go alone," he said, which was true.

"So what the fuck was so special about the club?" I asked him.

"She said she had to get rid of Trina," he said, causing my ass to choke on the smoke I had just inhaled.

"Nigga, you lying," I said.

"Man, on my kids', son. I am not lying. You been knowing me for years. When I ever played with my family like this, G? I love my jits to death," he said.

This was true, that nigga loved the fuck out them ugly ass kids. I wasn't just calling them ugly because I was on the verge of killing his ass. They was legit ugly as fuck, looking just like they ugly ass momma. She had some strong ass genes, bruh, because I never seen three ugly ass kids. You would think it would be at least one that came out decent looking. Closing out my camera system, I dialed up Giovania's number.

"You know if you lying, you just buried your entire family," I said as Giovania picked up the phone.

Giovania

Ring! Ring!

Seeing Jakeem calling me, my palms got sweaty as I hesitated to answer it.

Trying to calm my nerves, I said, "Hey, babe," in the best sleepy voice I could muster up, hoping he didn't sense anything wrong.

"Hey, baby girl. Did I wake you up?" he asked.

"Yes, I was sleep. What time will you make it back? I miss you," I said to him then held my breath as my body felt like it was going to explode, waiting any moment now for him to drop a bomb on me about the cameras.

Everything Momma Jackie said to me sounded good and all, but she was this fool's mom, so of course, her own son, whom she carried for nine months, didn't pump fear in her heart, so she could do anything to him. The rest of us weren't so lucky.

"I miss yo' fine ass too, girl. Listen, I'll let you go back to sleep, but first I need you to do something for me," he said as I smiled widely releasing the breath I was holding.

"As long as it doesn't involve too much lifting or driving because your kids a handful already and have made me extremely lazy," I said, laughing.

"Naw, you know I wouldn't have you lift a finger, and you don't have to drive. I need you to run in Roy security post real quick and grab something for me that I left. You can FaceTime me when you get there so I can see where it's at," he said.

"Oh, baby, why not just tell Roy and have him grab it?" I asked him, wanting to keep my distance from Roy right now.

He didn't do anything to me; I'm just trying to keep him alive, and staying away from him right now might help.

"I called that nigga, and he had went got some food for his baby momma. Her cravings worse than yours right now," he said.

"OK, baby, I'm getting up now," I said as he hung up.

Getting out of the bed, I threw on my robe, not bothering to put on any clothes. I wasn't worried about running into Roy because knowing Katrina, she liked foods from different stores, and Roy would no doubt go to six different stores if he had to just to see her smile. So I knew he would be a while, and I wouldn't run into him. I planned on being in and out his post quickly.

Calling Ashanti up, she answered on the first ring. "Bitch, what's wrong, you dead?" she asked me groggily.

"If I were dead, I wouldn't be calling you, now would I?" I snapped.

"Fuck. OK, well, call me back when you half dead then shit. I'm tryna get some sleep," she said.

"Ja just called me," I said.

"OK. Did he mention the cameras?" She asked me.

"No, but—"

"But nothing. Damn, Giovania, you really would snitch on your damn self like Momma Jackie said. If he didn't mention it, then it's all good. Yari came home and didn't say shit either, so quit stressing. I'm going back to sleep. Me and this big-head ass boy have had enough adventures for one day," she said, hanging up before I could say anything else.

Deciding that she was right, I walked out of the room, slipping my feet into my bunny slippers once I made it downstairs. I put the alarm code in and stepped outside, quickly making my way toward Roy's makeshift home.

Once I was inside, I called Ja's phone back so he could tell me exactly what I was looking for. Hearing music begin to play toward the back of the house like it was a phone ringtone, I moved toward the sound, thinking maybe it had something to do with what Ja wanted me to retrieve.

Opening the door, I almost threw up all the food I had earlier as I came face-to-face with a badly beaten Roy tied to a chair, while Ja sat unbothered, smoking a blunt in a chair facing me.

"W-Wha-What's going on here, Jakeem!" I asked in a shaking voice, but I already knew the answers judging from the condition Roy was in.

"No, baby girl, that ain't the real question here. The real one is, why you felt like it was OK to run over here naked with nothing but a robe on? What, you thought Roy was here and you was gone get some dick?" he asked.

"Hell no. I would never cheat on you," I said.

"Yeah, so you said last time until I was hit with a picture of you with a dick down your throat eagerly about to give my pussy away," he said.

"Really, Jakeem? You going there," I said, furious that he would even bring the Kyle incident up again.

"You know what happens when you call me Jakeem," he said, licking his lips and looking at me with lust-induced eyes.

"He hitting that pussy like I do?" he asked, looking at me with low, bloodshot bedroom eyes.

Even though I was in a sticky situation right now, I couldn't help the tingly sensation I was feeling right now looking at my husband. He was even sexier when he was mad. I wanted nothing more than to have him take me back to the house and have the same angry sex that we had when we made up about the picture. Just thinking about those angry, rough but pleasurable strokes had juices running down my legs. I silently cursed myself for not wearing any panties. Getting up, he walked toward me until he was standing directly in front of me.

"That pussy dripping wet. I smell her talking to daddy. You wore this robe for this nigga, Giovania? You want him to taste my pussy?" he asked very calmly and very low, barely above a whisper.

At this point, his entire aura had turned me on so much that I couldn't do anything but shake my head as I backed up until my back hit a wall. Leaning in close to me, I thought he was about to kiss me, instead, his hands around my neck as he choked me angrily. I knew it wasn't out of passion, but I couldn't help the moan that escaped my lips.

"Fuck, nigga can't even rough your freaky ass up," he said, laughing.

"You created a monster," I whispered.

"Yeah, a monster that was just supposed to be for me. I told you once before if you ever gave my shit away, I was killing that bitch ass nigga and making you watch. See, you the type of female you gotta show them better than you can tell them," he said, walking over to a case laying on the bed, opening it and pulling out a long sword.

"But I'ma fix you. Let this be a lesson from here on out. Any nigga you look twice at gone get the same treatment," he said as poor Roy squirmed and shook in the chair, trying to break free. With the duct tape over his mouth, his voice was muffling out the screams he was trying to make.

"No, baby! Please don't! It's my fault," I said as tears slid down my face. I couldn't allow Ja to kill this innocent man.

"You crying for this bitch ass nigga?" His voice boomed as he seemed to become even madder.

Making his way back over to me, he roughly grabbed me by my neck, this time lifting me completely off of my feet.

"You gone sit up in my damn face and cry for the life of another nigga? You got me fucked up, and if you wasn't carrying my kids…" he said as his voice trailed off and anger blazed in his eyes.

While I was struggling to breathe, I heard Momma Jackie's voice in my head telling me to be strong, stand on what I did, and dare him to get mad. Mustering up all the strength I had, I lifted my leg up and kneed him in the balls hard as I could as he dropped me to the ground, doubling over in pain.

"Run," he choked out.

"What?"

"Run fast, Giovania," he said, standing to his feet and mugging me.

On the inside, I wanted to cower away, but on the outside, I stood my ground.

"I'm not going no fucking where, but we are going to bed. Now, what you will do is untie Roy, and give him a raise. I expect ten grand in his account before we make it upstairs."

"Have you lost your fucking mind, bi—" He started, but I interrupted him.

"Say it and you'll lose that other nut sack, Jakeem Carter! Try me if you want to!" I yelled at him.

It may look like I had gained the upper hand, but I was really secretly praying for me and my kids' life because this crazy ass man could easily kill me at any given moment.

"Oh yeah?" He smirked.

Shit I knew it, he about to kill my ass, I thought. But instead, I said, "Yes, that's what I meant. Now I was wrong for opening my robe in front of Roy, but I was trying to get him to drive us to the club because I heard Trina would be there. Don't interrupt me," I said as he opened his mouth to say something. Looking at me, he kept smirking, so I continued talking while I still had confidence to do so.

"I killed Trina. I did it because as your woman, as a Carter woman, I had to step up and protect my family by any means necessary. I knew you couldn't get rid of the bitch, so I did it for you. Her testimony would not only hurt you, but our family. Family sticks together, no matter what. Besides, I refuse to raise these damn big-headed kids by myself while you get off scot-free of the responsibility of waking up with their asses in the middle of the night and losing sleep. Oh, hell no," I said as I waited for him to say something. The silence seemed to go on for a few hours, but it was really more like five minutes before he spoke again.

"So you killed Trina, huh, boss?" he finally asked.

"Hell yeah, I killed that hoe without even laying a finger on her, and I dare you to stand in my face and say something else about her," I said, getting in his face. *Jesus, be a fence and shield me from this demon because I'm surely pushing my luck*! I screamed inside of my head. Out of nowhere, Ja burst out laughing, doubling over in tears.

"Man, you better get yo' little ass out my face talking about you dare me to say something. You forgot who the fuck I am? Dick runs this household. You better gone on before I ball your little ass up like a pretzel," he said.

"You not going to do shit. Now untie him and come to bed," I said.

"Fuck that nigga. He better find his own fucking way out, and I wish the fuck you would help him. He got a pass to keep his life, but that's where it ends. I don't give a fuck what you did; he should have immediately hit me up when the shit happened. That's what a real nigga would have done. I would have told him 'preciate you for looking out, dawg, now follow her silly ass because she damn near five months pregnant doing dumb shit," he said as he moved to pack up everything he had brought to the room.

"We past that. I said untie him and give him a raise," I said.

"And I said, you better get your little ass out my face and go the fuck back in the house while you out here with nothing but a robe on," he said.

Raising my hand up to slap him, he caught my wrist in mid swing and forcefully pushed me back.

"Don't push your luck. Quit while you're ahead. That's the only warning you'll get," he said in a low voice.

I knew the game was over, so after I looked at Roy one last time, I turned and hurried into the house. If Ja said he escaped with his life, he meant that, so I couldn't worry about the rest. I mean, he's a big guy, he'll figure out how to get out of those ropes.

* * *

HAVE you ever had a wet dream that felt so real to the point where you thought you felt everything happening in that moment? That's exactly how I was feeling right now.

When Ja told me to go into the house, I went in and waited on him to come to bed. I figured we would have mind-blowing sex and pass out. After an hour passed, and he hadn't come to bed, frustratedly, I rubbed my nipples like he did and drifted off to sleep.

I was in a deep dream, and Ja was pleasuring me like never before. That devilish tongue of his was driving me wild and taking me to unheard of heights. It had been so long since I'd had a wet dream but never one feeling this realistic. This dream felt so damn real that it was like I could feel everything from the juices running down my leg to every flicker of his tongue. As my pussy gushed, I arched my back and moaned out in pure ecstasy.

"Fuck," I said in my sleep, still refusing to open my eyes for fear this would all disappear.

My husband was mad at me and probably would hold out on pleasuring me like this in real life, so I had to enjoy it any way I could. If you've ever been pregnant, then you know exactly how I was feeling. These twins had me ready for Ja to add one more to the bunch how much my hormones always up. Since I was having the best wet dream of my life, I might as well give in to the explosive orgasm I felt coming on.

I had never in all my life experienced a dream quite like this. When a finger was inserted inside of me, feeling too real to be a dream, my eyes quickly popped open only for me to look down and see Ja between my legs. He was devouring me so good, had we not been married already, I definitely would have gotten on my knees and proposed to him.

"Fuck! Bae, don't stop, right there," I said, lifting my hips off of the bed, pushing myself further into his mouth. At this point, he was eating me better than he's ever done before, and I was loving every minute of it.

"You like that, shawty?" he asked me as one finger quickly became two, and he began rapidly moving them in and out of me. Then he lowered his head back to my love nest and placed his entire mouth over me, sucking and slurping, willing my soul to leave my body.

"Yes!" I moaned out louder than before.

"You bodying bitches for daddy now, huh? I love that shit. You my rider, bae," he said before continuing his tongue assassination.

I lost all train of thought as I grabbed a fistful of his dreads into my hands, fucking his face with my head thrown back in ecstasy. Suddenly, the heavenly feeling was taken away from me as he abruptly pulled his fingers out of me and sat up. Placing his fingers into his mouth, he sucked my juice off his fingers.

"Wait! No, why did you stop?" I asked, breathing hard as my chest rose rapidly up and down.

"I don't have a problem with you riding for your man, but that shit you pulled was reckless and irresponsible. I talked to my T-lady, and she told me everything from it being her idea to the bartender you left alive. I love you to death, girl, and besides my mom, I've never told another woman that in my life. I appreciate you wanting to step up and handle business for your man, but I don't need a rider.

"Contrary to what my T-lady may have told you, I don't need my woman to mirror my mom. Grow a backbone and not let these bitches play with you? Yes. Hell, you can beat a bitch or two up if, and only if, you are provoked to do so, and I will be cool with that. But I don't need a woman to hold my dope, cook my dope, sell drugs, roll a blunt, and body niggas. I need exactly what I got, and that's you. I don't love you for what you not, I love you for who you are. Now your ass on punishment, no dick for you, good night. And Ms. Mary on vacation so a nigga better have breakfast ready bright and early," he said, moving over to his side of the bed.

This is why I loved this man. He could be the scariest man on earth in one breath, then make me fall more deeper in love with him in the next. I love the fact that this side of him was reserved just for me as well. Maybe he was right. He didn't need me in the streets with him, but after killing Trina, I felt a feeling I never felt and couldn't identify, but I knew I liked it. I'll chill out now until the twins are born, but I knew Trina wouldn't be the last person I killed.

"Babe, no. I'm sorry," I said, shaking him because I was so horny I could cry.

How dare he bring me close to the brink of a mind-blowing

orgasm, then deny me of the feeling? I was so turned on at this point that I couldn't even think straight. He knew exactly what he was doing, and I didn't like the shit at all. His only response was a loud, snoring sound.

Kicking my legs up and down in the bed, I grabbed a pillow and lay down with it on top of my face as I screamed into it. "Arghhhh!"

Removing the pillow, I put it behind my head as I tried to get comfortable and fall back asleep. What felt like thirty minutes later, but in actuality was barely three minutes, I was still sexually frustrated, and realized I wouldn't be able to get to sleep until I got the release my body yearned for.

I threw the cover off and glanced over at Jakeem, contemplating if I were bold enough to jump on top of him and take what I wanted. It was mine, right?

After having a back and forth debate with my brain, I said fuck it and wrapped my arms around his body from behind, as I licked on his ear. My hands then traveled down his body until I reached my target. BINGO!

Feeling that anaconda through his shorts, I slipped my hands inside his pants and began stroking him up and down, hoping to get a reaction out of him that would render me the release I sought. But nothing. He didn't budge or make a sound at all.

"Urghhh, I hate you!" I screamed and thought I heard a light laugh from him. "You're so damn petty and childish, Jakeem Carter," I said, hoping that would get him going.

He always loved when I called him Jakeem, and sex always followed. Still nothing. Throwing on one of his T-shirts and grabbing some panties, I got dressed and got back into bed. Half an hour later, I had slowly slipped back off to sleep when I was roughly turned over.

"Never feel like you have to scheme and sneak around to do shit. You almost cost a nigga his life for nothing, just because you wanted to be on some tough girl shit and get at Trina, not thinking about your kids or Ashanti's child. Don't do that shit no more, Giovania, because next time I won't be so understanding. Playing with my kids' lives is like playing with my emotions, and when that happens, everybody gotta die," he said to me as he brought his mouth down onto my lips.

At the same time, he ripped my panties off, lifted my legs up, and slid inside of me in one swift motion, causing my breath to catch in my throat. Damn, I loved this man.

Jakeem "Ja" Carter

"Tell Sade and Sage to let that lil' nigga Antwon go. Trina dead. I have no use for him anymore. I'm sure by this point his ass knows not to play with us. I'll kill that old bitch without so much as blinking."

"Damn, bruh. You'd kill an old lady?"

"I'll chop her head clean the fuck off. Wig will fly one way; her dentures will fly another way."

"You sick."

"Sick with a disease called, 'I don't give a fuck.' Just like I'm killing Detective Morris and Judge Thomas and won't give a fuck about the consequences coming behind it," I said to Yari as I passed him the blunt back as I looked on at target one.

We had been following Detective Morris around all day. Shit just wasn't sitting well with me seeing him leaving out of the judge's house. Especially ever since ole boy told me that Nancy and the judge had something going on, and his ass was the one who has been tryna kill me. I needed answers.

"I'ma be right beside you bussing," Yari said.

"Bitch ass nigga thinks he slick. Hold up, I'll be back."

"I'm coming with you."

"Naw, just stay here and watch my back," I said, getting out the car as I saw Detective Morris and his son in-law walking inside of a Cajun

Bistro. His ass wasn't the only one who did pop ups. Walking inside of the restaurant, I spotted they ass sitting down.

"Let me get a half sweet tea, half lemonade," I said to the waitress as I slid in the booth beside them. They both looked at me like they had seen a ghost.

"Can I start you off with an appetizer sir?" she asked, flirting.

"Naw, I'm good, love."

"I'll be right back," she said, yet she didn't make a move to leave.

"Damn, what the fuck you still standing your goofy ass right there for? Go do your damn job. Shit, you can't afford to get fired from the looks of it. Like, shawty, on the real, you too cute for your weave to be that nappy and stale and them knees look like you been breaking bricks with them hoes, just toe up, bruh," I told her, and she quickly left the table.

"I see you have a way with the ladies. Smooth," Jackson, Detective Morris's son-in-law, said, looking amused.

"Yeah, bitches love me. Ask ya wife. She couldn't stop swallowing my kids," I said to him as his smile quickly left.

"You black son of a bitch," he said through gritted teeth.

I put my hands on my chin. "Come to think of it, that's exactly what her ass used to say to me. She'd be like, 'you black son of a bitch. You so fuckin' deep inside of me,'" I said, laughing.

"Calm down, son. He's just trying to get a reaction out of you," Detective Morris said.

"Naw. I haven't even begun to get a reaction out of him. Oh, by the way, it's such a shame what happened to Trina."

"I know you had something to do with it, and it's just a matter of time before I prove it," Detective Morris said.

"Yeah? You gon' convince a judge and jury that from thousands of miles away, I managed to kill Trina and convince them of a testimony that she never officially gave is true?"

"I can be a very persuasive person, and I wouldn't worry about me convincing a judge if I were you. That part's squared away already."

"Oh right. Yeah, cuz you fucking with Judge Thomas now, huh?" I said as he choked on the juice he was drinking.

"Didn't know I knew that, huh? Both of y'all acting like some straight bitches. They said mad bitches link up when they have a bitch they don't like in common, but I didn't know niggas did the shit as well. Well, never mind, y'all both look like a bunch of bitches, so it fits you," I said.

"You think you invincible, but you'll get touched soon," he said.

"I can see your heart beating through your chest. I predict that macho attitude being turned down a notch real soon," Jackson said.

"And I can see me sticking my dick back down your bitch throat real soon, so I guess we both see visions like Raven Simone."

"You dead, Carter. It's just a matter of time. I promise you won't be breathing soon," Jackson said.

"Whenever you drop yo' nuts and wanna go toe to toe with the devil himself, I'll be waiting. I ain't hiding, bitch ass nigga, so come find me," I said.

Turning back to Detective Morris I said, "Tell your new best friend I'll be coming to see him soon."

"That isn't what you want to do."

"Oh, but it is," I said, placing two bullets on the table before I got up and walked off.

The bullets were clean; I just purchased them today, so he couldn't tie them to anything. However, I wanted him to get the message loud and clear—two bullets, two bodies. I didn't want them to have any surprises and know that it was me coming for their asses. They kept thinking I was my father and gave a fuck about going to jail or this bitch ass case.

Now that Trina was dead, and my family was free of all charges, since their star witness was gone, wasn't shit holding me back. I didn't plan on stopping until they ass took that dirt nap right along with her ass. Judge Thomas knows firsthand that the Grim Reaper finishes every mission, and they had just landed a free one on the house.

* * *

"MAN, I can't believe sis bodied Trina ass. Bruh, my baby momma got at Big John and Crystal, and yours got at Trina. These women these days ain't fucking playing. They'll lay your ass down with the quickness. Shit, I'ma start sleeping with one eye open and shit."

"Naw, I ain't worried about they asses at all. Giovania already know what it is this way. She knows to only try her luck so far with me. But I fucks with shawty even more now knowing she willing to kill for a nigga."

"Speaking of riding the long way, I think I've finally come to a place where I have decided who I wanna be with," Yari said.

"Who?"

"Shanti my baby momma, and I'll always love her and my son whenever he gets here. But even though I knew her longer, we still don't have the connection that I have with Danielle. Shit, once I accepted the kid, I guess a nigga just wanted to try and make my family work. I know this co-parenting shit can still work without us being together though. Hell, they'll have they own room, and I'll have my own room, just how things are right now. I'll probably get an even bigger place, though."

"So let me get this straight. You think Danielle gone be OK with your baby momma living in the same house as you?"

"Yeah. We ain't fuckin'. We just gon' be co-parenting."

"Nigga, you asking for these women to get off on your ass, and I'ma sit back and watch. I keep saying I want no parts in that shit and don't bring that my way. Hell, my wife already mad because she think you fucking both her friends and wants me talk to you."

"Who Giovania think she married? Yo' ass got hoes on every corner."

"Had."

"What?"

"Had hoes on every corner. My dick don't get hard for nobody but my baby now."

"Nigga don't want to hear about who or what your dick gets hard for, ole gay ass nigga. As a matter of fact, drop me back off to my car so I can go see my girl. Yo' sweet ass in here tripping, ole Prince looking ass."

"I know you not talking sitting up here looking like a gay ass Chris Brown. Get yo' ugly ass out my shit."

* * *

Ring! Ring!

"Who is calling you at this time of morning?" Giovania said.

"Probably one of my hoes who don't fart in their sleep. Yo' shitty-booty ass gon' start sleeping in the guest room."

"Fuck you, Ja. Don't try me like I done already got on my Dej Loaf. I'll fuck around and catch another body," she said.

Leaning up, I took my palm and hit it hard against the wooden nightstand, causing her to jump up, looking scared.

"Catch another body, huh, killa? Go yo' scary ass back to sleep; it's just Danielle on the phone."

"Fuck you."

"If you can go another round, gladly."

"Eww, get a room," Danielle said.

"Shut up. Now what the hell you want calling me this late anyway?"

"It's worth your while. You'll never guess who I found," Danielle said to me.

"Who?"

"Byron's wife," she said, causing me to pause in my tracks.

I had been looking for this lady for months now, killed her parents and a few of her friends, and still couldn't get her to come out of hiding.

"Where?"

"Well, since we been looking for her, I put tracks on all her credit cards, cell phones, social media, anything electric that I could have a trace on it. Anyway, she just used her credit card to purchase some gum at a 7-Eleven and another time at the donut shop across the street. Also, her cell just went back online, as well at the hotel beside the 7-Eleven about forty-five minutes from your house."

"Gum? The hoe purchased some gum with her card after all this time?"

"Yeah. Shit seem suspect as fuck."

"Send me the information. I'ma go check it out. It's more than likely a crackhead that stole her shit and using it," I said, throwing on some clothes. It could be a chance the bitch thought I forgot about her ass.

* * *

WALKING into the motel room door, a lamp was turned on the second I stepped foot into the door. There sitting in a chair was none other than Bryon's wife, Samantha. It's like the bitch was waiting on me or some shit.

"You either the smartest bitch in America or dumbest bitch in America. But seeing as though you obviously knew a nigga was coming, what's up, ma? Tired of this game you been playing?"

"That's where you wrong, I haven't been playing any games, but I did run to protect my kids. Regardless of my past life, I'm still a mother first."

"That mother shit not gone fly with me. I gave yo' ass a pass to keep your life, and you burned my trap down," I said.

"I didn't touch your shit."

"And why should I believe you?"

"Because I know who did."

"OK, who?"

"I don't know who lit the match, but I know who hired them. James."

"Who the hell is James?"

"Judge Thomas," she said, catching my attention.

This the second person that's accused this nigga of being involved in something, so I was gone listen to what the hell she had to say, even if I'm still killing her.

"And why would he do that?"

Laughing, she said, "You still don't get it, do you?"

"Shit, bitch, if I made sense of all this bullshit, I wouldn't be playing twenty-one questions with your alien-looking ass."

"Judge Thomas been in on everything ever since you killed his wife and didn't kill Byron. The day you let Byron live, he called James telling him everything and asking for his help. James told him all about you, I guess in an attempt for him to take you out. The crazy part is, Byron was the only one being played like a fool. He never was very bright. Byron and James knew each other, and James was aware of the alleged affair. Hell, it was his idea."

"And you just let your nigga freely fuck another man's wife?" I asked, thinking if I tried my life like that, I knew Giovania ass would likely kill me and the hoe.

"At the point that we were at in our marriage, we were just putting on a front for the kids, but the love was gone a while ago; it just was no hard feelings."

"OK, so how did Byron and Judge Thomas even get to be that damn cool for him to be fucking his wife? They don't even hang out in the same circles?"

"He and Byron's dad played golf at the same country club together. Anyway, I think the plan was for you to kill both of them, and when that didn't work, James suggested Byron get rid of you. In my past life, I used to be nothing nice to fuck with. I could kill a nigga in two point five seconds," she said, causing me to smirk. "What's funny?"

"You talking about some damn past life you was a killa."

"My past life is how you haven't found me until I decided to let you find me," she said, and I decided not to argue with her because she did have a point.

"OK, this don't explain why Judge Thomas been trying to kill me if the whole idea was to kill Byron from jump which I did."

"Because he figured Byron, being the little bitch that he was, told you everything he knew before he died. Byron knew a lot about scams, his wife's murder, and numerous of other things the dear old judge was involved in. I bet any type of money, he now thinks you know as well. He is trying to tie up loose ends."

"OK, so if you ain't been burning my traps, why you run?"

"I'm not new to the game. I'm true to the game. I've known men like you my entire life, so I already knew how this would end. Like I said, I'm a mother first. When Byron told me he was thinking of hiring a hit man to take you out, I knew it could go one or two ways; you would kill whoever he hired, or they would kill you. That wasn't a gamble I was willing to take with my kids, so I left. I knew to fall off the grid completely, and since disappearing was my specialty, it wasn't hard for me to do. You found me tonight because I wanted to be found.

"I'm not young anymore. I can't disappear with kids for very long. They tend to get antsy because they can't be in school, can't talk to their friends, and have to spend life on the road. I'm done punishing my kids for something they had no parts in. You wanted answers; those are your answers."

"Where Detective Morris come in at? And how I know you ain't working with the judge?"

"First of all, I don't need to work with any damn body. I'm a volcano all by myself. Besides, that nigga ain't too bright. He's the last person on earth I would even think about working with.

"So you just show up out of the blue talking this rah-rah shit, and a nigga 'posed to roll with it, instead of killing you right now?"

"Ask yourself, why would I be willing to get back on Danielle's radar?" she asked, letting me know she knew exactly who Danielle was.

"OK. Let's say I believe you, why you telling me this information?"

"Because I need answers as well, and if I wasn't all my kids had left, since you killed their dad and grandparents, I would go searching for those answers on my own. You think I want to be sitting here talking to the man who killed my parents? Hell no, but the enemy of my enemy is my friend. This all started with James; the affair, the hit, everything, so he needs to pay."

Giovania

"GiGi, do you think momma will ever go back to being nice?" Camille asked me.

I had been dreading her asking me about our mother because I honestly didn't have any answers to give her. I wondered myself everyday what happened to the woman that raised me. She had done entirely too much to come back from, and I knew that nothing but death awaited her. Still, with everything she's put us through over this last few weeks, I still loved her. I couldn't help it, and sometimes I hated myself because of it.

I think as kids, it's just inside of us to love our parents unconditionally no matter what. I just couldn't seem to catch a break in the parent department, though. I had a father who forced me to marry a man who turned out to be my soulmate and baby daddy. He used me to deliver God knows what to people and placed a hit on my husband and blamed it on me. Not to mention, held my mother and sister captive.

The crazy part about that was, Camille claims that he didn't harm them at all and was nothing but nice to them. She was a child though, so maybe she only saw what her eyes wanted to see, or maybe he didn't show her the bad. Then you had my schemed-out mother, who apparently has been playing a game all these years, plotting and scheming her way through life to get to this point.

The real question was, how specifically did New Orleans fit into this scheme of hers? I couldn't rest my nerves until I found out what she was up to. It would at least bring me some type of closure.

"I hope so, Camille. She's just really sick right now," I said to her. She was a kid, so I would never tell her the honest trust.

"I hope she gets better in time for my birthday. God daddy Ja told me I can have a My Little Pony Princess party, and he getting me a real pony," she said, clapping her hands together excitedly.

Ja spoiled her rotten, and I was in love with the bond they had already formed. On the outside looking in, you would have sworn he'd know her for her entire life. It's hard to believe someone so damn evil and mean could be so kind and gentle with kids. He knows everything about Camille, from her favorite color to her favorite snack, favorite food, and her birthday. My husband was one in a million, and truly God sent.

"All done," the stylist, Keke, said.

I had gotten Camille's hair in some kid-friendly, individual crotchet Senegalese twists to save everyone the hassle of dealing with that thick mess on her head.

"I love it," I said to Keke as she put the finishing touches on Camille's hair, applying edge control and styling it. Just then, we heard the chime of the door as Melinda and Angel walked in, causing me to roll my eyes in annoyance.

"Seems like somebody been eating everything in sight. Girl, that belly is getting on out there," Melinda said.

"Naw, my husband just been feeding his kids, that's all. Nut is really nutritious. Who knew?" I said, smiling.

"Husband? Girl, don't tell me you talking about Jakeem? Ha! You still with that nigga, huh? Still out here looking stupid," Angel said as a few ladies in the shop snickered.

It wasn't a secret Ja was a hoe before we were married, and a lot of women wanted my spot. However, I was long overdue on showing these hoes I'm here to stay.

"Naw, baby, not in my shop. You hoes gotta go, coming in here picking with this girl. I can't stand bitches who got they picks and chooses," KeKe said.

"It's cool. I got this, KeKe. They picked the wrong one today," I said as everyone got quiet waiting on me to respond.

Ever since our nail salon incident, Angel's ass has made it her business to stalk my Facebook and throw subliminal posts at me. She was carrying on like she actually slept with Jakeem, but he said he didn't sleep with her, and I believed him.

"Camille, put your hands over your ears," I said.

I didn't bother telling Kaine, my new security, to come get her because these hoes wasn't crazy enough to hit me, and KeKe wasn't dumb enough to let them. She knew like I knew that Ja would not only kill her, but everybody in this shop if some shit like that happened.

"And you still out here begging for that big dick, huh?" I shot back at Angel as everybody looked on in shock.

"Bitch, I can take that nigga if I wanted him."

"You couldn't even take the dick away from me, so how you expect to take the whole man?"

"Bitch, you think you got you something, and don't have shit."

"I have the nigga you want, got the ring other bitches want, and I'm giving him his first kids," I said, making sure to put emphasis on 'kids' as I rubbed my belly.

"You want a cookie, bitch?"

"Yeah, actually my pregnant ass do, chocolate chip if you have it."

"Pregnant bitches always talk the most shit, don't they?" Melinda said.

"Dumb and Dumber, you two bitches are salty as fuck, and I find it hilarious. Neither one of y'all have a man, nor can y'all keep a man for that matter," I said.

"Melinda, I can't even imagine how it feels to be with a nigga for years then *boom*, he gets a new woman, and that bitch got something he never gave you—his heart. Shit, I know Kosher be riding that dick every night like a soldier. How you out here giving relationship advice and couldn't even keep your own nigga?" I asked, laughing.

"See, little girl, where you wrong at is I fuck my man every and any chance I get," Melinda said, trying to act hard in front of the women in the shop.

I had a trick for her ass, though. Pulling out my phone, I called Kosher and put her on speaker phone.

"Cousin, what's up, baby?" she said all extra loud.

"Hey, cousin. Tell me why we at the shop and Melinda telling everybody she can fuck Sade anytime," I said, being messy I know.

"Oh, I know she fucking lying. He ain't touched that delusional bitch since we got back together. Tell that bitch quit lying on my man before I close that other eye up," Kosher yelled, going off as I heard Kemari joining in as well. I hung up on them and decided to call them back later.

"Why you ain't check her for telling you, you lying?" I asked her.

"Fuck you, ugly ass bitch," Melinda said.

"Now, girl, you know I'm not ugly. Quit playing," I said, laughing. "And Angel, girl, you are a joke. You attempted to suck my husband's dick, and he wouldn't even get on hard. Damn, that mouth rotten just like them walls, huh? Y'all ugly hoes funny, but I'ma need y'all to keep that same energy in about four months. Next time I bump into y'all, and I'm not pregnant, have it on your mind," I said, paying for Camille's hair, grabbing her hand, and walking out of the shop very unbothered.

* * *

"Move," I said to Ja as I slapped his hand away from my plate.

I had went to drop Camille off at Momma Jackie's house, someplace she practically lived at, and ended up getting a plate of food while I was there. I was so thankful that Momma Jackie had stepped into this grandmother role with ease because it was a huge help to me with her caring for Camille so much. Shanti said she thought it was because she was lonely since Pops was always gone. But I say it's because she really has grown attached to my sister.

"Give me a bite," Ja said again, reaching toward my plate.

"Hell no," I said, eating a forkful of my greens.

Since I found out I was pregnant with twins, soul food and wings was all these stubborn ass kids craved these days, and that's exactly what I was eating all day everyday.

"Damn, all I wanted was a piece of your pork chop, greedy ass girl. You better be glad you feeding my kids, or else a nigga would have straight jacked yo' shit," he said, laughing.

"And we would have to fight."

"This ain't what you want, wifey. I don't fight fair."

"Neither do I baby, zaddy," I said, picking up my knife, waving it at him.

"You killed one muthafucka, and now you think you a killa."

"I am too a killa, just don't push me."

"You a killa, just fuck you? Damn, girl. I mean I wasn't thinking about sex but if you insist."

"I said, don't push me. I never said fuck me."

"As long as I push deep inside of you? Shit, I'm with that," this idiot said, coming out of his shirt, and allowing me to see those rock-hard abs.

I forgot all about my plate as my eyes zoomed in on my best friend sitting on full display through his shorts and resting on his thigh like a damn arm. My mouth started to water just looking at it.

"Damn, you said you want to suck daddy dick? You nasty," he said.

Reaching out, I grabbed him by the waistband of his shorts and pulled him toward me. Next, I stuck my hand inside of his shorts, pulling my best friend out to play.

"Suck it? Don't mind if I do."

* * *

"MA'AM, I'm sorry, but without those transcripts from New York, we cannot register you in any master's courses. You will have to start over as a first-time freshman," the lady at the registar's office told me. Pregnant and all, I was determined to get started on my master's degree, and this was slowing me up.

"Urghh, OK," I said, walking away from the window because I had been arguing with her for the last twenty minutes, and I was tired and over it.

I was just going to have to call New York University and have them to fax all my information over. Headed home, I stopped to get gas and decided to pull my iPad out and log into my old student account; something I haven't done in months. Looking at all the messages they sent me, none stood out more than the urgent message from the on-campus post office.

Briefly scanning the email, it was saying how I had received a certified letter from a Guatemala hospital, and they had tried contacting me several times in regard to the letter. Since they had no forwarding address, they opened the letter, trying to see if a phone number for me was listed. They scanned the letter and attached it to my email below. It was from a hospital in Guatemala that I wasn't familiar with. It was basically saying how my mother was on life support, but they couldn't pull the plug without the next of kin giving permission. I didn't feed much into it since obviously my mother was fine now.

However, I would like to know what they gave her and maybe whatever it was caused her to act like she's acting right now. Replying back to the email, I asked the doctor to call me at his earliest convenience. I then put my iPad away as I got out the car to get gas.

"Go pay, and I'll pump," Kaine said, walking over to my car.

Nodding my head, I walked inside the gas station. I could have paid at the pump, but I wanted some Queso chips and a red Gatorade.

"Damn, it's raining hoes, I guess. Leave one hoe to run into another," I heard as I bent down to grab my drink. Hearing a voice I never thought I would hear again, I turned around and came face-to-face with none other than Kyle himself.

"I see it's raining bitch niggas as well," I said.

"I see that mouth done became slick. This ratchet ass city will do that to you though. What else has changed with that mouth?" he asked me.

"You'll never find out. Oh, and I know that was you that sent them pictures to my husband. You bragging 'bout some shit that didn't even last two seconds because you tried to rape me is lame as hell," I said.

"Is that the story you telling everybody? That I tried to rape you? Shit, how you freely giving that cat away, I doubt that story can fly," he said.

"The only person that freely gets pussy is my husband, and he's most definitely somebody you need to watch your back with."

"Fuck that nigga. I don't fear nan nigga walking this earth. You tell his bitch ass to watch his back. And I found the shit funny as hell I was online looking at the nigga fuckin' my bitch, and I saw you tagged in a family picture with his ass, cheesing hard as hell. He been fucking with my family, so I felt it's only right I fuck with his," he said as I looked at him with a confused look on my face. He either had to be talking about Yari or the twins, but what the hell did that have to do with my ass?

"I don't know what the hell your problem is with me, but I don't and won't argue with a guy. You can talk to my husband, though," I said, pulling my phone out and FaceTiming Ja.

"Yo, baby momma, where yo sexy ass at?"

"On my way home, but the man of the hour wants to speak to you because like I told him, I won't argue with no man when my man will catch all them problems."

"He can catch all these bullets."

"Where Kaine?" Ja said

"Outside pumping gas."

"Bet. I'm on my way, and tell that fuck boy keep that same fuckin' energy."

"Fuck you, bitch," Kyle said, yet he knew to hurriedly walk the hell away. *Just what the heck is he doing in New Orleans?* I thought as I walked outside to see a very angry Ja going off on Kaine.

Sade

"Unc still away on business?" Sage said as he texted away on his phone.

"Yeah, he 'posed to be coming back in a few days."

"Unc be gone too damn much these days. Shit, if we not fuckin' with Mateo anymore, where he getting re-up from?"

"Shit, maybe he fuckin' Mateo momma and getting the shit that way," Sage said.

"Nigga, really, though? His momma? That's sick."

"Shit, that's genius, ya heard me. I'll knock the lining and worms off that old ass pussy if it was me, so I know Unc in that shit makin' me proud."

"You got problems, you know that," he said. "Aye, Kemari was looking good as fuck in them shorts she had on the other day. Put me down with her."

"Shit, put yourself down, nigga. Fuck I look like?"

"Yeah, that nigga Ja would lose his shit if I started fucking Kemari. Hell, it's bad enough you done professed your love to Kosh ass and shit."

"Speaking of my baby, Melinda ass making my damn life hell. Kosher keep beating her ass, yet she keeps fucking with her. How do you keep getting beat the hell up but still fix your mouth to talk shit?

I'm doing things differently this time, though. I check Melinda ass each time I see it, and I continuously shower Kosher with love and affection, so she know it's real."

"Shower her with love and affection? Nigga, where you heard that bullshit from? Yo' ass is toe up and starting to embarrass me," he said, laughing as he picked up the mail, throwing me mine until he came to one letter.

Looking from the letter to me, he asked, "Damn, G, why you ain't tell a nigga you was applying for college?"

"My letter came?" I said, getting nervous all of a sudden. This was a foreign feeling for me because didn't nothing on earth cause me to feel like this.

"Yeah, I'm looking at it."

"I didn't tell you just in case I didn't get in so yo' ass wouldn't start with the jokes."

"I'ma clown yo' ass regardless, but that doesn't mean I wouldn't be proud of you. Shit, what happened to us doing everything together? You don't think I can be a college man? I ain't smart enough?"

"Man, it wasn't shit like that. I took Kosher the other day to get her books; she just got accepted into the community college. She kept saying shit like I should apply and study business management and expand my money and shit. That's the same shit Ja always preaching to us about anyway, so I felt it was something I should look into. We already got our GED, so that means we can't be that dumb," I said.

Ever since Kosher agreed to be my girl again, we had been going stronger than ever. She was the smartest, coolest, most down-to-earth chick I'd ever met. She didn't judge a nigga by what was in my pockets, and my clout in these streets didn't faze her one bit. She genuinely liked me as a person, and not because of what I could do for her. When we linked up, we always had fun together, from hopping on the Xbox together, hitting a movie, or just Netflix and chill and really chilled, not just fucked. I felt like, with her, I could be my laughing, cracking jokes self, and could also go deep with our shit. We talked about any and everything, and she's never judged a nigga off my past. She always listened to what I had to say and even responded with solid advice.

So when she suggested I apply for school to further solidify my position in the game, I did. True, it's the same shit Ja been saying for years, but the shit coming from my girl, while she was blessing me with the best head of my life, made more sense to me than coming from my cousin. Opening businesses didn't mean I was going legit, far from it. Shit, just meant I was moving smarter and could back all my funds up like Ja do when Detective Morris be bringing his ugly ass around.

"Well, if your non-reading ass can get in, they gotta accept a playa like me. Smart hoes be the freakiest hoes."

"Hell yeah," I said, nodding my head in agreement because that shit was true as hell. It's always them smart, goody-goody, home before nine type girls that will do an entire gymnastics routine on ya dick.

"Gon' open it, shit," Sage said.

"You open it."

"Getcho scary ass on, ugly ass dude," he said as he opened it.

"Damn, nigga. Fuck, bro," he said.

"What? What?" I asked.

"Shit," he said.

"Fuck it. I know they ain't accept me. I ain't fucked up about it," I said, but really I was real fucked up about it.

"Naw, they actually want your ugly ass. You got in," he said.

"Damn, nigga. You the worst person to deliver a message."

"Heart was beating fast as fuck, huh?" he asked, laughing.

"Fuck you, bitch," I said, snatching the paper out of his hands. I read over it for myself before taking a picture and sending it to Kosher. I sounded soft as fuck, but this shit was all possible because of her ass. I loved the fuck out of that girl, and I didn't plan on letting her go again.

* * *

"I'M TELLING YOU, Melinda ass is stalking me," Kosher said.

"Did you see her?"

"Hell naw, but I know when a muthafucka switching lanes just because I'm switching lanes. Then she keep saying y'all still fucking, sending me pictures of you laid up in her bed and shit. You did leave me and go back to her."

"That's because you was playing games with a nigga like I was a damn toy. And that bitch is crazy. Don't listen to her ass. All them pictures is old."

"That hoe ain't too crazy. Hell, Trina was crazy, but that's because Ja was still fuckin' her, paying all her bills, and bought her a car."

"I'm not Ja. I ain't even bought the hoe a KitKat since we stopped talking. I'm telling you, the hoe is crazy, and she just wants your attention."

"Uh huh. For your sake, you better hope that's the case, and where we going?"

"Thought you was chilling with me tonight?"

"I am."

"Bet. We headed to my crib, though."

"What's wrong with my house? Why you never want to spend a night with me, Sade?"

"Shit, because I'm not laying my head in that neighborhood."

"But you trap in that neighborhood."

"Trapping and living are two different things."

"So what you saying is you too good for my house?"

"Shit, hell yeah, that's exactly what I'm saying," I said, laughing.

"Fuck you," she said, laughing as she kissed me.

* * *

> I came up from nothing, nigga; you can't tell me shit
> Yeah, did it on my own
> Check out my neck, check my wrist.

As YFN Lucci's "Everyday We Lit" played over the speakers, me and my niggas popped bottles in our VIP section that was getting more and more packed by the minute. Sage had applied for college and actually got accepted. We both were incoming freshmen, majoring in business management with a minor in accounting, so it called for a celebration. Once Ja found out, he rented out the club, invited all our friends, family, and crew, and we was turning this bitch out.

"What's up, Thing 1 and Thing 2? I'm proud of y'all niggas, bruh," Yari said, walking up and dapping us up.

We had long since got over that warehouse incident. That was my brother from another mother, so that nigga know we stay clowning.

"'Preciate it, ya heard me," I said just as Kosher danced her fine ass up to me. Walking off from them niggas talking, I pulled up to an empty side of our VIP, so I could tongue her down properly.

"Damn, you looking good enough to eat tonight," I said, bending down and sucking on her neck.

"Keep talking like that and make me find a dark corner and show you what this mouth do," she said.

Not giving her a chance to change her mind, I took her by her hand and damn near drug her to an empty room. As soon as I closed the door, she wasted no time dropping to her knees, unbuckling my pants, and pulling my dick out. The first feel of her tongue almost took a nigga out; I was so horny. This weed combined with alcohol had me ready to lay up and fuck her ass all night long. Raw. We had to try for another baby since she killed my last one.

"Oh shit! Suck this dick, bitch, and you better not gag." I huffed vigorously, shoving my dick in and out of her mouth and watching it disappear down her throat.

Kosher's hands down had the best sex I had ever experienced, and I wasn't saying that cuz she my girl. I was saying the shit because it was the truth; her head game had me hypnotized. The way she can swallow a dick should be illegal. My toes were curling, throwing up all types of gang signs as I felt my nut brewing.

"Yes, daddy, feed me this dick," she moaned as she nastily and hungrily swallowed all of these inches like it was her last supper.

That shit sounded so sexy how she said it, that it had me shooting off all my kids in her mouth.

"Arghh," I growled as I bust a big ass nut.

Opening her mouth to show me my kids on her tongue, she then swallowed it all up as she licked her lips.

"Fuck! I'm marrying yo' ass, girl."

Danielle

Waking up on the floor, I forced myself to get up as I handled my hygiene and walked downstairs to fix breakfast. I wasn't even that far along, yet this pregnancy was already kicking my ass. I'm so glad Cassandra, my good friend and Safari's god mom, had her for a few days giving me a break.

It felt like I had mentally checked out on life, and I needed to get myself together. I was running around mad at Yari and Ashanti like this was my boyfriend. When, in actuality, he never gave us a title. He simply said he wanted me to give him a chance to prove he was a good nigga and wouldn't hurt me. I can't say his actions hurt me. Shit, I hurt my own damn feelings when I got dickmatized and just made this man my boyfriend. Fucking with a New Orleans nigga will do that to you. They will have your ass tripping hard as hell and experiencing every different emotion all at once.

In the middle of me fixing some grits, I heard knocking on my door. Turning the stove down, I went to open the door to see Yari standing there looking good as hell in some stonewashed True Religion jeans.

Cocking my head to the side, I asked, "You lost or something?"

Yeah, I was happy to see this nigga, but I wasn't telling him that. I was done wearing my emotions on my sleeves when it came to this nigga. I've been down this road before with Bull, and I made a promise that I would never be that weak bitch again. We all slip up every now and then and fall back into the web of these niggas, but the key is to get the fuck out before you get swallowed up.

"Man, gon' 'head with that, bruh, ya heard me? I gave you time to calm down. Nigga just came over to check on your mean ass. What you cooking?" he said, bending down and giving me a juicy kiss before he sidestepped me and invited himself into my house.

"Damn, this shit smell good, and a nigga hungry as fuck. Yo, fix me a plate real quick. I'm tired as hell, I'm about to go lay down," he said, making himself comfortable as he kicked off his Jordans.

"Nigga, I know you fucking lying! This not your fuckin' house, and who the hell I look like?" I asked him.

"You look like my lil' sweetie. The woman that loves a nigga, and who 'bout to go ha fine ass in the kitchen and fix a real one a plate, ya dig," he said.

"Nigga, who said I loved you?" I asked him with an eyebrow raised.

"Oh yeah? So you don't love a nigga, Danielle? Shit, last night a nigga was hittin' yo fuckin' cervix, making you hit them high notes, you sholl loved a nigga then," he said, laughing.

Shaking my head at his ass laughing like he was Kevin Hart funny, I said, "When we was fuckin' and I said I loved you, I wasn't talking to you."

"Who the fuck you was talking to then?" Yari said as his smile left and was instantly replaced with an angry face.

"That dick," I said, sticking my tongue out.

"You better give that answer because you almost got fucked up," he said, laughing as he headed upstairs.

Walking back into the kitchen, I finished my grits, before I cut up some potatoes into small cubes and throwing them into a pan, frying them up. Finally, I dropped some fish into my deep fryer. You haven't lived yet if you've never had New Orleans style fish and grits. I usually prefer my fish I eat with my grits to be baked, but this morning I had a craving for fried fish.

I hoped I kept all of this down because everything looked so damn good right then. My stomach was growling loud as hell as all the aromas hit me at once. After I had plated everything up, I put it on a serving tray and headed upstairs. As soon as I made it to my room, the smell instantly caused Yari to turn over and jump up.

"Hell yeah, that's what the fuck a nigga talking about," he said as I sat down on my chaise directly in front of my bed. He looked confused when I picked my fork up and dug into my food.

"What the fuck, D? I thought that was for me. Where mine at?" he asked, looking mad.

"Downstairs," I said, pouring more hot sauce than I should have been consuming on my fish.

"Why you ain't fix my plate? You wild as fuck, man," he said.

"Because your legs don't look broke to me, and you ain't my man," I said to him.

I was done giving husband privileges to a nigga that wasn't even my boyfriend. I had to boss up, realize who the fuck I was, and recognize my worth. This house we was in was bought and paid for with my money that I worked hard as hell for. My bank account was courtesy of me, not a nigga. Granted, I got the money from Ja, but it wasn't just handed to me; I worked for that.

"It's like that, though?" he asked, getting off the bed and coming to sit beside me.

"Yeah, it is," I said, taking a bite of my fish. "Hmmm, sooo good," I taunted him, rubbing it in his face.

"It damn sure is, and a nigga hungry as fuck," he said, looking me up and down.

"Well, you should gone eat then," I said, picking up the crescent roll I made. Before I could even take a bite, his ass had snatched the roll out of my hand and stuck the entire thing in his mouth.

"You ugly muthafucka!" I yelled angry as hell as he chewed my shit in my face.

"Damn, that shit was good as fuck, and just what I needed. Now it's time to eat," he said.

"That's what I been telling you to do for the longest," I said as I picked my fork up. Before I could even take a bite, this nigga had grabbed my entire fucking plate.

However, instead of eating it, he sat it on my breakfast tray, then turned back to me and said, "That's what I'm about to do," with a devilish look in his eyes.

Before I could protest, he had already stood up, bent down, grabbed me by both of my thighs and lifted me off the chaise. It didn't help the fact that the only thing I was wearing was an oversized T-shirt either. Skillfully putting me on his shoulders, he wasted no time diving into my happy place as he walked with me until my back hit a wall. Not missing a beat, he continued feasting on my body like he was on death row and this was his last meal.

I didn't want to enjoy this because each time we had sex, I lost part of my mind, my rational thinking, and hell, all of my common sense. You ever tried to hold back while a nigga eating you, but then his tongue touched a part of your body that causes you to lose your mind? Shit, that's exactly how I was feeling right now. I know I went retarded for a moment, that's how good this nigga was eating me. Shit, I felt like ole dude off *Get Out* when, each time the momma tapped that spoon on that cup, he slipped further into the sunken place.

With each stroke of Yari's tongue, I felt my soul leave my body more and more. Shit, I was headed straight to heaven to kick it with God. Yari has eaten me before, but never like this. This time felt different like he was expressing his emotions through sex. I just hope my dumb ass didn't fall for it again.

"Oh my God!" I screamed as my breathing picked up, and my legs began shaking.

"That's it. Let that shit go, bae. You gone come for daddy?" he asked before sticking his tongue inside of me and jabbing it, mimicking a penis. It instantly drove me wild.

"No! I don't want to," I said, shaking my head as my stomach became tight as I felt pressure building up inside of me.

Him sticking a finger inside of me and fingering me at the same time as he was sucking on my clit, drove me insane. I damn near pulled my own hair out.

. . .

YARI PAUSED HIS MOVEMENTS. "Didn't I tell this lil' pussy to cum?" he asked sternly as he popped me on my clit as it jumped.

As my eyes rolled into the back of my head, my body betrayed me as it instantly responded to his voice, cumming on command. That hoe don't know how to listen to me when I told her we not giving in to this nigga anymore. I told my pussy one thing, and she did the complete opposite!

Smiling, he went back down and continued feasting on me, instantly pulling another earth-shaking climax out of me.

"Fuck boy! Shit!" I moaned with a tight grip on his head, grinding my pussy into his face, making sure he didn't miss not one drop.

Looking up at me with my juices coating his face, he smirked and instead of stopping, he kept going.

"No, Yari," I moaned.

"I need you to cum for daddy one more time."

"I'm tapping out," I said, completely drained of energy at this point. I was pregnant, tired, and needed a nap.

Ignoring me, he began licking around my pussy, and kissing on my thighs before he dove back in to claim his prize. This time, he switched it up and started French kissing my mound ever so gently, making love to me with his mouth. Turning around, he began walking with me still on his shoulders toward the bed never pausing the slow torment he was laying on my body as he placed me on the bed. Using this as my opportunity to escape, I scooted up a bit, only to be dragged back down.

"Where you going?" he asked me.

"Away from you, I can't take this," I moaned.

"You can't, but you will cuz I want your soul," he said.

That shit sent chills down my body when he said that. Flipping me over so that I was on top of him, he brought me down on his body sliding me down until my mouth was within reach. Leaning up and kissing me at the same time as I felt him opening his jeans, I got excited thinking about the dick I was about to be blessed with.

As soon as I felt that anaconda hit me, I hopped up and rushed to the bathroom, barely making it in time before the vile vomit left my mouth. Once the vomiting started, I couldn't stop.

"Damn! What the hell wrong with you? I'm glad I didn't eat that shit, got your stomach tore up," Yari said, coming into the bathroom and holding my hair as I emptied everything I had eaten today and green shit I didn't even consume.

"It-it wasn't shit I ate," I managed to choke out.

"Shit, it gotta be something. It could be some shit from yesterday, or you caught a bug from somebody," he said.

"I know exactly what it is," I said.

"What?" he asked me.

"I'm pregnant."

* * *

"YOUR HONOR, the defendant never even told my client about his child before he moved away. Since he has returned, he's made numerous attempts of reaching out to Ms. Walters to see his child, and she has denied each attempt. Our only concern is the safety of his daughter," Bull's lawyer said to the judge.

After Bull had asked me to help him take over Yari's operation, and I refused, he hit me with a custody order. That was almost two weeks ago, and here we were on this Tuesday morning in court! I don't know how the shit moved so fast, but we were at a hearing, and his lawyer was really laying it on thick. Thank God Ja pays me really well, and I was financially able to obtain a good lawyer as well. I wish I had access to Ja's attorney, Stan, but I know he's busy dealing with Ja's case right now.

My lawyer wasn't bad though, and so far, he was doing a damn good job. I wish someone was with me right now for moral support, but I knew everyone has their own problems right now. And ever since I told him I was pregnant, Yari has been avoiding me like the plaque, but I couldn't focus on that shit right now.

Tuning back in, trying to take everything in, I put my game face on and listened to every word being said, trying not to miss anything. All throughout the court hearing, I kept it calm, cool, and collected. But when the judge told us to break for recess, I broke down as soon as I made it to a private room with my lawyer.

"I can't do this. It's no way in hell he's getting near my baby," I said, crying.

"I hate to say this, but as your attorney, it's my job to advise you on how things will go from here on out. They struck first blood, and it'll only get worse. They'll question your ability to financially provide for Safaree," he said.

"I provide for her just fine! What the fuck you talking about? I'm not on government assistance, and my child goes to a private school!" I yelled out.

"I'm not the enemy. I'm on your side. That's all true, but what check stub do you have to prove any of this?" he asked me.

He knew about my income, but I never told him how I got my money. I didn't trust him as much as Ja trusted Stan.

"A check stub wouldn't be hard to obtain," I told him because by tonight I could have about eighty check stubs dating back a few years if need be that will all check out as credible. My lawyer better recognize I'm the best to ever do this computer shit.

"I'm just saying, this process can and will get nasty and could draw out for a few months, or even years. We already on recess for two weeks, next time, it could be two years. The truth of the matter is, custody battles are unpredictable with time and outcome. You do not have a criminal record and appear to be doing fine financially. However, the plaintiff is married, has children, and businesses. If he were a convicted felon that was working a dead-end job, I could, with confidence, tell you, you need not worry. However, you need to prepare yourself for the worst-case scenario of him winning joint custody."

"Over my dead fuckin' body! I'll kill his ass first!" I screamed, causing him to look alarmed.

"I'm not saying is this case. I'm saying it's a possibility. Now, I met with the plaintiff and his lawyer before court, and they agreed to settle out of court with supervised weekly visitation, and overnight weekend visits. I would advise you to consider it, being that he could possibly end up being awarded far more time than that. I've seen cases where the father gets the child from Thursday until Monday, and every summer and holiday," he said, looking at me as if to say "bitch, this your only option so you better take it."

"And I would advise you to stop discussing my child with that snake ass nigga. Only thing you need to advise me of are ways to win this case, that's it. I'm not paying your ass to do anything that falls outside of that category, and that included the dumb shit that just left your mouth. I don't know if I made myself clear when I retained you or not, but Safaree Janae Samuels is my one and only concern. I'm the only parent she'd ever known, and over my dead body will I ever give her up, even for a night to a muthafucka who asked me to abort her.

"I don't care what a damn piece of paper may or may not say; the shit ain't happening. I carried her for nine months before sixteen hours of labor, took care of her when she's feeling bad, sad, or happy. Fed, clothed, educated, and nurtured her like a mother should. She's the sweetest, funniest, smartest child you'll ever meet, and I'll be damned if he come in and reap all the benefits of my hard work. I raised her alone, and I'll continue watching her grow, alone. Now, to avoid me getting ignorant and fucking shit up, I retained you to bring me a happy ending. If you feel like you can't do the one task you were given, let me know right now so I can look into finding someone who can," I said to him because I didn't want to hear that shit he was talking about.

The nerve of him to meet with them bitches and discuss a settlement. He can settle these nuts. Fuck out of here! I said I was going to keep shit on the low and handle this one myself since the gang has their own issues, but I might have to break down and tell Ja what's going on and get help.

Hell, hopefully once he knows that Bull is trying to take over, he will kill him, and that will help me out. Shit, I'll kill him myself before I let him take my baby away from me.

"No, we don't have to mention the offer again. I'm not here to harm you, simply help. Look, emotions are high. I'll take a step back and go get us some coffee," he said, not even bothering to wait until I replied before he walked out.

Putting my head down, I tried get myself together. Feeling an object drop on my head, I immediately thought a spider or roach was in my hair. I jumped up, flinging my hands around just to spin around and come face-to-face with Bull at the same time as my hand made contact with the intruder in my hair.

"What the fuck yo' bitch ass want?" I asked him, pulling the object toward my face to see what the hell was in my head.

When I saw the locket, all the color drained from my face as recognition set in. Looking from the locket to him, I couldn't even form a sentence as memories of the locket came flooding back to me full force. The locket was given to me by my stepfather, Boon, and he used to call me his special girl. Having never had a father, I was excited that he thought of me as his special girl and used to cling to him, hoping to fill that father-daughter bond I was missing. Things between us were going great until the sexual abuse started. His "special girl" went from a term I moved to hear him use to one I cried each time I heard.

"Just put the tip in your mouth. We only playing a game, baby girl. Remember, you are my special girl, and you don't want to make me mad now, do you?" he would say before forcing himself on me. That went on for a few months. Him giving me oral, forcing me to suck the tip of his dick, which really meant let me stick my dick down your throat. Besides fingering me, or using toys on me, he had never penetrated me until one night he decided I was ready. All day he had been hinting around to taking our "relationship," as he called it, to the next level.

I didn't know what level that was, but I knew it couldn't be good. so mustering up all the courage that I could, I told my mother in detail everything that Boon had been doing to me. I begged her to save me from him because I didn't want to experience whatever he had planned for me. To say that I was hurt by her next actions would be an understatement. That shit broke me when she told me I was lying and didn't want to see her happy. I decided that the only person that could save me was myself, so I packed a bag of clothes and a knife for protection because New Orleans can be dangerous at night. As I walked outside, I felt a hard blow to my head, causing me to pass out.

When I came to, I found myself face-to-face with Boon. Let's just say, he raped me so much that night that I kept passing out from the pain. I don't know how I managed to do it, but when he finally passed out, I struggled, on shaking legs, to pick myself up, half crawling, half dragging my feet to try to get away from him.

Once I made it out of the abandoned house he brought me to, I cried a silent but deadly cry for all of five minutes. I was so hurt; I couldn't even cry out loud! Something snapped in me as I turned around, walked back into the house and grabbed the knife out of my bag, stabbing him about fifty times. I buried his body along with the knife, locket, and my clothes I was wearing, and decided to return home.

People go missing in New Orleans every day, so it wasn't a big deal to some. My mother, however, blamed me and my accusations as the reason to why Boon had left us. I met Bull shortly after that and eventually confided in him my secret, and I even took him to the spot where I had buried Boon at. He told me from that day forward he would never let another soul hurt me, and he kept his promise. The only person that hurt me throughout our entire relationship was his ass.

"Didn't expect to see that again, now did you?" he asked me.

"What the fuck do you want from me?" I said barely above a whisper. It was hard being strong when you had to be strong solo.

"I've already told you what I want; you need to make things easier on yourself and start cooperating." He smirked. "Regardless of the shit I asked you to do, I do want to see Safaree. I know it was fucked up for me to say abort her, and I can't change that. The kid looks just like me and my other kids. My blood's pumping through her veins. That's my seed, and you won't keep her from me anymore. Hell, if you would have told me you went ahead and had her, I probably would have been took her ass away from you. All my kids live under one roof, that's how it will always be," he said.

"Bullshit. Cut the fucking 'father of the year' act, Bull. You can put on for these people, but bitch, I know you in real life. You'll never take my child away from me, and I put that on your kids' heads, bitch." I snarled.

Gone was the scared kid that he left, the one was that was scared to look him in the eye as people in *Harry Potter* were scared of saying Lord Voldemort's name. That Danielle died a long time ago, and I rose in her place. As mothers, we will do anything to protect our babies, even gain strength we never knew we possessed.

"Tread lightly bringing my kids into anything, because I don't give a fuck about the fact we inside of a courthouse; you know how I give it up. Make me remind your ass who runs shit. Now I don't want to take Safaree from you, but I will if you don't tell me everything I need to know about the bitch boy Yari and Ja. Are they worth losing your child over? I'll even drop the custody case, and you can keep Safaree, just let me see her every now and then. I might be a fucked-up individual, but I ain't no damn deadbeat."

"And if I say 'suck my dick, bitch,' then what?" I said.

"Then you go to prison for life, and I take Safaree and kill ya little boyfriend anyway. You don't have to tell me where his bitch ass lives, just tell me about his traps, and I'll take it from there. You choose. Oh, just in case you thinking about warning them, I gave my lawyer all the evidence from that murder. If I turn up missing, you loose Safaree anyway, and since my wife is my power of attorney, and I left her guardianship over the kids, so she'll get Safaree as well," he said just as my lawyer showed back up.

"Make your next move, your best move," Bull said before winking at me and walking out the door.

* * *

I KNOW I was gambling with my life by telling Ja about the Bull situation, but after weighing all of my options, this was my only one. I wouldn't tell him about Bull trying to take over, but I would tell him about this custody situation and using Boon's death against me. Since I had some new information about Samantha, I called Ja up to tell him.

"What you got for me?"

"I just sent you everything I have on Samantha, and so far, everything she told you is checking out."

"Bet, and what you found out about the Kyle situation because that little nigga gotta go?"

"I'm sending you everything I found on him since he got in town," I said.

"Bet that up. I'm glad you back to your normal self and on top of things."

"It's something else I want to talk to you about," I told him.

"What's up?"

"I had a court hearing, and Bull is trying to take get joint custody of Safaree. I need help with this matter, Ja. I can't do it on my own. My lawyer talking about Bull wants to settle out of court with weekday visits supervised, and weekend visits unsupervised." I cried, feeling a slight weight being lifted off my shoulders, knowing I had told someone about what was going on, and didn't have to keep it bottled up. I figured Ja would be just as outraged as I was being that Bull hasn't been there for my baby all these years and told me to abort her.

Instead, he said, "Listen, bruh, you making this shit more complicated than it needs to be. Why go through this long ass court process getting the white folks involved when they agreed to settle?"

"Fuck that! Over my dead body will he ever get my child or have her around that bitch!

"Don't ask me for my advice, then get mad when I give the shit to you. If all the nigga wanna do is see his kid, let him."

No, he also wants to take over y'all territory, but if I tell y'all that and y'all kill him, my secrets will surface, I thought to myself.

"He's evil, Ja, and I don't want my child around Jewels's because —" I started until he cut me off.

"Don't be bitter about the situation when you the one chose to sleep with a nigga that had a girl. You gotta take whatever comes with that. That's a decision you made, and you can't blame nobody but yourself. If that nigga moves wrong and tries to harm you, then let us know, and we'll take it from there. But if he tryna see his kid, don't be a bitter baby momma. But check it, nigga got bigger problems to take care of than this shit, so one love," he said, hanging up on me.

It was at that moment that I realized I was on my own and had to do whatever I needed to protect my child. Dialing a number, I listened to it ring about five times before the person picked up. "What's up?"

"I'll do what you asked," I said, hanging up. Bull gave me an out, and I was taking it. He didn't ask for no addresses, just trap houses and weaknesses. I figured I could give him what he wanted and still keep my baby. He would see that I was cooperating and destroy the evidence against me. I would make sure it was gone before I told him everything. I was confident in the fact that Yari and Ja would no doubt kill Bull, but I was willing to gamble with their life in the process.

Nobody would be put above my child's safety for their own. I didn't trust Jewels around my child because she's still mad I fucked her nigga and had a baby by him. Does that sound like a person who would welcome a baby with open arms? I just hope when this all ends, Ja will understand.

Jakeem "Ja" Carter

"You better fuck me back because if I have to fuck you solo, I'm murdering this pussy, Giovania," I said to her before I found my way back inside my warm, happy place. It's something about this pregnancy pussy that I just couldn't seem to get enough of.

Her hormones always had her horny, and my ass was always there to drop dick off. When I didn't feel her fucking me back, I held onto her waist and started plunging deeper into her like I had a point to prove.

"Ahhh! Jakeeeem!"

"Fuck me back, ma," I said, hitting the jackrabbit on her ass. Catching the hint that I wasn't playing, I felt her start throwing her ass back on me.

"That's what I'm talking about. Take all these inches, ma. It's yours," I said, going deeper than I normally go, hitting her with death strokes.

"It's too big, baby," she said, trying to run.

"Don't run. Take this dick," I growled, pulling her back down, not missing a beat.

She reached back and put her hand on my leg, trying to push me out some, but I grabbed her hand, twisted it behind her back and went even deeper. I felt my nut forming, and I started standing up in that pussy. Her knees gave out, and she fell on the bed, so I went down with her, still stroking.

"Fuck," I growled out. "You ready for daddy to cum?"

"Yes, cum for me," she moaned.

"Sike!" I said as I flipped her over, back onto her back and went back inside that heavenly place.

"You always saying how much you want the dick, so take all this shit, babe," I said, slowing my pace down as I leaned down and kissed her pretty ass. I can't believe she turned me soft as hell because I never used to like kissing in the past. Now, I couldn't stop kissing this juicy, soft lips.

"I love yo ass, girl," I said, grabbing her face and pulling it to me as I slow stroked the wettest place on earth.

* * *

NOTICING YARI HAD HIT me up earlier, I hit him back to see what's up.

"I know. I just heard. I'm headed to the restaurant now," he said the minute he answered the phone.

"What you talking about, nigga?"

"Momma Bee's. Somebody burned it down; I thought that's why you was calling me," he said as I zoned out and hit a U-turn on the highway, speeding back toward my T-lady shop with fire dancing in my eyes as I called her repeatedly.

"Fuck!" I yelled, punching my steering wheel over and over again. As soon as I pulled up, I noticed fire trucks and ambulances blocking the entrance. Hopping out my truck, damn near forgetting to put it in park, I ran full speed toward the front.

"Whoa, sir, you have to stay back," an officer said, stopping me.

"Get yo' hands off me, bitch. This my momma shit. Where she at?" I barked, looking around wildly for her as I saw bodies laid out everywhere. Some were customers, some workers, but none was my T-lady.

"Momma!" I yelled, running around as the fire rose higher and higher.

Taking my jacket off, I was prepared to dive into that shit headfirst if I had to if my momma was in there. She usually restocked the inventory in the basement and maybe she got trapped down there. I was either running out with her or gonna die trying. That's my fucking best friend, my heart.

"Sir, I'm going to have to ask you to stand back," an officer said to me.

"If you don't get yo' bitch ass out my damn face," I said as my hands went to my gun. I was about to get to airing this bitch out.

"We can't allow you to go in there, sir," he said as backup came to help him.

"Fuck y'all! If my momma in there, I'm going in there! Which one of you bitch ass niggas gone stop me?" I asked, ready to take on an army right now. I was losing my mind and becoming unhinged.

"Look, my brother, let help me help you, sir," a black officer said frantically.

"Nigga, you ain't my fuckin' brother, I'll knock yo' bitch ass out too. If you can't tell me where the owner of this restaurant is, get the fuck out my face," I said.

"Jackie Carter, right? Sweet Jackie Carter," he said.

"Yeah," I said, calming down a bit.

"She's gone," was all I heard before I started laughing hysterically as I pushed off him and walked away as he yelled after me. Yari, Sage, and Sade all pulled up just then as I was walking to my truck.

"Yo, Ja, what's going on?"

"I'm killing everything moving and breathing. Every fucking thing moving is dead," I repeated.

"I just got a text from my shawty at the hospital. Momma Jackie and a child was just brought in on stretchers. She right up the street," Sage said as I jumped into my truck and sped off toward the hospital, praying the entire way there.

* * *

"Say, I need to know what room my momma in. They brought her in here a few minutes ago. Jackie Carter," I said to the girl at the front desk, but instead of the bitch typing the information in, she just batting her eyes at me.

"What's her name?" she asked.

"Bitch, I just told you—Jackie Carter."

Again, instead of her typing the name in, the bitch was sitting there, staring at me in these grey sweats pants like she wanted to pull my dick out right here and start sucking it. Not in the mood, I pulled my gun out and held it at her head,

"Bitch, I'm not in the mood. Every second that passes by is time I'm not with my momma. If you want to see tomorrow, you better get to fuckin' typing. Now I said Jackie Carter, bitch," I said, not giving a fuck who saw me with my gun. I was liable to air this whole hospital out at this point.

"Jackie Carter is in ICU 311, and the child she was brought in with, Camille Santiago, is in stable in room 510," she said.

Pushing her head, I walked off headed toward the elevators. Once they opened, I saw Pops stepping off.

"You been up there already?" I asked him as he looked at me with a confused look on my face.

"Already been up where?"

"Room 311, where Ma at," I said, stepping onto the elevator as he got back on with me.

"What you mean your mother in room 311? What the fuck happened?"

"That's what I'm tryna figure out," I said as I rushed off the elevator heading to ICU. Pressing the buzzer to get buzzed in, the lady on the intercom chimed in and said we couldn't come in right now.

"Fuck you, bitch! Open these doors," I said.

"Son, calm down for me, I'm about to go find a doctor," Pops said, walking off.

Walking over to the wall, I punched it repeatedly becoming angrier by the second. Taking a seat in the waiting room, I sat with my hands in my head praying my T-lady would pull through. Hearing loud voices, I stood up and walked toward the commotion seeing my father and a doctor arguing.

"What the fuck you mean you can't tell me shit about my fucking wife? Y'all got me fucked up in here! Y'all better tell me something right fuckin' now!" Maxx Carter said.

He rarely was mad, so when he did get mad, bullets started flying next. Once he hemmed the doctor up by his neck, the weak ass security ran in, and I damn near flew over there to them and immediately started swinging haymakers, knocking they asses out. It was seven of them and two of us, and together, we was beating shit and knocking they asses down each time they ran out.

"Aye," I heard as I looked up and saw Yari, and the twins running up to us, trying to break everything up.

"Come on, y'all. If y'all go to jail, who gon' be here for Momma Jackie? Y'all all she got and the only ones who can make medical decisions for her," Yari said as Sade and Sage grabbed Pops.

"Fuck that. Sade, get off on that nigga," Pops said, referring to the guard he was fighting.

Being that the twins looked at him like a father, Sade instantly let Pops go and rocked the fuck out of the guard as an all-out brawl started. One that even I knew we had to stop because Yari did have a point.

Managing to get everyone away from the fight, we headed downstairs for some fresh air and to calm down. Walking outside, we passed a nigga mugging us before he started talking shit to Pops who just smirked at him. I knew that look; Pops was done swinging. He was ready to drop bodies.

"Thought you wasn't gone see me again."

"Keep on and you won't see you again. Don't let a nut be the cause of your momma burying you," Pops said.

"I buried my momma a long time ago, so I ain't got shit else to lose," dude said.

"Man, Pops, stop arguing with this bitch ass nigga." I jumped in, not knowing who dude was but ready for all smoke that was coming my Pops way.

"Like father like son. Both y'all tryna wife these hoes."

"Lil' nigga, today not the day. You'll get yo' ass whooped out here," I said.

"Nigga, shut yo' ass up before I stick my dick in Giovania's mouth again," he said.

"Hell naw. Who the fuck this knockoff Mista Cain-looking ass nigga is, bruh?" Sade said.

"Nigga will get off on your ass, fuck you talking about," Sage said.

"Oh, so you the nigga Kyle, huh? Same nigga that I told to keep that same fuckin' energy when you saw me," I said to him before I hauled off and hit his ass with a clean ass left hook.

Even though I was tired as hell from beating them security guards asses, I was still fucking this nigga up. Yari managed to pull us apart before the nigga said this wasn't over and took off inside the hospital.

"What the fuck going on around here?" Yari said.

"Yeah, man. If somebody else come looking to fight you, we shooting they asses," Sage said.

"Shit, I really don't know," I said as I thought popped in my head.

"What's really good, Pops? And it just hit me that yo' ass was here when I got here, yet I was the one told you 'bout Ma Dukes. If you wasn't her for Ma, what you was doing here already?" I asked him as everyone looked at him for answers.

He was quiet as hell for a moment until he said, "I don't know how to tell you this, but I fucked up. I was fuckin' with this broad from New York until she got pregnant, and I cut her ass off quick as fuck."

"Damn, Unc, you still out here stroking, breaking these bi—"

"Shut up, fool," Sade told Sage, cutting him off.

"Anyway, I told her it wasn't my seed and stopped all communication with her. I think she followed me home because last night when I stopped to grab some food at the drive-thru, she hopped in my car. We got into a fight this morning, because even though I got us a room, I still wasn't fuckin with her like that. The argument got heated, and I pushed her ass down, forgetting she was pregnant. Her water broke, and I had to rush her to the hospital. Kyle is the nigga she was fuckin with before I came in the picture, or shit, while I was in the picture.

She told him it was my baby and not his, and the nigga been in his feelings ever since," he said.

All I could think about was the fact my mom was fighting for her life while a new life was being brought into this world. I needed to get away from this before I violated and murdered his ass. I knew he fucked with different bitches, but my number one rule was don't shit where you sleep, and don't hurt my mother. The news of this baby gone crush her, if she ever wakes up.

Ashanti

Breathing heavily, I struggled to get my big body inside of the cute maternity sundress I had picked out. I was bubbling with excitement because Lexx had texted me that he was in town today and wanted to see me. I didn't know why he was here, and I didn't care. I was just ready to see him. Never before has a man ever stimulated my mind with just conversation like he did. It was different and refreshing. Mainly because he didn't let me have my way and give in to my pouting faces. No matter how many times I asked for a naked picture and FaceTimed him with a sad face, he refused to give in to my demands. That was a new one for me, but instead of being turned off, I was extremely turned on.

After the struggle to get into my clothes was over, I sat down to take a break because that took a lot out of me to do. Once I got my breathing together, I started on my hair, curling it to perfection before moving on to my makeup. With each stroke of the brush, I smiled a little bit more on the outside and inside. It had been a while since I looked and felt beautiful and I was loving every minute of it. I went from never leaving out the house without a full face beat to the gawds to not caring how I looked these days.

Before I moved in with Yari, he had never before seen me without makeup because I always wanted him to see me at my best. Now, my ass was always walking around looking like who shot John and forgot to kill him.

After I was done getting dressed, I stood up in my floor-length mirror and admired my work. Besides looking like a big ass Barney in my purple and green sundress, I looked cute. A big ass cute Barney. Grabbing my things, I made my way downstairs running into Yari on my way out of the house.

"Damn," he said, taking in my appearance. The way he was looking at me caused me to blush.

"Where you going, girl, looking good enough to eat?" he asked.

"To hang with a friend," I said, omitting the fact that that friend was Lexx.

I didn't have time to hear Yari's mouth about the situation, because I already knew where he stood on the topic. He got mad every time he saw me FaceTiming or talking on the phone with Lexx and didn't mind verbally expressing the shit. Yet I didn't trip off anything he did with Danielle. His childish ass needs to grow up.

Yeah, I'm the last person that needed to be talking, but life and this past year had forced me to grow up way in a major way. I may still be petty and with the shits, but at least I'm also understanding and tend to mind the business that pays me. I don't wild on anyone that Yari entertains, nor am I a bitter baby momma.

Shit, I know his ass out here fucking everything that moves, and I'm not fucked up about it. I just want us to co-parent Tariq and be the best parents we can be, that's it. He do his own thing, and I do my own thing.

"What friend?"

"Shit, mine," I said, brushing past him and out to my car.

* * *

"So TELL ME THE TRUTH, you came out here to see me, didn't you?" I said to Lexx.

Flashing me that panty-dropping smile, he said, "Seeing you was just a plus that made this trip all the more better. But naw, baby girl, my brother wanted me to come out here and sit in on a business meeting of his. I didn't want to come, but that's my kid brother, and I'ma always have his back. Regardless if I think his ass doing dumb ass shit or not. Feel me?"

"Why you think he doing something dumb?"

"Because I was built for this life, and he thinks he about this life, but it's a difference. This ain't a joke, this grown-man business, and he'll fuck around and get killed. Then if that happens, the monster in me—that I hope you never meet—will turn this bitch into Afghanistan with no problem," he calmly said.

Even though he said the shit in such a calming tone, I still felt that shit. I've been around drug dealers my entire life and could usually spot a thug from a mile away with one damn eye. Lexx, however, didn't look nor act the part, and that's the part that drove me wild. The mystery of it all.

He blended in with a square ass good boy to the tee, but really, I know he was moving major weight.

I catch on to code talk very easily, courtesy of Big John, so I know he a boss, and that this meeting was more than likely concerning drugs. I promised my son we were done with drugs dealers, and I meant it. But that still didn't stop my body and mind from wanting the fuck out of this man. Hell, for him I was willing to make an exception.

"Yo' ass needs to lay down before you try and get back on that highway heading home," Lexx said, his voice slicing through my thoughts.

"I don't need a nap, but I do want to lay down and rest my feet. They so swollen and sore," I said, looking down at my feet. Well, trying to anyway.

"I would have picked you up from the house. You don't need to be driving as big as you are," Lexx said, instantly reached down and pulled my feet into his lap, massaging them.

We were currently in his penthouse suite where we've been talking for a few hours now. We had opted for room service instead of going out to eat, which I was grateful for because that drive to his hotel had drained the energy out of me, and I had gotten lazy.

"Oh God," I said as he worked his magic on my feet. I felt like I had died and gone to heaven. It was feeling so good. Yari may cater to my food cravings, but he never once asked to massage my feet or body.

"Hmmm," I moaned with my head thrown back in ecstasy as I closed my eyes. I swear to God this shit felt like an out-of-body experience. It felt so good.

"Stop that, bruh," he said, laughing.

"Stop what? Ohh shit!" I gasped as he worked his fingers in between each of my toes.

"That, bruh. Quit moaning like that. I may be a respectful nigga, but I'm still a nigga at the end of the day. Shit, I be catching all the subliminal messages throughout the day you throw at me. Naw, I'm not sending you no damn dick picture through the mail. I'm a grown ass man, not a lil' boy like you used to dealing with.

"They brag on they shit all the time, and they quick to whip that shit out. A real nigga, a grown ass nigga, ain't 'bout no talking, straight square business. However, as long as you got that nigga seed in you, you can't see no dick, touch no dick, taste no dick, or feel this dick rearranging ya spinal cord. However, if yo' ass keep that moaning up, nigga might have to make an exception and see if it taste as good as it smells," he said.

Normally, I would have a nasty ass comeback to that shit to keep this conversation going, because for months, that's all my freaky, horny ass been trying to do, have sex talks. However, he wouldn't breach the topic for shit, and would always side step that shit like the plaque.

They say the things we can't have, we crave the most, and I craved him like I craved food. All that waiting and right now, I was in a massage-induced coma, and couldn't do anything but lay here with my eyes closed as I felt the darkness engulfing me. Before I knew it, I was fast asleep.

* * *

WAKING up not even a few hours later to sharp pains ripping through my body, I sat up, looking around and realizing I was no longer on the couch. I threw my legs off the side of the bed with the intentions on getting up and getting a glass of water when another pain surged through my stomach. This one worse than before, causing me to scream out in agony. Rushing into the room with his gun drawn, Lexx looked around, wildly searching for the source causing me to scream.

"What's wrong, shawty?"

"Baby," I choked out as his eyes grew big.

"Whoa, you sure?"

"Yes, nigga, I'm sure!"

"You can't hold it in a little while?"

"Urghh! Get me to a hospital, Lexx!"

"Damn you know I hate those—" He started saying until I cut him off.

"Alexx, if you don't drive me to a damn hospital, right fucking now so help me God, I'm fuckin' you up!" I screamed as he just looked at me.

"Keep talking to me like that, saying my government, and watch you don't get shit but this dick for the next few hours, long and strong. Now I done told you, I don't know how the fuck you talk to the fuck nigga that impregnated you, but that hot ass mouth not gone fly this way," he said.

I was in pain, but I wasn't crazy, so I shut the fuck up for now.

Just as I had gotten myself calm, another sharp pain hit me that was so unbearable that I could barely breathe as it ripped up my side and shot down my back, causing my knees to give out as I went down.

Before I fell, however, Lexx had scooped me up bridal style, like I weighed five pounds, and rushed out of the room with me. He ran full speed into the living room, placing me on the couch. Thankfully, I had left my phone on the couch. I immediately snatched it up calling Giovania and letting her know what was going on. I wanted to call Yari, but another wave of pain hit me, causing me to drop my phone. I knew Giovania would relay the message for me.

Lexx ran back into the living room with a bag in his hands as he picked me up bridal style again, and we headed toward the elevators. I could feel him shaking and knew that he was more nervous about going to the hospital than me having a baby. He hadn't stepped foot into a hospital since his parents died in one, that's why he had a hospital built into his home. The fact that he was willing to go for me really spoke volumes to me. When this was over, and it was all said and done, I was coming for my man.

Yari

Shit been crazy ever since we found out Pops knocked up a bitch who talked to a nigga that beef with Ja over Giovania. The family was divided, Momma Jackie still hadn't woke up yet, and Ja ass was out here killing everything that moved. Shit was making my job even harder trying to push drugs successfully. The police came around every two days all over this city because a crazy, deranged killer was on the loose.

I had tried talking to Pops to get him to step in and intervene, but really, the only person who could stop that nigga was Momma Jackie. Not even Giovania could get him to think rationally. He was hell-bent on the streets talking about what happened. The fire department already ruled that it was arson, so somebody intentionally burned Momma Bee's down. They killed twelve customers and three workers, yet everybody that Ja killed claimed not to know who lit the match.

I had men out searching day and night for answers, because at the rate he was going, and with the case Detective Morris was building against him with Judge Thomas, Ja was either gone be in jail before the month was out, or dead. Well, OK, not dead, but definitely in jail because had already gotten picked up by the police three times. Each time Stan had to come get him, and that shit had to be getting hard to keep getting him off.

I paid a hefty price for a tip from a little bitch I used to fuck with that told me she overheard a nigga bragging about the shit. Said he had skipped town, but he was back since he thought everything was gravy now. The nigga gotta be a trained killer or the stupidest nigga I know to come back after pulling some shit off like that!

* * *

WALKING INTO THE WAREHOUSE, I noticed Danielle had called me twice. I debated on calling her back or not because I hadn't spoken to her since she sprang the news on a nigga that she was pregnant. I wasn't mad at her or no shit like that. I was mad at my damn self for carrying on recklessly without a care in the world, like it wasn't gon' be consequences to my actions. I fucked with D the long way, but her ass needed somebody better than me, and at least I could admit that much. Figuring I'd call her back after this meeting, I went in and took a seat.

"So run that by me again. How three of my houses got hit this week?"

"Boss, we don't know how these niggas getting in. It's like they got inside information or some shit," Johnny said.

Pulling my gun out, I lit his ass up. Ja was a torturer, but me, I got straight to business.

"Anybody else got any better answers than that bullshit?" I asked. I was in rare form today and likely to shoot all of their asses.

"We think somebody on the inside snitching. I think we should switch all the traps up and switch everybody to a different houses and not tell them the new locations. So when a house gets robbed again, look and see if any of the niggas was in the house robbed in the past," Charles said.

"Nigga, who about to be doing all of that work? Shut your ass up," DoBoy said.

"Naw, I can fuck with that idea," Sade said.

"Yeah, makes sense to me," Sage said.

"And that's what we gon' do. Next up, how everybody numbers looking for the week?" I asked each of my lieutenants.

"You know our shit straight," Sage said as Sade just nodded his head in agreement.

"Yeah, we good this way," Mark said.

"Our shit was short, but I got everything under control. I'm getting on everybody ass," Doboy said.

"Yo' ugly ass can't have everything under control if yo' shit short. I don't even know why yo' ass in charge of that trap. You softer than Angel Soft Tissue. Nigga, don't take your Bubba Gump-looking ass serious," Sade said.

"Right. Peter Griffin-looking ass," Sage said.

"Fuck both of y'all Kermit the Frog-looking asses. Niggas always worried about the wrong shit," he said.

"Bitch, my money is the right shit, and instead of arguing with niggas who got they shit together, you need to be telling me just why it is I shouldn't put two in ya dome right now," I said.

"Fuck all that. Ain't nobody about to be talking to me crazy. Nigga don't give a fuck about that shit you talking about. What y'all niggas tryna do?" he asked, standing up as a few of the men who worked in his house stood up as well.

"Bitch ass nigga, you standing up like you wanna catch a fade," Sage said.

"Shit, I'm 'bout all that dumb shit, my nigga. Fuck y'all two bitch boys. Y'all pump fear in them other niggas, but ain't nobody scared of y'all bitch asses. Y'all bleeding like I'm bleeding," he said.

Before any words could be exchanged, Sade had hopped across the table with no hands, hit his ass with a mean two piece, and they all started fighting. I had my own shit going on, so I sat back for a second and just watched the shit.

Looking up, I saw Ja running in like the Undertaker, popping niggas in the arms and legs. I had forgot his ass said he was gone be at this meeting.

"Fuck! Nigga shot us," one of the dudes said.

"That's what yo' ass gets for wanting to be Boosie Bad Ass. Nobody told you to jump up behind that clown ass nigga," Charles said as I still sat calmly.

"Pussy, it's a flesh wound. If I wanted you dead, you would be dead," Ja said as I calmly got up and walked over to all three of them.

Without saying a word, I shot all of them in the head, walked back and sat down. Deciding meeting was adjourned, I dismissed everyone but Charles because I wanted to holla at the lil' nigga.

"Damn, nigga, you could have warned us before you starting shooting. I got blood on my Forces," Sage said.

"Shut y'all asses up," I said.

"Aye, don't start with us, ole crying ass nigga. We'll tag team Danielle ass and buss them wall up with twins," Sade said, laughing. I knew they asses wouldn't let the shit go because that's how we all are. I can't fall off in my feelings when it's my turn.

"Beat y'all to the punch; I shot my seed deep inside that good pussy already."

"So you telling me Danielle pregnant? Damn, nigga, you running them bitches back-to-back, huh?" Ja asked, laughing as he passed me the blunt. It was good to see the nigga actually crack a smile.

"Man, fuck you, bruh."

"Don't get mad at me because yo' ass got two women pregnant at the same damn time," he said, laughing.

"Can't neither of y'all niggas talk shit. Y'all both 'bout about to have two damn kids and shit," Sage said.

"Nigga, I know you ain't talking. You know Karlena ugly ass baby she just had yours while you running around here denying ya seed," Ja said.

"Hell naw. That *Predator vs. Alien* ass child ain't mines," he said.

"Who the fuck jokes on their own seed?"

"Shit, me. Fuck y'all thought this was," Sage said.

"Anyway, back to business. Charles, as second in command, don't you double-check the re-up bread behind Doboy? So why y'all was short?" I asked him. I wanted to hear his response before I made my decision to give the trap to him.

"We was short, but the nigga didn't know I had replaced the shit," he said.

He had really stepped up and been putting in more and more work lately, and that's why I think it's time the nigga got a raise and promotion. I see the hustle in him, and I respect the fuck out of that shit.

"Word? What y'all was short, blood?"

"About five racks, I put eight back," he said.

"Damn. I'm overpaying your ass if you put eight back."

"Naw, I just don't splurge my money on bullshit. I don't need to impress some hoes I could still hit wearing some Jordan flip flops and a wife beater," he said.

"I can respect that," I said, getting up and going to my office. Closing the door, I walked over to the wall and put a code in as the picture slid to the left revealing a safe. Putting my palm on the safe, the locks clicked, then swung open. Grabbing two stacks of money, I took it out then closed everything back up as the painting slid back into place. Walking back into the room, I placed the money down in front of him.

"Consider this a bonus, and 3rd Ward House is yours. One fuck up, and you'll be vacationing with DoBoy ass, though," I said.

"Aye, Giovania just hit me up, yo' baby momma about to have the baby," Ja said as I panicked and took off running toward my car with my heart beating fast as fuck.

I knew this day was coming, but it's different from knowing and experiencing it.

* * *

"SIR, this room is for the parents only. I don't think the mother requested to have anyone in the room with her," a nurse said, trying to usher me out.

"Shit, well, tell that bitch ass nigga to leave, then because I'm the one nutted all inside that pussy, and that's my seed she pushing out," I said in a matter-of-fact tone as soon as I saw this nigga Lexx in the room wiping sweat off her forehead.

Giovania had already told Ja that Lexx had brought her to the hospital. I took a wild guess that this was the friend Ashanti ass went to go chill with. Why she keep testing my gangsta? I don't know.

"Excuse me?" the nurse asked.

"You excused," I told her ass as she looked at me as her face turned a few different colors.

"Who the fuck you calling a bitch ass nigga, fuck boy?" Lexx asked calmly, never looking up at me.

Shit pissed me off but wasn't no bitch in my heart, so I said, "Shit, it's obvious who the fuck I was talking to. Fuck you going to do about it? They said parents only, so you didn't make the cut, nigga. Bye." Being petty, I waved him off.

I don't know why Ashanti big forehead ass thought it was OK to have this nigga in here, and I wanted to curse her ass out, but right now, she was in the process of delivering my son, so my anger toward her temporary subsided.

Smirking, he said, "We done been done this road before. You know like I know I'm 'bout whatever you 'bout."

"Them idle threats don't move me, my nigga."

"You know I can damn sure back up everything I say," he said.

"Y'all stop," Ashanti said barely above a whisper as loud beeping noises sounded off and more nurses rushed in.

"Look, baby, I don't know what the hell y'all got going on, but both of you can either stay and get along, or I'll kick both of y'all asses the hell out and will beat anybody ass who wanna fight," the black nurse, who had just come in, said, snapping on our asses. Just then, the monitors that Ashanti were hooked up to all started going off at the same time.

"What's wrong with her?" Lexx and I said at the exact same time.

"Both you idiots are making her stress levels rise. That's part of what's wrong," she said, pushing past us and rushing to the bed, checking the monitors and calling some code in. As more nurses rushed in, they pushed us out into the waiting room.

"Aye, y'all asses better do something!" I said in a panicked voice, banging on the door.

"I'll kill everybody in this bitch if my seed don't make it," I said, feeling myself flashing out.

"You think that shit helping right now? Chill the fuck out, nigga,"

Lexx said, taking a blunt out his pocket and sparking that bitch up like we wasn't in a damn hospital.

"Nigga, you can't smoke that shit in here," I said, shaking my head cuz this nigga had heart. I'll give him that.

"Shit, says who? I don't see a sign that said I couldn't," he said, really looking around.

It wasn't a sign, but everybody knew you couldn't smoke in a fuckin' hospital, especially a blunt. Taking two more puffs, he put the blunt out and put it back in his pocket.

Running his hands down his face, he sat down in a chair and said, "This ain't how I saw my day going," as he started laughing.

I just looked at his ass for a second, before I took a seat as well. "Shit, you ain't never lied."

For the next hour or two, I surprised myself by having a conversation with the nigga, and he wasn't bad at all. Did I like him, though? Fuck no, but if Shanti liked the nigga, I was gone step aside and let her do her thing. My only concern was my child. The nurse eventually allowed me to go back in the room with Ashanti who was screaming at the top of her lungs.

"Oh, damn. I'ma come back," I said.

"Urghhh!" Shanti yelled.

"It's time," the nurses said as a doctor ran into the room. I slowly eased over to the bed and as soon as I was in arm's length, her crazy ass snatched me to her and grabbed my hand in a death grip.

"Get. This. Big-headed. Ass. Baby. The. Fuck. Out. Of. Me. Before. I. Cut. It. Out!" she screamed, squeezing my shit like something was gone come out.

"I need drugs! Please give me an epidural."

"Ma'am, it's past that point. It's time to push."

"Say, bruh, if you don't loosen your grip on my shit," I said, struggling to snatch my hand away from her ass.

"This is your fucking fault, you bastard! I hate you!" she screamed.

"OK, somebody looks to be in labor," the doctor said.

"Naw, you think?"

"Just get this demon out of me!" Ashanti screamed.

"OK. On the count of three," the doctor was saying, but her stubborn ass gripped down on my shit again and started pushing hard as hell, pausing to take a few deep breaths, then pushing again.

Ten minutes later, Tariq Deshawn Johnson made his way into the world, and I immediately fell in love with his little ass. Damn, a nigga a dad now.

Giovania

Coming out the bathroom, fully naked, I came and sat eagle style on Ja's lap as he kissed on my stomach. Rubbing his head, I just held him close. I had to be strong for him because he was strong everyone else.

"It's going to be OK, baby," I said to him as I felt him slip inside of me.

Grabbing a handful of my hair, Ja started pumping in and out of me at a fast pace. We both needed this release, given everything that's transpired over the last two weeks. I matched his pace, meeting him stroke for stroke as I bounced up and down on his dick.

"Get this first nut off me so daddy can beat this shit out the frame." He hissed at me.

I clenched my muscles down on him, locking him in place as I started bouncing up and down in his lap harder, feeling every inch he was giving me.

"Baby!" I screamed as I threw my head back in ecstasy. Reaching out and grabbing me by my neck, he choked me as he put his other hand on my hip, bouncing me up and down roughly.

"Fuck," he said as I felt him pulsating inside of me before he shot a bucket full of nut inside of me.

Thankfully, I was already pregnant. Standing up with me in his arms, he laid me down on the bed and walked into the bathroom. I heard water running, and a few minutes later, he came back and began wiping between my legs with the towel.

Tossing it to the side, he raised my legs up by my ankles, like I was a baby about to get my pamper changed, then bent down and started eating the booty like groceries. Something he loved doing.

"Mhhh," I moaned out. When he let go of my ankles, I spread my legs as far apart as I could, giving him more access. This probably how I messed around and got pregnant in the first place—being so flexible.

"Ohh, shit!" I screamed, feeling my nut rising.

The slurping noises he was making was enough to drive me insane. A few seconds later, the floodgates opened, and I started gushing all over the place. Being the nasty nigga that he was, he proceeded to catch every drop, before he shoved his dick deep inside of me. Grabbing me by my neck, he started jabbing in and out of me as deep and hard as he could, really working with what he had.

"This dick good, huh?" he asked.

"Fuck yeah, baby," I said, thrusting my hips up, meeting him stroke for stroke. We went at it for almost an hour until we both were too tired to do anything but close our eyes and go to sleep.

* * *

"CAN WE GO SEE GRANDMA JACKIE" Camille asked me.

"Not right now, baby, but in a little while."

Since the fire happened, I had not let her out of my sight, not once. That was the worst day of my life when I got the call that someone had set Momma Bee's on fire. It's crazy because I had literally just gotten off the phone with Momma Jackie, so I thought I was as being pranked when I got the news. That really rocked me to the core because Momma Jackie was like the mother I wish I still had.

Speaking of my mother, I didn't know how I was gone tell Ja about my plans to go to Guatemala, but this was very important to me. The doctor had emailed me back after I asked him what he gave my mother when she came off life support because it altered her mindstate completely. I refused to believe she was acting in her right state of mind. I just couldn't erase all the years of hard work and sacrifices I personally watched her make.

I could see if I had been in America all my life, and I didn't witness any of this. But up until a few weeks ago, my mom was my hero. The strongest person I knew, and I only hoped for half her strength and dedication when I grew up. Now, all I'm left with are memories and anger in my heart. I need answers, and I need to forgive her for me so I wouldn't project this energy off on Jakeria and Jakeem Junior, or Ja and JJ.

"OK," Camille said with a sad face. I don't think nobody was taking this harder than her, because her and Momma Jackie were literally inseparable.

"We can go see your baby cousin," I said, referring to Tariq, Ashanti and Yari's baby.

"Yahh," she said, jumping down and running upstairs to get her shoes.

I never told her we were leaving at this exact moment, but whatever caused her to smile, I was happy with. Camille recovered faster than Momma Jackie because when the fire happened, Momma Jackie threw herself on top of Camille, essentially shielding her from majority of the fire and debris. Momma Jackie herself didn't suffer any major burns, but a lot of heavy debris did fall on top of her, one leaving a nasty deep gash on her forehead.

Ding! Dong!

"Ms. Mary, can you get that for me?" I called out to her as I made me way into the downstairs bathroom. These kids were really sitting heavily on my bladder right now. After I handled my business, I opened the bathroom door and came face-to-face with Detective Morris.

"What the hell are you doing on my house!" I yelled, walking out the bathroom to see police all over my house. Hearing Camille screaming, my maternal instincts kicked in as I tried to take off toward the stairs, but Detective Morris grabbed me. I tried to fight him as best as I could as more officers came over to detain me, one even going so far as to strike me.

Feeling the blow to my back, I calmed down instantly as I saw Camille being dragged down the stairs by the last person I ever expected to see again; Nancy, my mother.

"You've got some balls, bitch, to come into my house. I promise, on my kids, I'm fucking you up as soon as I get free1," I yelled, struggling to break loose.

"Mrs. Carter, you are not the legal guardian of seven-year-old, Camille Santiago. I have paperwork signed by a judge to remove the child from your home and a social worker behind you placing temporary custody to her real mother, pending investigation. But seeing as though no investigation is needed because you stole her, I doubt you'll be getting her back. Now, as for you, you are under arrest for kidnapping, and you are a prime suspect in the death of Trina Hill. Take her away," he said as I fought and kicked as hard as I could to get away. This couldn't be happening to me right now; it just couldn't.

"Call Ja!" I screamed out to Ms. Mary as Kaine followed behind us.

"I'll meet you at the precinct, Giovania," Kaine said.

"That won't be necessary; we have enough evidence to hold her by law forty-eight to seventy-two hours."

Jakeem "Ja" Carter

Since my mother has been in ICU, I've had more bad days than good days. The only good news I've had was my mother was expected to make a full recovery, and the surgery I paid for was for a success. She didn't sustain any major burns, just tissue scarring that they already operated on. I didn't think it was possible, but she looked even more beautiful than before. Pops ass hasn't left her side not once, which gets awkward for me because I'm always at the hospital seeing my T-lady, so I have to see him too. I still had beef with that nigga, especially since I learned that bitch named her baby Maxx Carter Jr.

So for him to be a Carter, Pops either got a blood test before he signed the birth certificate or thought he didn't need one. And if that's the case, then he lied about not believing the baby was his and not fuckin' with her like that. Shit, he used to preach to me about running in these hoes raw, then he turned around and did it is the shit; I can't respect. Until his baby momma and that fuck nigga are ruled out as suspects in the fire, I'ma forever be beefing with Pops.

Today was the only other good news I had gotten because Yari finally found a good lead, and he told me I could come with him to question the nigga. We had already snatched his ass up and put him in the warehouse. I had gotten here extra early to have some fun with the nigga by myself for a while. I promised Yari I wouldn't kill him, and I won't. That don't mean he won't beg me to kill him when I was done with him. Walking into the room, I dapped Charles up, who was watching the nigga for me.

"Good looking out, ya heard me. I got it from here."

"Bet," he said, dapping me up again and walking off.

"Damn, nigga, you stank. And I know you didn't shit yourself," I said, pulling a chair up to the table. He was currently tied to a chair and seated at the table.

"Why yo' ass looking at a nigga like that? This some gay shit."

"Oh, so he does speak?"

"Yeah, I speak. I'm just not telling yo' bitch ass shit, so you can shoot me and get it over with," he said.

Laughing a sinister laugh, I said, "Shoot you and get it over with, huh? Naw, see I'm a beast with a gun, but I don't prefer to use them. But if I did shoot yo' ass, I'd also bring a doctor in here to retrieve the bullet and save yo' life. Give you blood transfusions if you needed it. See, that way you could die every day and come back to life. You ever watched *1000 Ways to Die?* A nigga like me loved that fucking show, best thing they ever came up with."

"You crazy as hell, bruh."

"About my momma, yes I am. Speaking of Momma, Momma Bee's, who paid you to burn it down?" I asked.

"I don't know shit about that, and even if I did, I wouldn't dare tell you."

"Wouldn't dare tell me, huh?" I asked, laughing as I stood up and grabbed the bag I brought in with me. I calmly grabbed my Katana sword out of its casing and turned back toward him while he was still talking shit. Taking the sword, I simply cut his arms loose that were tied behind the chair.

"Damn, so you did all that to untie me? Damn, when I took the job, they told me to watch out for Ja Carter because he wasn't shit to play with. They must got your soft ass confused with somebody else," he laughed.

Swoosh!

I grabbed the sharp blade with ease and precision and sliced his right arm clean off.

"Arghh!" he yelled, looking from his severed arm to the place where his arm was supposed to be that now was gushing out with blood at a rapid speed.

"I don't know what they told you or what the fuck you heard, but clearly, you're mistaken. Allow me to introduce myself, I'm Jakeem Carter, bitch, your worst fucking nightmare," I said as Yari walked through the door. He took one look at dude and shook his head at me as dude screamed like somebody was murdering him.

"What? His ass ain't dead. We having a friendly conversation," I said, turning back to dude.

"How it's friendly with his bitch ass screaming like that?"

"It is friendly because I was just kindly introducing myself. Now, where were we?" I said with my hand on my chin. "Oh yeah, right, I'm Ja. Nice to meet you," I said, sticking my hand out toward his severed arm.

"Oh, my fault," I said as I reached down and grabbed his arm off the floor, and I shook his hand.

"You sick, bruh," Yari said, shaking his head. "How you gone shake the fuckin' arm you chopped off?"

"Just like the fuck I just did."

"Look, tell this crazy ass nigga what the fuck he wants to hear before yo' kids open the gift box we gone send them with your body in little pieces," Yari said.

"Yeah, cuz we can do this your way, or we can do this Grim Reaper's way. Now if you choose your way, you can make shit less painful on yourself. But if you choose Grim Reaper's way, then you're in for a brutally, long, painful day. I'll cut your ass up limb by limb, and make sure I have my doc in here to keep your ass breathing for a few weeks. You'd be surprised how long the body can last with no arms, legs, feet, or tongue."

"This cat name Bull hired me and my men to hit a few trap houses and burn Momma Bee's down. He said he and his girl was taking over New Orleans and eliminating the competition. Said it was only room for one sheriff. I was there, but I didn't light the match. My men did. I can tell you where they at right now," he said in a rushed tone.

"Bull? Why the fuck would Bull burn Momma Bee's down? Everybody knows I'm not even in the streets. Only our men know I call the shots. If he wanted to take over, he wouldn't have assumed I had anything to do with it? And why Momma Bee's of all places? Shit not adding up, it's something else to this story," I said.

"I told you all I know."

"What you know not good enough," I said.

"What's that?" Yari said, pointing to a box I had almost forgotten about. Picking the box up, the contents of it immediately started hissing.

"Nigga, the fuck you got in that shit?"

"A gift for our friend," I said as I unclasped the box and turned it upside down, shaking the contents all over his body. I watched closely and a bit fascinated as the poisonous snakes, wild rats, and spiders immediately started running and crawling over his body.

"I wonder who will succeed in eating him the fastest."

* * *

"WHY I'M JUST HEARING about this!" I barked, speeding toward the police station. Kaine had called me telling me Detective Morris came to my house and drug my pregnant fucking wife out of our home and threw her in jail. Pissed wasn't even the proper word to describe how I was feeling right now.

"I called you a few times, but your phone went to voicemail," Kaine said. I hung up on him as I called Stan.

"Danielle called me already. I'm up here now. Don't come up here, Mr. Carter. You won't make things better for her. Meet me as my office."

"What the fuck your mean don't come up there? Muthafucka, that is my fuckin' wife. I'll shut that entire fuckin precinct down! My T-lady already laid up in the hospital, they snatched my fucking daughter and my wife, and you telling me that coming up there will make it worse! You wanna die with them, Stan? Because, bitch, you headed on that list right along with their asses!" I screamed, banging my fist on the steering wheel repeatedly as I weaved in and out of traffic, barely escaping three wrecks, driving like a bat out or hell. I was in rare form and there was no calming me down right now.

"If you come up here, both of you will end up in jail. You built to withstand it, but do you really think your six-month pregnant wife can?" Hearing this, I knew he was right, even though I didn't want to admit it.

"You better meet me at your office with my fucking wife and daughter," I said, hanging up.

Sparking a blunt up, I tried to calm myself down before I had a meltdown. At times like this, I wish I could call my T-lady, but she was laid up. I wasn't fucking with Pops right now still, so I hit my brother Yari up.

"Yo, what's up?"

"Bro, I need you to meet me at Stan's office. I feel like I'm about to flash out and lay everybody in the police station and courthouse down. From police to lawyers to judges, every fucking body!"

"Whoa, what's good? I'm on my way. We can ride out. You know if you rocking, I'm rolling," he said. I heard the baby in the background, and immediately felt bad I was asking him to leave his newborn kid for me.

"Naw, bro, handle your business with your family. That's my bad asking you to ride out. Ashanti and Tariq need you."

"Hell no, fuck that, I'm coming."

"Naw, I'm good," I said, hanging up as I pulled up to Stan's office.

Parking, I sparked a blunt, and took a very long pull from it before I let my seat back and laid my head back. About thirty minutes passed by before I heard a tap on my window. Grabbing my gun, I sat up at the same time as I pointed my gun in the direction of the intruder. Seeing my Pops, I unlocked my door and got up with my gun still drawn.

"What the fuck you doing here?"

"Yari called me concerned about you. Danielle also told me what happened."

"OK, so why you here?"

"Because you my fucking son, that's why, muthafucka. I left your mother's side, somewhere I've been faithfully since she got to the hospital to come see about my fucking son! I don't need you doing anything irrational and landing yourself in a situation that Stan or no amount or money can get you out of. Think about your kids. What you gone do if you can't raise them? And you know your mother would lose her mind if she woke up and yo' black ass was in jail. Hell, she would beat my ass as well, like I had something to do with the shit. You know anything that you do, I get punished for it. When she found out Giovania left because of Trina's ass, I slept on that damn couch damn near a month. Hell, my back still hurting from that shit," he said, causing me to laugh because my T-lady does punish his ass for anything I do.

"Now let's address this baby situation. You running round here acting like a white kid or some shit acting shocked I been cheating on ya momma. Hell, you a better man than I've ever been. I love ya momma more than life itself. I would give my left nut sack for her, and she knows this. But I love bitches too. The difference is, them hoes know they place. That's the number-one leading lady in my life, and that won't ever change. Cara is some groupie bitch that was thirsty for the dick, so I gave it to her a few times while I was in New York on business. I actually met Cara at a business meeting.

"The lil' nigga she fuck with named Kyle got a brother name Lexx that's running shit out that way. He had retired; but got back in the game for some reason. I was securing a distribution deal with him, which by the way Mateo still like clockwork sends my re-ups. Anyway, I saw Cara with Kyle and didn't pay her no attention until she knocked on my hotel room door, then swallowed my dick right there with the door open," he said.

"Damn, that bitch raw," I said, temporary forgetting I was beefing with the nigga.

"Right, but the bitch got clingy, so I had to cut her off. She trapped me when she wanted to fuck one last time. I think the hoe poked holes in the condom. I didn't need a blood test for Maxx Carter Jr. Nigga look exactly like me."

"Damn so I got a little brother."

"And I finally got a cute son."

"Fuck you. Bitches love me. I'ma teach baby bro all the ropes," I said as we shared a laugh that was long overdue and much needed. After the laugher, I got serious again.

"I'm killing Morris tonight," I said.

"I got your back. He violated when he touched my daughter-in-law and my cockblocking ass princess. Camille be blocking her ass off, but I love the fuck out of that girl."

"Her bad ass don't do nothing but block. It's like she know exactly when some shit 'bout to get popping. She'll wait right until nigga 'bout to slip in and punish shit to try and come in," I said, laughing before I got serious again.

"Pops I can't live without my girls. I need all three or them. I'm losing my damn mind, bruh," I said, trying to hold it together because I felt myself getting emotional, and I wasn't built to be no crying ass nigga.

"Your momma gone be OK. She just acting stubborn right now, but she'll wake up. And we definitely gon' get Camille and Giovania back. I bet my life on it. They officially brought Maxx Carter out of retirement, and they damn sure can't handle two Carter men at the same time.

* * *

"Where the fuck my wife at?" I asked Stan.

"We've ran into another problem that Detective Morris knows about. You told me that situation was under control when I talked to you last week," he said as he pressed play on the TV in the room. At first, I didn't understand what was going on until I made out Trina walking through the crowd followed by Ashanti and Giovania.

"Is this why you don't have my fucking wife? Dont play with me,

Stan! Go get my fucking wife now! Her fingerprints nowhere on the scene, and this don't prove shit. Giovania never denied being there or speaking to Trina. But she didn't touch that girl," I said, which was the truth because she didn't actually touch her at all. I had even doubled back and killed the bartender; no face no case.

"I know, but it looks—" He was saying until I cut him off.

"Nigga, I don't give a fuck what it looks like. My wife ain't touch that hoe, and besides, she pregnant with twins. What the hell could she have done?"

"I understand that, but understand the prosecution at this point is desperate, and will spin this anyway they can."

"We don't give a fuck how they spin it," Pops said.

"Right. I know my wife better be at home before midnight. She too pregnant to be in a filthy jail."

"The judge who signed off on the warrant also signed the warrant for kidnapping. They know it won't stick, but by law, they have probable cause to hold her for forty-eight hours."

"They won't last that long."

"I'm with whatever you tryna do, son," my pops said.

"I don't advise you to kill them because it wouldn't—"

"Shut the fuck up talking to me. You already treading on thin fucking ice. Like I said, them bitches won't last that fucking long. But since you seem incapable of doing your job the legal way, I'll do it the illegal way," I said.

* * *

Miss Mary told me that one of the officers hit Giovania, and that shit just added fuel to an already burning fire. He definitely was dying tonight. I sent Pops back up the hospital to sit with Ma Dukes because I didn't need any help killing this bitch. This became personal the minute he put his hands on my queen. I had already had Danielle break into the alarm system and disable it, so that enabled me to not only creep in undetected, but also the cameras wouldn't be active.

Creeping into his son's room, I put my hands over his mouth, snatching him up first, dragging him downstairs, then duct taping his mouth up. I did the same to his daughter and wife. Next, I went around the house trashing it and taking anything valuable to make it look like an actual robbery. Finally, I took me a seat on the couch, kicked back, and waited for my prey.

About two hours later, the door opened as Morris came in. I heard him in the kitchen moving around like he didn't have a care in the world as I heard him warming up the plate she left him, oblivious to what he was about to walk in on. Getting up calmly, I walked in the kitchen and listened to his conversation as he had his back to me talking away.

"Yeah, I roughed her ass up. That nigga thinks he's so tough. Let's see him get her out of this. We holding her for seventy-two hours, and tomorrow, she'll be in a cell. It's only going to take one guard to turn the other cheek, and I got some girls lined up willing to do anything with the hopes of getting out. He gon' lose those kids and his wife, and then he'll truly understand my family's pain," he said.

"OK, I'll come over later," he said and hung up.

"Damn, you was gone do baby girl like that?" I asked as he quickly turned around and reached for his gun, but I shot him in the hand before he made it to his weapon. I'm glad I had my silencer on so the shots were silent.

"So this what it's come down to? You think you tough with that gun," he said. His voice was trembling, but he still tried to play it off.

"You had all that mouth before, and even just now, and that's all you can come up with?"

"You really making shit worse on your wife now. If I don't check in, they won't release her ass at all. I hold the cards to all of this shit. She won't get out unless I authorize it. Hell, my men probably on the way here now since I haven't checked in," he said, trying to sound tough.

"Nigga, you don't run shit. You just a damn detective. The same judge that signed off on the shit gon' sign off on her release," I said.

"You think Thomas gone do that shit?" he asked, laughing.

"You think you making it to tomorrow?" I asked him.

"Yes, if you want yo' wife to get out. You think they gon' let her out if I'm dead?"

"Nigga, I don't need you alive to make that happen, but since you know something that I don't, call and have her released right now," I said as he started laughing.

"Oh, I'm Kevin Hart funny, am I? OK, nigga, here's how this will work; your entire family in the living room tied up, and I'll kill their asses one by one until my wife is home."

"You bluffing," he said. The color drained from his face as he rushed into the living room.

"Babe," he said, trying to run to his wife until I paused him.

"Dial or I'll chop your fucking son into bite-sized pieces." I said, pulling out my Katana.

"You dead, you hear me? You dead! That's why I took pride in punching your wife in her throat," he said.

Walking over to his wife, I slid the sword across her neck chopping her head off.

"You hit mine in the throat; I hit yours in the throat," I said.

"You son of a bitch!" he screamed.

"Dial before I move on," I said.

He quickly called Judge Thomas. While he was doing that, I called Stan to get my wife, and we all waited until Giovania called me from the car. I answered and heard her crying, but I immediately hung up.

"Now let my fucking family go," Morris said.

"No. I never said that."

"Wha—" was all I let him get out before I sliced his head off.

Grabbing his head and his wife's head, I put them in a bag. Next, I walked to the kitchen then paused. Last time I let a family live, I thought Byron's wife was coming after me, making me kill other people in the process. Doing an about-face, I walked back and shot them both in the head before I headed home to be with my wife. Judge Thomas was next.

Danielle

Walking into the warehouse, I typed a few codes in the safe and got the money out. I was gambling with my life, I know, but this had to be done. After that was done, I went to where I knew Ja kept the re-up drugs, and I pulled them to the front. Getting a ding on my phone, I pulled it out seeing that it was Bull. Hurrying to the door, I opened it for him as he rushed in.

"Damn, girl, you wasn't lying when you said it was money and drugs everywhere. Shit, I feel like a kid in a candy store up in this bitch," he said.

"Enough talking. We don't have a big window. In about thirty minutes, more than a few workers will be here to count this shit up," I said as he pulled his phone out.

"Let me tell my girl to get out the car so we can move this shit faster."

"Damnit. I said no people," as he went to go let her in. He returned with the last person I expected to see.

"What the fuck you doing with this hoe?" I asked him, pointing at Melinda.

"This my man, bitch, that's why I'm here."

"Girl, you dick hop a lot, don't you?"

"Don't get cute, bitch, before the deal is off the table, and we take your fucking child."

"You won't take shit, but these hands, hoe."

"Ladies, ladies focus. Let's get this bread, and we'll disappear. You won't see me again, Danielle; I'll send Safaree a postcard."

"What happened to some you want your child bullshit you was spitting?"

"Why you bringing up the past, bruh?"

"And where does your snake ass fit into all of this?" I asked Melinda.

"I'm the reason why Bull is here. We go way back."

"I'm not surprised, girl. Who haven't you fucked?"

"Yari, but I could if I wanted to," she said, causing me to laugh.

"Bitch, he may be a hoe, but he damn sure ain't desperate."

"Whatever, girl. I'ma let you think that. Anyway, that nigga Sade thought he was tough shit, but his punk ass was content with the position that he was in in the game and had no intentions of dethroning Yari. Then he thought he could shit on me for that ugly bitch Kosher, but the joke is on them. Fuck him. I wanted a boss anyway, not a worker, so I hooked back up with Bull and told him we could take over this shit together."

"OK, but I only told Bull about old traps. How y'all hit newer ones?"

"Y'all call me a hoe all the time, but this lil' pussy got some power, that's how I found out."

"So he pimped you out to niggas for his gain only? Cuz bitch, I know you ain't think he was taking you with him? Girl, that nigga ain't leaving Jewels, yo pussy ain't got the much power."

"Sholl the fuck don't," Sade said, walking in with Sage and Yari.

"You bitch!" Bull yelled, reaching for his gun.

"Damn, them dry ass walls don't get tired, do they?" Sade asked.

"Fuck you, Sade. You was sprung for a while, so my pussy can't be too dry."

"Don't act like K-Y Jelly wasn't our best friend. You can take dick like a champ, though."

"Shit, probably because her shit deep as hell," Sage said, laughing.

"Y'all bitch boys came to talk, or y'all gon' make some shit shake?" Bull asked.

"D, this what you doing?" Yari asked, looking at me as if he was hurt.

"No, this ain't what I'm doing. This what I'm fixing," I said.

I was ready to own up to my mistakes and right my wrongs. I had already confessed to Ja what was going on with Bull after I made sure Bull got rid of the evidence he had against me. Ja was pissed off at me, and it will probably take a while to gain his trust back, but it was either that or make a run for it like I had originally planned. I figured honesty was the best policy. He knew about everything going down tonight, and I guess this was the first step to proving myself.

As far as Bull went, I agreed to the settlement he offered my lawyer, and we had a new custody decree drawn up, stating he got her every other weekend, but her guardian and power of attorney, in the event of our death, was her godmother. That's all I needed on my end. I never told Bull anything important about Ja or Yari. I only told him about trap houses that don't even make money like that.

Simply telling him, however, got him to believe I was down for his scheme. When in actuality, I was one step ahead of him. He was a monster, and he would never ever get my child, no matter what. After hiring somebody to burn Momma Bee's down, he had to go, so I had set up the perfect plan, and just executed it.

"See you in hell, bitch," Bull said.

"Oh, I'll be there, bitch, just not right now. In the meantime, make sure you say hey to Boon for me," I said, walking off. I heard all of their guns going off as I opened the door and walked out with a smile. I was headed home to my baby and that was something to smile about.

Giovania

Waking up in bed, I struggled to drag myself to the bathroom. I had went from jail to the hospital. I was dehydrated, my stress levels were up, and my blood pressure was through the roof. I had been crying since I got to jail, so I can understand why my blood pressure was up. I just wanted my sister back, and I felt like this time, our mother would really harm her. Ja promised me he would, once again, get her back, but I wasn't so sure how.

I felt like the biggest failure in life because it seemed like I could never protect Camille. If I couldn't protect one child, how was I going to protect three? Walking downstairs, I saw Ja sitting on the couch talking to Yari, the twins, and Pops. They all instantly stopped talking when I walked into the living room. It's like now I was excluded from all plans and news.

"Don't stop talking. I want to know what y'all discussing."

"It's not important," Ja said.

"Jakeem Carter, we are a team."

"Just show her, son,"

"Yeah, cuz I'm ready to see what's on the shit," Sage said.

"Hell naw, fool. It had Giovania name on it and was marked urgent. It could be Camille on that tape getting hurt," Sade said as I gasped.

"Play it!" I yelled.

"You gone upset my kids. Doc already put you on bed rest since your jail visit. Let me look at it first, then if I find it's OK, I'll show you."

"You don't get to make those decisions for me, Ja."

"Yes, the fuck I do. I won't risk my kids' lives by showing you a tape that could possibly be my baby getting harmed."

"You protecting me or you?" I asked him because everybody knew Camille and him were best friends.

"Both."

"Look, we are a family, dawg, so whatever happens, we will get through it as a family," Pops said as everybody looked to Ja.

You could see the battle playing out on his face on whether to put the DVD in or not. Finally, he handed it off to Pops and signaled for me to come over to him. Sitting beside him, I grabbed Ja's hand with my right and Yari's hand with my left. It seemed like we all held our breath as the DVD started and a doctor came into view.

"Hello, Ms. Renaldez. I am Doctor Jose. I received each of your emails, but I'm sorry I did not understood them," he said in broken English. "As I said before, your mother is on life support, yes," he said, walking down a hall as the camera person walked with him. Stopping in a room, he entered, and there laying in bed, hooked up to machines was…

"It can't be," I said, standing up.

"What the fuck?" Ja said.

"What type of *Iyanla: Fix My Life* meets Oprah found my long-lost sister is this bullshit?" Sade said.

"Shhh! I can't hear," I said, turning the TV up.

"Right now her condition hasn't progressed, but it hasn't gotten worse either. We have limited resources here to determine what is really wrong, so for now, until you come, she remain on life support. We can't keep her much longer though. It gets expensive," he said as he looked to his left.

"Oh, Mr. Renaldez, I am making tape for her daughter. I am trying to explain in my best English that her mother is here," he said as Mateo came into view.

"Oh hell naw," Yari said.

"If you are seeing this Giovania, then that means you are under the impression Fancy is your mother. It honestly took me awhile to figure it out. I had my suspicions, because try as she might, she doesn't exude the same love, dedication, and compassion as Nancy does. It was never my intention to bring you harm. It was the truth that the first day I thought of or seen you was the day you barged into my meeting.

"I started noticing signs, and once I figured it out, it was too late; Ja's men had already performed the rescue mission, killing one of my sons in the process. The worst thing I ever had to do was bury a son. Hey, I wasn't a saint in all of this; I've killed people here and done other stuff, but that had nothing to do with this war that she has going on; I had no parts of it. It took me a while but I finally found your mother, and I haven't left her side since then," he said as the camera cut off. I think we all just sat there in shock, trying to absorb everything we just heard.

"On the cool, we still getting re-up from that nigga, so he cool in my book," Yari said.

"And I'ma man of my word, so I still give him his guns."

"What the fuck? Why y'all ain't told us we still getting re-up from that nigga?" Sade said.

"What the fuck?" he repeated.

"Yeah, is me and my brother the only ones left out the damn loop about some shit we pushing out everyday? That's fucked up. And damn, so ya moms ain't a schemed-out, dusty-feet bitch that we gotta kill after we pass her around to the crew? I ain't wanna say nothing, but she got a badass shape. I wanted to knock the cobwebs off that pussy," Sage said.

"Nigga, it's too early," Sade said.

"Well, excuse the hell out of me. Nigga never been in a *It Takes Two* type of situation. Shit, why we ain't never think of no twin shit like that?" Sage said as I got up and walked off while their dumb asses went back and forth. Halfway to my room, I got a phone call from a private number.

"Hello?"

"Giovania," I heard Camille say.

"Camille!" I screamed as the phone was snatched from her.

"Here's how it will go, I need three million by midnight, or you'll never find her body. Three million... midnight... only bring your little lap dog, Ja, and that's it. Anybody else, and she dies," Fancy said, hanging up.

It all was starting to make sense why I could never accept her behavior! That's because that really wasn't my mother! I knew it! I'm so glad I didn't give up on my mother. Breaking down once I got to the room, I cried for my mother, for Camille, and for this evil ass auntie that was making my life a living hell. Once I shed my last tear, I picked myself up and went to get prepared to get my little sister back. First, I had to prepare myself for Hurricane Ja though because it wasn't no way in hell he was letting me go without a fight.

* * *

"WHERE IS CAMILLE?" I asked as soon as I saw Fancy.

"Damn. No, 'hey, Mom. how are you?'"

"Bitch, cut the act. We know you not her momma, Fancy, with your ugly ass," Ja said.

"Cat got your tongue?" I smirked at her.

"So you finally figured it out. Good, because the worst thing in life is pretending to be that bitch. Her gullibility rubbed off on her kids in the worst way. I mean, I hadn't seen the bitch in years, then I pop up out the blue, and she thought we was about to be one big ass happy family. The second happiest day for me, besides killing our mother, was getting rid of Nancy."

"You evil bitch."

"I'll wear that crown proudly. Enough talking. Where my fuckin' money at?"

"Where is my sister at, bitch?"

"Yeah, you not getting shit until we see Camille," Ja said.

Pulling out her phone, she texted somebody, and a few seconds later, Judge Thomas came into view with Camille.

"Camille," I said, wanting to run out to her. She had her mouth duct taped, but you could still tell she was screaming behind the tape.

"Just the nigga I been looking for," Ja said.

"Get in line. A lot of niggas be looking for him," Fancy said.

"Ja, it was business, nothing was personal."

"Naw, nigga, when you try to kill me, I take that shit very personal. I had a chat with Byron's wife, and apparently, you told Byron to put a hit on me, and gave him very important information about me. Now why would you wanna go and do that for?" Ja asked calmly, not bothered by the gun Judge Thomas or Fancy were holding.

"And how did it come about that y'all two hooked up?" I asked as I looked on, waiting for answers.

After a pregnant pause, Fancy said, "I'm not hooking up with that booty bandit. That's probably the secret he didn't want you knowing about with elections coming up and all. But I did know about his little secret, I've known for some time now. See, I used to talk to Damion Morris back in the day, Chad Morris' brother. And he told me all about the judge, and he even suspected he used to touch on little boys, nasty muthafucka. Probably touched on Chad, that's why he was always at his house. Anyway, I just used him because I needed a judge in my pocket, and he used me to get to Ja. I guess we used each other," she said.

"Hell naw, don't say to get to Ja like that. Nigga better not come this way with that shit. Damn, nigga, yo' old ass like boys' booty holes?" Ja said in disbelief. Damn, I didn't see that one coming either.

"Not to get you like that, as in fuck you, or at least I don't think so. Shit, I really don't care," Fancy said.

"I thought Byron had told you before you killed him, that's why I wanted to get rid of you. It was a long time ago that me and Byron used to hook up," he said.

"So was that why he was sleeping with your wife? What, did you tell him you'd rat him out, that's why he did that shit? Damn, nigga, who else you fucked?"

"Enough about who he has and hasn't stuck his dick in. Where is my money?" Fancy asked, pointing the gun at Camille.

"Damn, bitch, hold your horses," Ja said as he walked off and returned with the bag of money, throwing it at her. Still, with the gun pointed at Camille, she bent down, unzipped the bag, and revealed the money.

"Release the brat," she said.

"If I give him her, he'll get away, and he knows too much," Judge Thomas replied.

"Nigga, you want me? I'll come to you," Ja said as he took off walking toward Judge Thomas, who pushed Camille out of the way and pointed his gun at Ja, at the same time that I raised my gun that I had secretly pulled out.

Pow! Pow! Pow! Pow!

Epilogue

Two months later

If she a baby momma, she gone do that baby momma.

Dancing to the baby momma song with Jakeem, we enjoyed our baby shower, laughing and smiling amongst our closest friends and family. Two months ago after that fateful night, when the smoke cleared, only Camille, Ja and I walked away. When Ja walked toward Judge Thomas, he pushed Camille to the side and started shooting at Ja, but Yari, Pops, and the twins all jumped out shooting as well. I had dropped my gun and ran toward Camille. Fancy made it to the car before they gunned her down. A few days later, we got a call from the hospital saying Momma Jackie had come out of her coma. Leave it to her to raise from the dead talking shit. I've always heard that people can hear everything you say in a coma, and I guess that was true, because when she woke up, the first thing she started fussing about was Pops's new baby. She hasn't fully regained her strength, but she's getting stronger every day.

Sade and Sage are still crazy as ever, but surprisingly, they are doing great in college. Who would have thought they be honor students as much as they always cracking jokes? Sade and Kosher are still going strong.

Check out *Double Dosage of A New Orleans Savage: Sade and Sage's Story* to delve more into their crazy lives.

Ashanti and Lexx are taking things slow with dating, although I have a feeling their lives will be turned upside once he knows that it's his little brother, Kyle, that's been a major pain in everybody's asses. I don't know how we managed to miss that one. Yari has come to the terms that Danielle is really pregnant, so they are trying to make their dysfunctional relationship work.

Ashanti, Lexx, Yari, and Danielle's crazy saga will also spill over into *Riding For My Savage.*

Everyone's favorite parents, Momma Jackie and Maxx Carter, are still very much a match made in heaven because they both are batshit crazy, and made for one another. I've never seen a person in a wheelchair beat somebody ass like Momma Jackie. She went upside Pops's head once she gained strength to do so, and it was the funniest thing I've ever seen. I personally wouldn't take him back, but if she likes it, I love it.

I can understand what she obsessed with, because like father, most definitely like son. Those Carter men were sent down straight from God. Now, as for my little family, Camille is super excited that the twins are on the way, and after talking to her, I finally explained that was not our mother who tried to harm us. It helped that Sage and Sade are really identical, and they helped out with explaining, in true twins' fashion.

Sade pushed Camille down, and she thought Sage had done it since they were both dressed alike. That made it much easy for her to grasp Nancy and Fancy. As for my real mother, Ja had her moved to the States, and she's currently getting the best treatment money can buy. Her progress hasn't changed, but I'm keeping my fingers crossed. Mateo has been by her side the entire time. I still don't like him, and still keeping my eyes on him, but for now, I've put my hatred of him to the side for my mother since he was with her, even in Mexico, watching over her in my absence.

Jakeem Carter is the same ole Ja. Either the New Orleans Police Department didn't want any smoke, or they really didn't believe it was him behind the murders, because we haven't had any more problems out of them. Stan told us the case had officially been dropped, so business was back booming for everybody, and Ja had returned to his own crazy job.

As for me, well, I'm at peace right now. These days, I'm enjoying my husband, my sister, my family, and my friends while patiently awaiting the birth of Jakeria and Jakeem. When I first came to New Orleans, I knew I was going to be married to Jakeem, but I never imagined I would fall in love and be starting a family as well. Funny how life works, but the best thing that ever happened to me was getting Married to a New Orleans Savage.

THE END... SIKE keep reading, kinfolks!!! No, seriously, cousins, the book ain't over yet, y'all. It's just getting good.

Jackie Carter

My red bottom heels echoed throughout the quiet house as I made my way up the stairs, carrying the baby and a bottle in one hand and a gift-wrapped present in the other hand. Walking inside of my husband's study, I smiled brightly as I laid eyes on his fine ass. Even at almost fifty-three, Maxx Carter was still undoubtedly the finest man I had ever seen. I loved him more than life itself. Sure, we had our problems, but with as long as we've been together, a few bumps in the road are to be expected. You show me a perfect relationship, and I'll show you a lying ass bitch

"Hey, baby," he said.

"I got a gift for you," I said as I placed the box in his lap before walking over and sitting down in a chair with the baby as I gave him his bottle because he was screaming to the top of his lungs.

"What is it?" he asked, shaking the box to his ear trying to guess the contents inside.

"A present I picked up for my wonderful husband," I said as I continued to feed the baby. Eagerly ripping the pretty bow off and opening the gift box, he immediately pushed it out of his lap as Cara's head rolled out, landing in a position where her face was staring up at him. Smiling to myself, I looked at Little Maxx. He was just the cutest baby I had ever seen.

"What the fuck wrong with you, Jackie!"

"Hunny, you don't like your gift?""Hell naw I don't like that shit."

"We worked really hard on that gift, didn't we, Little Maxx?" I said to him in a baby voice.

"I've always wanted another baby, and since your mother just tragically and suddenly died, I have one. Little Maxx Carter Jr, you look just like your brother Jakeem. Yes you do, yes you do," I said.

"You crazy as hell, Jackie," Maxx said.

"That's Mrs. Carter to you, and don't you forget it," I said, winking at him.

THE END

BEFORE YOU GO, be sure to head over to Amazon, and check out the rest of the books that I have to offer!

NOTE FROM THE AUTHOR

I've come such a long way since my first series, and I'm forever humbled and blessed by this amazing journey. I still cannot believe that I am a national best-selling author, but God said speak it into existence, and since my first book, that's exactly what I've been doing! With God on my side, I plan to drop hundreds of books! To everyone in the author world, I encourage you to continue to walk by faith and not by sight, staying steadfast and unmoving in this industry. If God is for you, who can be against you? Always trust your craft and belief in yourself. If you understand time and season, then you'll know yours is coming. Just wait on it, and trust the process! Your best is yet to come! As always, you can follow me on my social medias listed below.

ABOUT THE AUTHOR

Author Carmen Lashay born Jasmine Miller, is a native of Monroe, Louisiana. The young author has since relocated to North Richland Hills, Tx with her husband. The national best selling author has to date written 19 novels and doesn't she herself slowing down anytime soon. Carmen Lashay has been in love with books since her 4th grade teacher, Mrs. Joyner, introduced the class to Harry Potter and the Sorcerer's Stone. Since then, her love of books has grown to a passion for reading as well as writing. In her spare time, she enjoys traveling, thrift shopping, binge watching, and relaxing at home with a glass of wine, and her kindle. Her favorite tv shows are NCIS, Criminal Minds, S.W.A.T and Big Bang Theory. Carmen Lashay hopes to produce books that will have capture the hearts and attention of readers all over the world, as well as keep them on the edge of their seats coming back to enjoy more stories.

STAY CONNECTED:
Facebook Reader's Page:

Authoress Carmen Lashay

ALSO BY CARMEN LASHAY

WHAT IS LOVE

WHAT IS LOVE 2

WHAT IS LOVE 3

IN LOVE WITH THE KING OF HOUSTON

READY FOR LOVE

READY FOR LOVE 2

AIN'T NO LOVE LIKE A GANGSTAS LOVE

COKE GURLS DALLAS

LOVE AND HENNESSY

LOVE AND HENNESSY 2

LOVE AND HENNESSY 3

LOVE AND HENNESSY 4

GIOVANIA & JAKEEM: MARRIED TO A NEW ORLEANS SAVAGE

Royalty Publishing House is now accepting manuscripts from aspiring or experienced urban romance authors!

WHAT MAY PLACE YOU ABOVE THE REST:

Heroes who are the ultimate book bae: strong-willed, maybe a little rough around the edges but willing to risk it all for the woman he loves.

Heroines who are the ultimate match: the girl next door type, not perfect - has her faults but is still a decent person. One who is willing to risk it all for the man she loves.

The rest is up to you! Just be creative, think out of the box, keep it sexy and intriguing!

If you'd like to join the Royal family, send us the first 15K words (60 pages) of your completed manuscript to submissions@royaltypublish-inghouse.com

LIKE OUR PAGE!

Be sure to LIKE our Royalty Publishing House page on Facebook!

CPSIA information can be obtained
at www.ICGtesting.com
Printed in the USA
LVHW091331280319
612176LV00001B/243/P

9 781797 495927